TWISTED FAITH

WILD SPACE SAGA BOOK 3

TWISTED FAITH

BRANDON HILL & TERENCE PEGASUS

4 Horsemen
Publications, Inc.

4 Horsemen
Publications, Inc.

Published By: 4 Horsemen Publications, Inc.

4 Horsemen Publications, Inc.
PO Box 417
Sylva, NC 28779
4horsemenpublications.com
info@4horsemenpublications.com

Cover Illustration by Oxford
Cover Typography & Typesetting by Autumn Skye
Typeset Design Niki Tantillo
Edited by Joseph Mistretta

Library of Congress Control Number: 2025939732

Paperback ISBN-13: 979-8-8232-0908-3
Hardcover ISBN-13: 979-8-8232-0909-0
Audiobook ISBN-13: 979-8-8232-0911-3
Ebook ISBN-13: 979-8-8232-0910-6

DEDICATION

As always, Special thanks to our Patrons and 4 Horsemen Publications.

Special thanks to Bayou Pen 2 Paper for all your helpful insight!

And as always, thanks to our DeviantArt, and IRL followers. You're what keeps us going! Keep following the Northwest Passage with us!

THE UNIVERSE OF
WILD SPACE SAGA
Jakarta's Pride
Icona
Hemlock IV
Xiao
SECOND IMPERIUM
Knives of Blair
Dionysus Major/ Minor
DISPUTED ZONE
Tantagel I
FELYAN EMPIRE
Tophanavar
An're'hara

MAELSTROM
NEBULA

Hana IV

Holsk

Haven

Mandela I

Siberna

Dorado

Sepra

Zade

lo
ridian

Columbus

Zynj

Beauvior
III

COLONIAL
ALLIANCE

Bartholomew VII

TABLE OF CONTENTS

PROLOGUE

XIAO: XING YENG DISTRICT, UPPER LEVELS, FUJI 29 PROCESSOR TOWER

Snow leaned against the steel railing and looked out at the pale blue sky above. It was a rare clear day on Xiao and the sprawling continent-sized city was bathed in the pale light of its nearby star.

Actually, "City" was a loose term; Dì Yi Chéng was more a collection of settlements built onto the sides of mountain-sized atmosphere processors that kept the former moon habitable. In the sky, Snow could make out the tumbling pieces of the planet Xiao Prime, destroyed during the centuries-ago Imperium Wars.

Snow's moment was interrupted as her wrist comm buzzed. She didn't even look at it; she knew who it was and what they wanted. Turning away from the view of the immensity of metal and concrete, Snow headed through a narrow corridor toward the inner parts of the level, marveling along the way at how the areas she walked through could look so ramshackle considering they were attached to one of the most advanced pieces of technology in the galaxy.

As she exited the tunnel, the area opened out into a large atrium lined with shops and cafes, Snow's white eyes fixed on her destination, a noodle bar about 30 meters away. Through the window, she spotted him waiting. She ran a hand through her white, almost translucent hair and sighed. She had hoped to arrive first and get something to eat before having to talk business.

Absently, she scratched at the tattoos on her forearm: simple Greek symbols, each representing a kill, as well as the target's importance. Snow was a tank and, like most Imperial soldiers, had distinctive paper-white skin and a muscular build. However, she was cursed, born a 'blank' where a quirk of the random sequencing process meant her entire genetic code had been set to a default of some kind. It meant that along with her skin, Snow's hair, irises, and even the inside of her mouth were as devoid of color as an ancient early-generation cathode ray tube display. She was fairly certain her organs were white, too.

Steeling herself and shaking her mind from its self-piteous reverie, Snow entered the noodle bar and sat down opposite the man who waited there. He was always in that damned suit with never a mark or scuff anywhere to be seen on it. Snow could not have looked more different, wearing a simple rainbow tie-dyed t-shirt, khaki shorts, and, like most tanks, a solid-looking pair of combat boots.

She took a seat opposite the man and nodded. He gestured to a device on the table that appeared to be plugged into his neck via a thin cable. Another identical cable was attached to the side that faced her. Snow brushed her hair away from her right ear, revealing one of her cranial interface sockets just above it. Deftly, she removed the protective cap and plugged the cable in.

Snow picked up the menu on the table in front of her and studied it as their conversation began. Direct neural links would make it as private as possible, free of wireless networks that could be hacked. To an outside observer, they would appear to be sitting in total silence.

Good morning, Snow. How have you been? The words took on a sound in Snow's head, and she frowned. Agent Four always insisted on this senseless small talk, and she wished he would get to the point.

Straight to business, huh? Four shook his head and smiled, her emotions coming across the neural connection as clearly as his words had. *After all these years, I thought you'd have learned to loosen up a little.*

Just because I focus on the task at hand doesn't mean I have totally disregarded the things you taught me, she said, rolling her eyes, *but there is a time and place, and this is not it.*

Very well then. Snow felt Four's amusement through the connection. *To business.*

Images formed in Snow's mind. Images of a slender, white-haired young woman with piercing blue eyes. Each image depicted her in various black coats and outfits. These flashed in sequence across Snow's vision.

Kumiko? Snow said. *I know of her.*

You should, Four replied. *She's a tertiary. Child prodigy of Subject 182.*

Snow's eyes widened. *The survivor of the Blair incident?* She then started to giggle quietly. If he had been about to ask her to do what she thought, then the galaxy truly had gone mad. *You're joking. This is one your 'wind ups,' right?*

To her chagrin, Four's face remained impassive.

She's become a threat to the security of the Imperium. ISID has learned that through a form of alien technology, she can travel instantaneously to any point in the galaxy just by willing it. You can imagine how that makes those at the top nervous.

And what do you expect me to do? Snow said, unable to do much else but fix him with an incredulous glare. *This is the most powerful psion known across the entirety of the Colonial regions. And much of that is thanks to your agency friends' experiments on her mother. Wouldn't your blue-haired friend be more suited to this task?*

For the first time, Four returned her gaze.

That is precisely why she is unsuited for this task. No one can get close. Your skills as a sniper are uniquely suited for this.

Snow placed the menu flat on the table and stared at Agent Four, a part of her still unwilling to believe that he was actually serious. A few moments passed before she decided to respond.

This is a bit of a reach even for the Imperium, she said at last. *Frostbyte is not just high profile; she's on the Felyan High Command payroll. This could precipitate a war.*

So, you've done your research.

Agent Four tilted his head, still expressionless, but he was clearly impressed, especially with how she addressed Kumiko by her nom de guerre.

I keep tabs on potential targets, Snow said, eyeing Four suspiciously. *You know that.*

Four snapped his fingers. *Aha, so you have a strategy for this target!*

I might have worked out a potential plan. Snow shrugged, leaning back in her chair and folding her arms. *It's not exactly watertight, though. Kumiko's abilities create a lot of variables that cannot be completely accounted for, after all.*

That seemed to be all that Four needed to come to his conclusion.

So, you accept the mission?

Snow only gave a knowing look.

TOPHANAVAR: TERTIARY HANGAR BAY, *RECKLESS*

From the day that wily pirate blood came into her life, then pursued her until, partly out of ardent passion, partly out of sheer exhaustion, she'd agreed to become Mrs. Paraska, Neela had learned that ordinary was a word that would no longer define her life. But even their most outrageous happenstances always felt like controlled chaos of a sort with her husband at the reins. Today, however, she began to believe that things had truly gotten out of hand.

Falling asleep without him beside her in bed was not uncommon whenever he would pull late nights with the crew on *Imani*, or if he was out drinking with friends or family. But rare were the times that she woke up without him there. And even then, she would usually find him asleep like an alley cat on the scaffolding in the hangar, or in his office. But today, he was absent from even those places.

"And you're sure none of your crew saw him yesterday?" Neela asked Paige. The look of the *Shadow Star* captain was just as concerned as hers was, which was of some comfort. At least Neela knew she wasn't alone in her worry. Alexa's unbridled confidence and reassurances during their communication had been almost irritating.

"Not since yesterday," Paige said. "My crew and I took the opportunity for downtime after all the business with the Doctor and her copycats, just like you. Last I saw of him was when we went our separate ways. I've been aboard the ship since then, and my crew hasn't seen him either. I'd help you look, but we've just packed up *Tiberius* and are getting ready to head off. We have business on Dorado and then we're headed back to Siberna to drop off *Tiberius* in Pit Town. And even Pip has her hands full right now, so I can't spare anyone." She then snapped her fingers. "Oh, but Xerx did shoot me a message last night. He asked me to keep a look out for a ship."

"Oh, yes, *that* ship," Neela said, recalling her discussion with Alexa, and then Rinkya and Rati, who had first informed him about the vessel that shouldn't exist: the one that her husband's escaped quarry had fled Tophanavar in. Small wonder that he had sent out a message to Paige and Alexa to keep an eye out for it, in spite of the fact that the Doctor had most likely long since ditched it. But that had been the extent of info they'd had for her husband. Neither their cousins nor the Pirate Queen had seen him since yesterday, either. Mobola, Pepper, and Var had been with her at the Purring Princess the last time she'd seen him, while

Salt had sneaked off with that bartender, Ti'Niya—no surprise there. But even he hadn't seen him when he returned to the *Reckless* that morning, and neither had Ti'Niya, who had been with him all night. It was too early to file a missing person report, but Neela would not have wanted to do that unless she truly suspected foul play. Besides, Xerx was too resourceful to let himself get kidnapped.

She hoped.

"I see," Neela said. She let out a sigh that expressed anything but relief.

"I'm sure he's all right," Paige said. "Besides, think of all the times he's found himself in a spot. He'll probably be back looking like a cat that had been in a fight and lost at least two of his nine lives."

"I hope so," Neela said. She tried to sound optimistic in spite of Paige's false confidence, but she couldn't help but shake the feeling that something had happened. "Thanks anyway; I'll keep you posted."

"Please do; I dread to think what trouble Chook has got himself into now," Paige said before the comm ended.

Pushing back her fear of something more serious, she leaned against the railing that lined the captain's dais. Closing her eyes, she steadied her breathing and ran her hand across the top of her head and down to the back, then along the texture of her single thick braid. Mobola was busy accessing backdoor subroutines and camera feeds across the colony, but Tophanavar wasn't small, and she wasn't a tech tank like Pip, who would have been a big help right about now. Even Salt, Pepper, and Var, who were busy securing *Imani*, would only be able to do so much. That left Neela to figure out what to do next.

Xerx had always been the better one at making plans. She was always the better one at running a tight ship with her crew. Now she was the one who needed to plan something, and she was struggling just to keep it together and not worry.

Neela turned around, ready to sit down and try to settle her nerves, when Mobola's voice startled her back to stressed alertness.

"What was that?" she asked, more than a little confused and overwhelmed.

"I said that we have a visitor," Mobola said, speaking up from her station below. "It's Tyger. He's comming us from outside the *Reckless*. And he's got someone with him."

"Tyger Ral?" Neela said, not quite understanding why he would be here, and not aboard his team transport.

"It ... looks that way," Mobola said, her voice faltering, as if she thought that she'd said something wrong. "Should I let him in? He says he needs a lift."

"To where?" Neela asked.

"To An'Re'Hara."

Perhaps Xerx's disappearance was making her antsy, but Neela found something off about pretty much everything here. After all, come to think of it, Tyger had his own ship, didn't he?

"Put him on the main holo," she said.

The standard stat monitors vanished partly, replaced with a view of the *Reckless'* landing gear, and two figures standing beside it. Instantly, the image switched to a close-up, revealing Tyger, holding a satchel slung over his shoulder. He was one of the more unusual hybrids that Neela knew; he never seemed to change or age, with his shaggy brown fur and black slicked-back hair. And that fur-lined leather jacket made him look more like a refugee from a space gypsy fleet than a champion Gestalt pilot. Standing beside him was someone whom Neela had not seen in a long time, but whose presence at Tyger's side was anything but surprising. Akiko was a tank, like the triplets in Paige's crew, but with strange black scars in circuitry patterns marring the monochrome gray skin of nearly the entire left side of her face, making even her sclera a disturbing black surrounding her intensely blue iris. She tried to hide it behind her banded black and white dreadlocks but to little effect.

"I see you have your better half with you," Neela said after having Mobola open the comm to the bridge. "What's wrong? Paige wouldn't let her aboard?"

A wide grin crossed Tyger's muzzle as he glanced at Akiko, who wore a confused look. "I figured you'd find it weird that I wasn't taking off with them," he said, "but truth is, I'm not going back to Siberna. I'm going to see my mom."

"And the *El Tigre*?" Neela asked, inquiring about his eponymous Mallethead. She hadn't seen the ship when they'd arrived at Tophanavar, but she supposed that he'd docked with the *Shadow Star* somewhere along the way. Wasn't it built for long-range travel?

"Back on Siberna as well," Tyger said, rolling his eyes. "My dad made a lot of mods to the ship, one of which was a Takome condenser. Efficient as hell, but they only make 'em on Hana IV. Couldn't get it in time for the tourney, and Paige wasn't going my way afterward. I ran into Alexa, and fortunately, her royal pain-in-my-ass was nice enough to tell me that you guys were headed to An'Re'Hara. Thankfully, she didn't want her usual 'payment' for the info."

It was as she figured. Tyger's reputation as the Pirate Queen's favorite reluctant "boy toy" was well-established in the Gi. He always tried, with varying degrees of success, to stay scarce whenever she was in heat—which explained why he was nowhere to be found until his match against her Gestalt, *Steel Dragon*, and why he had been so unusually aggressive during the actual fight. In better times, she might have found it amusing.

"And your shadow?" Neela said, gesturing toward Akiko, aware that the visual communication was only one-way.

"Why are you questioning Tyger in such a fashion? Are you not friends, like he suggested?" the tank asked testily. But Tyger gave a placating gesture.

"Happy coincidence," he said. "I was headed here; Aki heard I was on Tophanavar and came looking for me. Turns out that we happen to be going the same way."

Neela let out a breath, realizing how she must have sounded to both of their potential guests. At the same time, she felt a sense of shame in the back of her mind unnecessarily playing inquisitor. Xerx hadn't been missing for even a day.

"Sorry about that," Neela said. "I've ... been on edge. Come aboard; we can discuss fare." She nodded toward Mobola, who deactivated the outside security protocols. As she did so, the comm beeped once more.

"It's from An'Re'Hara," Mobola said.

"Probably Izz checking in on us," Neela said, a knot forming in her stomach. She'd dreaded this.

"No, not from Isibar," Mobola said. "The code says it's ... coming from the royal palace?"

"*What?*"

"Should I put it on main holo?" Mobola asked. Neela nodded back.

"Hi, *Kipenzi*."

Unbelievably, it was her husband.

Impossibly, he was on An'Re'Hara. Neela's jaw hung open wide.

"*Kidege?*"

"*How?*" Mobola spoke the word that hung between both of them.

"Spin up the drive and set a course for An'Re'Hara," Xerx said as Kumiko stepped into view. At least she now knew why Akiko was headed to the Felyan homeworld. "Have I got a story to tell you!"

TWO

AN'RE'HARA: ROYAL PALACE

Xerx, having finally been able to contact his wife and crew, exhaled as the last of his peace of mind winnowed away his former frustration and worry. Despite him not yet fully knowing the reason why Kumiko had spirited him away to An'Re'Hara, Neela seemed to have accepted it overall, though she had not been happy about it—not that he'd expected her to be. He didn't blame her. But according to Kumiko, answers would come soon enough. The young silver-haired girl was taciturn, but not stupid.

It didn't make the wait for learning this reason any more annoying, however.

Now, with a moment to breathe, he took in An'Re'Hara's almost seamless amalgamation of natural beauty and contoured architecture in his surroundings, mixed with a near-overload of pleasant scents. Despite the few times that he'd visited, he always saw the Felyan homeworld as something as close to paradise as a planet could get. Even the Royal Palace, formed from asteroids brought into the lower atmosphere and maintained by modulated antigravs, used no planetary land resources, remaining a floating archipelago of terraformed gardens above a garden world.

Minarets stood like towers amidst terraced rivers and ponds, arched over with miniature suspension bridges, all wreathed with hedges and vines surrounding willow-like trees with leaves that shimmered in hues that few Colonial plants could match, where flocks of spotted *deekl* swam and fluttered, flapping their butterfly-like wings as they swooped in to catch fishlike creatures in the water.

He wondered if Felyans knew exactly how blessed they were with such an unspoiled world. Shepherded by the enigmatic Vlissians from a time when they were still hunting with spears and arrows, they'd been safely guided away from their baser tendencies, while human history was etched in rivers of blood, ultimately leading to the overcrowding and environmental strains on old Earth that forced the Great Exodus to the Colony worlds, and then the devastation of the Imperium Wars of two centuries ago. One trip to An'Re'Hara was all it took for any human to see that there was a distinctive difference between their respective worlds—many still recovering from that time of madness—and the planet the Felyans called home. Even the most beautiful images of lost Earth couldn't compare to a world like this.

"You know, it seems that just about every human I encounter here ends up standing around like you, mouth agape, catching flies," Kumiko said, approaching from behind. "Is it really that fascinating?"

Slowly, Xerx looked away from his meditative spot, fixing the silver-haired woman with an unreadable expression.

"I sometimes wonder if you're the single most jaded woman in all the Colonies," the captain of the *Reckless* said, giving a rueful shake of his head. "I mean, New Kyoto's meditation gardens might come vaguely close to this, but even Hana IV is no An'Re'Hara."

"And I wonder how you don't get tired of it," Kumiko replied, her tone dispassionate, as if she truly was as eternally bored as she sounded. She shrugged, as if he'd just told her about the water being wet, then inclined her head, gesturing to the largest building. "The Empress is ready to see us. Did you get hold of your wife?"

"Yes, and as I said to you before, she doesn't like surprises," Xerx said, pushing himself from the bridge's wood and marble railing. He then followed Kumiko as she led the way. "And she especially didn't like me not knowing exactly why you brought me here. And neither do I, for that matter."

"I'm sure she'll understand," Kumiko said, "as will you, soon enough."

"Just like I had to 'understand' when I was forced to wait until ten minutes ago for the palace to connect me to a secure channel to my ship after I've been here half the day?" Xerx asked, buoyed on a note of annoyance that he'd kept a tight lid on until now. "What is it with royalty and secrecy, anyway? I mean, Alexa has cloaked bodyguards with her nearly everywhere she goes, even though most folks are scared shitless of her. And by the way, I still need to get hold of Izz and his family."

"You're rambling," Kumiko answered, not looking back. "And you can ask the Empress about all that."

"I just wish you wouldn't leave me in the dark."

"I didn't."

"You said you needed me for a top-secret mission, and that was it."

"So you see? I didn't leave you in the dark."

"Not funny."

"Who said I was joking?" Kumiko said, her usual deadly serious expression unchanged.

"It's always hard to tell with you," Xerx said, heaving a loud sigh. "And yes, I know that you aren't at liberty to say any more about this 'mission.'"

"I expect you'd know this by now," Kumiko said.

"Kinda hard not to." Xerx frowned. "I'm beginning to feel like I can read *your* mind too."

"Who knows?" Kumiko replied. "If you shut your mouth long enough, you might actually hear my thoughts after all."

"Why Kumiko Zero," Xerx said in mock surprise, "I do believe you actually made a joke!"

Kumiko paused, still facing only their moon and lantern-lit path. Then a moment later, resumed walking.

"I do actually have a sense of humor," she said. This time, there was a vague quality in her voice that betrayed something that sounded almost like hurt. "Once, mum even said I smiled."

A sly smile crept across Xerx's face. "Come on, now. What about Remli?"

Again, she paused, a shudder passing though her.

"How did you know that name?"

Her question came out with the sharpness of one whose nerve had been touched.

"It was—"

"Tyger."

Kumiko, having clearly read his mind as tertiaries were wont to do with surface thoughts, whispered her half-Felyan father's name in a brittle tone, as if she were holding back disgust. He knew that she didn't exactly see eye to eye with the eccentric man, and for reasons that both he and Tyger had agreed were fairly petty. But both he and Kumiko were adults, and this spat was something that Xerx was happy to stay out of.

"You know your dad's a storyteller," Xerx said. "He'd pick up on it sooner or later."

"He's not that sensitive," Kumiko said. "He shouldn't have picked up on ... private things."

Private indeed. Based on what Tyger had once told him over a pint back on Siberna, Remli, some Felyan pleasure boy on Haven, was the closest thing to a boyfriend that Kumiko had once had. Emphasis on *was*. Though that was all he knew. Private things, like this clearly was, tended to be associated with strong emotions, so there was little surprise that even Tyger could pick up on this. Still, Xerx felt that he'd crossed a line.

"I see it's personal," Xerx said, contrite. "I won't say anything more about it."

There was another long, silent pause, then Kumiko answered in a quiet voice.

"Thank you."

With the exception of Kumiko informing him that the building where they were headed was the palace keep, the rest of the trip there was uneventful, allowing

Xerx to once again be caught up in the beauty that surrounded him. An'Re'Hara had two moons, Erufi and Kela: the former terraformed to a habitable state, and the latter a rust-red airless ball, like Siberna's three satellites, but below the surface lay extensive subterranean mining cities. Both shone bright and full in the night sky, making the lanterns' light superfluous.

All the palace guards he spotted were *Hara'Kya* Felyans, Xerx noticed as the sleek shapes prowled the ground on all fours in scant armor and personal force fields. Two of them standing at the entrance rose to two feet upon their approach. A set of spears extended from a device they held in their hands, similar to the vajra weapons that Imperial tanks carried. They stood before a massive door, which appeared to be made of some kind of wood, with a portrayal of Felyans on a ritual hunt, led by an icon of Trisii, their patron saint, carved into its façade. Xerx paused at the sight, noting its level of detail with some surprise. As far as he knew, Felyan icons of their patron saint rarely portrayed her in any way beyond the most generic, as to show respect to her memory and not her image, but this carving was a grand exception to the rule, featuring a beautiful *Re'Kya* in flowing robes and a bow without arrows, flanked by *An'Kya* disciples, and guiding a pack of *Hara'Kya* through a forest to a deer-like animal that had been caught in vines by its antlers. It shared the theme of peaceful acquisition common to Felyan iconography, and Xerx could not help but be curious as to how old it was.

The door opened with a swiftness that belied its size and thickness, and Kumiko led him inside. Beyond, everything seemed to stop with a single room, with walls of white.

"Her majesty bids you welcome," the guards said in unison, speaking in Felyan.

"I humbly accept the invitation," Xerx replied along with Kumiko, as she had coached him after their arrival.

"Recognition: Kumiko Zero," a digitized voice said as they passed across the threshold. "Recognition: Xerxes Paraska, Thane of House Paraska. Destination: audience room."

Xerx raised an eyebrow at his formal title: something he had not heard since the last time he'd visited Rhoma nearly fifteen years ago, as the court heralds announced him at his cousin Iriid's coronation and wedding to Alexa.

"So we walked through a castle door into a ... closet?" Xerx said, nonplussed at what appeared to be a dead end. But right on the tail end of his question came the sound of some kind of turbine cycling. The light in the room, at the same time, grew brighter.

"Close your eyes," Kumiko said, and Xerx obeyed. At once, the noise rose to a crescendo, as the light beyond shone bright enough to shine through his eyelids. Suddenly, there was a thunderclap—or perhaps it was the sound of a balloon popping through a stadium speaker set at maximum. Immediately afterward, the turbine died down amidst a ringing in his ears that quickly died away.

Kumiko let Xerx know that he could open his eyes. The light was now significantly lower, but there was enough to make his dramatically changed surroundings visible. The floor was still white and shone with the same inner light as the room from before, but before him now was a hallway with a series of what appeared to be wooden columns rising from grooves cut in the ground, appearing like tree trunks. They even branched out near the ceiling, but their boughs ran in geometric patterns, converging on orbs of light set at intervals into the ceilings and upper walls. At the end of this grand hallway was another set of doors with a symbol etched into it that Xerx did not recognize.

"Did we just use a teleporter?" Xerx asked.

"There are too many rooms in the palace keep to make stairs and lifts practical, except for outside the building," Kumiko said as she led the way down the corridor. "Teleporters are easier."

"You could've just teleported us here yourself, couldn't you?" Xerx said. Kumiko shook her head.

"I've been there before, but I don't know exactly where 'there' is, inside the castle. I could still teleport there, using the Vlissian map I absorbed, but it would be more difficult." She then gave a small shrug. "Besides, there's the subject of manners to consider. If I did it that way, it would just be rude."

"Good point," Xerx said, feeling no small sense of disquiet over the level of technology the Felyans could so casually wield to move people around rooms in a building. He eyed the edges of the hallway, which appeared to be glass, but as he and Kumiko passed them by, he noticed that inside were entire water ecosystems, with plants and swimming things that resembled a combination of fish and snake. They cast rippling patterns of shadow and light on the walls, giving a peaceful, almost meditative quality to his surroundings.

"Do you remember what to do when you meet the Empress?" Kumiko asked as they reached the door.

"Yes," Xerx said, his tone betraying his impatience. "It's not my first time around royalty."

"Indeed, but that royalty was your own family," Kumiko replied. "They give you some leeway. A faux pas here would be far more embarrassing. And the Empress is a stickler for protocol, especially for new guests. So, mind your P's and Q's."

"Yes, mom," Xerx drawled, already somewhat nervous enough about this impending meeting, but hearing Kumiko's tone of voice betray an apprehension of her own made him want to add levity to the situation. But the silver-haired girl's reaction revealed that she was less than impressed with the reply. She made a flicking motion with her finger, and Xerx received the sharp sensation of someone plucking him on the forehead.

"Snide remarks are right out," she said. Then she paused, and did something rare: something that tertiaries hardly ever did, except in very intimate moments. Turning fully around, she took him by the hands, physically touching him.

"Xerx, *please*." Her expression softened into a look of actual concern. "The Empress has placed a great deal of trust in me to even mention this to you. You know Felyans don't have the best relationship with pirates, so think of the pride she has to swallow for this."

Xerx only stared, stricken. This was about as close to pleading as he'd ever seen Kumiko get. And she *never* pleaded. Whatever this was all about, to have dragged him all the way from Tophanavar, leaving his crew to find their way here on their own, made him realize that this was more than just important.

"I'll be on my best behavior," he said, his words spoken with as much earnestness as he could muster. And this seemed to set Kumiko at ease. Even her permanent case of resting bitch face had relaxed to the point where he could see that she was actually human.

As if sensing the conclusion to their conversation, the featureless wooden doors ahead of them swung open, this time slowly, as if they were truly made with the dense wood they appeared to be constructed from. The light inside was the same as that in the hallway, except the chamber beyond was circular, and the rows of tree-like columns wove their geometric branches into formations that resembled a massive chandelier laden with bunches of the glowing orbs. At its far end, on a dais, stood a black-haired human that Xerx was surprised to actually recognize from newscasts of years ago. He wore a spotless green three-piece suit, along with the maroon sash of an Alliance emissary. Alongside him was a throne of wood that Xerx would have thought grew out of the room's floor, had it not been for the lovely arrangement of stained-glass panels at its back.

Upon the throne sat the Empress, holding an infant in a blue quilted blanket.

THREE

Though Neela maintained a smiling outer image, she could not help but feel especially drained when speaking with Tyger. Oddly enough, however, his tendency to slip into his usual tall tales about his past or his late father's exploits helped to put her somewhat better at ease for a change. Perhaps it was the comforting regularity of it all. Still, she suspected that Tyger was at least nonplussed that he hadn't been met with her usual reply of "not right now, Tyger," once he'd begun his yarn about the time he'd evaded a clawbeast in Sepra's deep jungles while trying to pilfer wild dilkin pods for a client. And, as usual, neither she nor Tyger—nor Akiko, for that matter—could recall exactly where he'd gone off on that tangent.

Oh, wait.

"So, the price is fine?" Neela asked once the chatty hybrid had wrapped things up. She opened the deposit function on her credstick and Tyger transferred his funds.

"More than adequate," Tyger said, shrugging his backpack more securely on his shoulders. His long tail wrapped securely around Akiko's waist, and Neela suppressed a grin, knowing that they'd be mostly pre-occupied during the journey, as little as they saw of each other. "And yours was a pretty interesting story, if I do say so myself."

"Little surprise that it was dear Kumi involved," Akiko said. Neela suppressed a bemused expression. Kumiko was perhaps more of a free spirit than she believed even her mother knew.

"Wait. How can it not surprise you?" Neela asked, considering the tank's tone of voice.

"We run into her at the uncanniest times," Tyger said. "Trust me, this is far less surprising for us than it is for you. Like that time when—"

"Not now, my furry fighter," Akiko said. She pressed a finger to Tyger's lips, much to Neela's relief. She patted her sizeable luggage bag slung across her chest. "I'd like us to find our quarters, so we can shrug off this weight and relax." She absently stroked Tyger's tail, which still encircled her waist.

"No doubt you do," Neela said, and flashed them an understanding grin. "Since my husband is, of course, indisposed, I'll have to bring you to your quarters. Let's just get the ship off the ground and on the way, alright?" She then switched on the comm. "Salt, is *Imani* secured?"

"Var and I are finishing up the last of the locking clamps now," the older Felyan replied amidst a background noise of massive servos. "Should be done in a minute or two."

"Good. How are the engines, Pepper?"

"Singing like a choir," Pepper answered. "Hyperdrive's on standby, waiting to get us on our way."

"Once your father is finished with loading *Imani*, we'll be go for takeoff," Neela said, more eager to be reunited with her husband than she believed any of her crew were eager just to be on the proverbial road again. "Standby."

The loading manifold was secure as anything, but the last few locks, for their sheer size, often felt like they took forever, Salt thought as the frame moved over *Imani*'s house-sized ankles with glacial inexorability. But eventually, the resounding *clack* that he could feel in his sternum resounded through the main hangar, signifying that the Gestalt was at last fully secure. And not a second too soon, as Var loped over to his side, then stood upright.

"We good here, Kyori?" Var asked.

"Good as it'll ever be," Salt replied. "All the small stuff's secured?"

"If there's a cabinet or drawer that isn't, we'll know after takeoff," Var said.

"Don't jinx it, now."

Var hacked out a sandpapery laugh before heading off to the comm console to inform Neela. He could relate to how anxious she was to get this tub moving to where her lifemate was. Like Neela, before Alsai had passed, he always had the feeling of distance between himself and his lifemate when they were apart.

He felt the vibrations of the *Reckless'* engines starting up just when his personal comm signaled an incoming caller. The ship swayed gently as it rose through the orbital shaft, inertial suppressors not having yet kicked in, and Salt kept himself steady as he switched the device on.   The image in the holo was just the person whom he'd been thinking about.

"Hey there," he said, feeling an almost boyish glee at the sight of her. And he could see the smile on her slightly graying muzzle that seemed to hold back a combination of nervousness and longing.

"Hi." Ti'Niya spoke softly, even meekly.

"I'm glad you called," Salt said. "It's a shame we couldn't hang out longer, but I'll be sure to try and get back whenever I can scrounge some vacation time."

Ti'Niya's smile broadened, and she looked away, her red-orange fur concealing any blush she might have had. Salt found himself longing for that flash of increased warmth in her touch, which now seemed to be on the other side of the universe.

"Maybe you won't have to," she said.

"You planning on visiting me first?" Salt said, hopeful, but keeping his voice from betraying the burst of hope he felt at that possibility.

"Maybe."

"A little secretive, are we?" he said, not fully under-standing, but loving her playfulness nevertheless.

"Let's say that I might miss you even more than you miss me," Ti'Niya said.

"Enough to cross half of known space for a visit when I get back to Siberna?"

"We'll see."

With no further explanation, she leaned forward into the image and cast Salt a coquettish wink, her tongue half-sticking out of her mouth.

"You're still quite busy, aren't you?" she asked.

"Not as busy as I was a few minutes ago," Salt said.

"But still busy?"

"Sort of," Salt admitted, knowing that it was actually best not to linger on a personal comm during takeoff. He flashed a sad smile.

"I'll leave you to your work for now," Ti'Niya said. She brushed her hand up against nothing, as if touching an invisible window between them.

"I miss you already," Salt said.

"I miss you more."

They were reaching the end of the launch shaft and would be joining Tophanavar's orbital traffic soon. In the background, Neela could hear Tyger regaling Akiko about An'Re'Hara, which she had never visited, in spite of her keeping with space hippie fleets. She tended to go where the work was, and the fleets found better business hopping around the Alliance, and sometimes the holdings of the Second Imperium, if their laws weren't too restrictive. This was one of the few times that she saw the dreadlocked tank actually captivated by Tyger's stories. But enough tall tales were told of the Felyans' Edenic homeworld to make those whose only experience of it being through StellarNet videos and cybersims wonder if these truly did it justice.

"Orbital traffic reached," Pepper said over the ship's comm. "Skies are clear; intertial suppressors engaged; setting a trajectory for An'Re'Hara in twenty."

"Wait!" Mobola nearly squeaked out the word as a sharp miniature klaxon sounded from her console. "All stop! A ship just appeared on sensors. It's … de-cloaking?"

Neela felt the ship give a slight lurch as Pepper responded to Mobola's exclamation. Even inertial suppressors could only do so much with an emergency stop out of a hyperspace trajectory. She heard Tyger and Akiko give a yelp. Out of the corner of her eye, she saw Akiko, being the more sure-footed of their two guests, grab Tyger by his tail, breaking what would have been a nasty tumble. Over the comm, Salt and Pepper's voices spoke over each other, basically asking variations of what the hell was going on.

"I'm so sorry!" Mobola said, then swallowed against apologizing even more profusely. "It's just that it appeared right on top of us."

"Is it still in front of us?" Neela asked, now more than a little miffed at this sudden turn of events that seemed to be preventing the expediency of her being reunited with her husband. Mobola nodded, and without waiting for an order, put the image up on the main holo.

Neela clutched the railing at the dais' edge just a bit more tightly as the image appeared.

Quandisa's massive blue-violet sphere dominated the view as a cacophony of sparks erupted over what seemed like nothing. Then, seemingly right above their heads, the sleek hull and ring-shaped hyperspace drive of a Felyan Cruiser appeared before them. Like a mirror, it seemed to reflect the black of space and the swirling colors of the gas giant's atmosphere, along with the harsh unfiltered glint of the system's main star.

"So the fleet ships weren't hiding after all," Tyger remarked with an approving noise. "They were here the whole time."

"I thought it was strange that they were nowhere to be found at first," Akiko added. "We're at the Empire's front door, after all."

"They're hailing us," Mobola announced. Neela then stepped over to the console beside the captain's chair and switched on the comm herself.

Before she could speak, a loud voice broke out over the speakers.

"Breaker nine-nine, this is the cruiser Ol' Furball's Revenge hollering at ya with the hand of friendship. Come back."

"Uh, what?" Neela blinked, confusion creeping across her face. It seemed like they were trying to approximate the CB lingo that had grown popular among Alliance and pirate ships, but speaking the words in Felyan made it damn near unintelligible.

"Felyan vessel, this is Neela Eweke Paraska of the *Reckless*," Neela managed to reply, composing herself. A slight shake lingered in her voice due to her scant experience with this. Xerx had helped her to become familiar with the controls, but she was not normally gregarious with strangers. "Identify yourself. Why have you blocked our exit trajectory?"

"What? No Old Earth lingo?" A gruff voice sounded over the comm, now speaking in Alliance standard. "That's something of a disappointment."

Neela had been about to reply but heard someone hiss faintly in the background, then say something in a reproachful tone. Her grasp of the Felyan language wasn't quite as good as her husband's, but she knew a few rather unpleasant words in that conversation. When the voice (male, and with a slight accent and very jocular tone) spoke again, it was a bit more formal and subdued.

"Warship *Reckless* of the First Imperium, please accept my sincere apologies. This is the Felyan Imperial cruiser *And'Arra's Vengeance*. Please power down your engines. As of now, we're placing you and your vessel into our custody."

Snow stood at yet another handrail, this time overlooking the gargantuan docking station near the top of the city stack attached to the atmospheric processor. She'd stopped off on her way to port and changed into a black and gray skintight flight suit that she wore underneath a baggy white t-shirt emblazoned with a splash-style logo for Seascape Aquaculture Corp and a pair of long, dark green shorts.

Ships of all shapes and sizes moved in and out of the station. The larger vehicles lay docked in large bays like oversized honeycomb cells in a beehive. She watched as port crews swarmed over the myriad vessels like similarly insectile creatures. There was a loud, dull *clunk* as huge clamps released above her and a monstrous cargo vessel began to move slowly past, with multicolored cargo containers locked to its rust-colored, box-like hull. Snow sighed impatiently when finally, the light gray form of her own ship came into view. The *Hammerfall II* was a slab-sided beast. It was designated as a Tiger

Shark Assault Carrier, with a massive cargo door that dominated its forward section, which swept backward in an overhang. The aft section swept into four exhausts surrounding the cylindrical core and ridged sails of a rift hyperdrive, commonly used by Imperial military vessels. Its most notable features were the large swept "hammerhead" wings that flowed from the dorsal section of the hull, finishing fully halfway along its length. A tall fin stood proudly atop.

"Hello baby, did you miss me?" she said quietly. A grin started to crease the sides of her mouth as she began making her way toward it. As she approached, the maintenance crews were just finishing their removal of the various fuel and power umbilical lines, readying it for takeoff. She gave them a brief nod as they hurried past, exchanging anxious glances toward her before continuing on their way. Their behavior came as no surprise; the presence of a tank, even one not clad in her usual armor, made most Imperial citizens nervous. As military constructs, tanks were often a head taller than most standard humans and much more powerful. Here, on one of the Imperial core worlds, to see one dressed as Snow was, let alone be acknowledged in such a manner, must have been rare indeed.

Snow passed into the shadow cast by the *Hammerfall II*'s immense port side wing and approached an entrance hatch located near the forward section. She placed her hand on the biometric panel at its side and then pushed down the handle that emerged from the door. The door slid inward, and she stepped inside. She then paused, taking a deep breath and savoring the metallic, industrial smell of the hangar bay. As she moved further inside, lights began to turn on high above, bathing the bare metal walls of the bay in a stark white light.

High above, the angled walls of the observation deck provided an unobstructed view through large trapezoidal windows. Catwalks attached to the rear wall provided access via ladders set into the bulkhead. Halfway down was a mezzanine floor loaded with a number of lockers and weapons crates. On the hangar floor itself, multiple vehicles were secured underneath protective covers.

She turned and ran toward the nearest ladder. Moments later, in a rumble of antigravs the ship began to lift off the landing pad and moved toward the exit.

FOUR

The formal bow was an elegant, curtsey-like motion that surprisingly did not appear effeminate when Xerx performed it alongside Kumiko.

"Empress and protector of the sacred home, I stand at your service," both he and Kumiko recited, Inwardly, Xerx was thankful that Var, noting its possible necessity in their line of work, had taught him the rarely used, more formal dialect of the Felyan language.

"I congratulate you and your mate on a successful birth," Xerx added. "Blessings and health on the royal scion."

When the Empress said nothing at first, merely shifting somewhat in her chair, her dark gray tail twitching, Xerx thought with horror that he'd committed some kind of faux pas. Then, at last, she turned to face the man at her side.

"You were right, my *li-ah*," she said. "He did impress me."

"All because he knew protocol?" the man said, seeming to suppress a laugh.

"You'd be surprised at how many pirates I have invited who were not quite so courteous," the Empress answered, her voice betraying a tinge of remembered annoyance. "But this one even knew the formal recitation for congratulating a royal birth."

The infant in her arms squirmed, then yawned, falling back into her peaceful slumber. A slight impatience mixed within Xerx along with a hint of annoyance at her remark, but he kept stolidly silent as he waited to be addressed.

"Pirate royalty is a cut above the rest," the man said, giving a bemused expression, which seemed to put the Empress in better spirits.

"I no doubt imagine you're wondering why I had you dragged from the edges of my domain all the way to its heart?" the Empress said, at last speaking directly to Xerx.

Xerx, gave a vague shrug. "Her Majesty has her reasons."

"Let's not be too deferential now." The Empress shook her head, her tone cooling slightly, and Xerx suppressed a wave of embarrassment. He'd thought the question might have been some kind of political double entendre, but it seemed that the Empress was being genuine. "Nevertheless, I will get to the point. As you were on Tophanavar, you'd no doubt heard of our daughter?"

Xerx grinned, now more relaxed. "It was definitely hard to avoid the news."

"Did you know that she is the first hybrid of royal blood born since the arrival of humans to the Colonies?"

All expression fell from Xerx's face, coalescing into a look of genuine surprise.

"Actually, no. No, I didn't," he said. "I would have thought—"

"Ever since your arrival in this part of the galaxy, our relations with humans have been cordial, sometimes intimate, but never formal," the Empress said, then smiled at the infant in her arms. "Until now."

Her gaze then shifted back toward the human beside her, with a more intent look. Taking the cue, he stepped to the front of the dais. He was a familiar face, but Xerx still could not place from where. It was the kind of face that most would call handsome, but not in any way that particularly stood out: black hair and green eyes like Xerx, but of a darker complexion. Features were unmistakably Doradan, as was his Espyan accent. He momentarily paused to lift the sleeping child from her mother and take her into his arms. The entire time, she remained sleeping soundly.

Then it hit him.

"I don't know how closely you follow Alliance politics," he began, "but my name is—"

"Ramirez." Xerx nodded at the man's nonplussed expression. "I know who you are. Wasn't there kind of a big to-do on Dorado when you were elected to the Alliance embassy here?"

Ramirez gave a nod, seemingly pleased with his recognition. "My people don't trust Felyans as much as they do on most of the other Alliance worlds. I was the odd duck. Then I was assigned here, probably to keep me from ruffling any more feathers back home. And ... well, I fell in love." His smile widened as he sneaked a besotted look at the Empress. "The only thing I regretted about the whole affair was that we could never become lifemates."

"Yet you still had a kid?" Xerx said, phasing the question as a statement as to make it not seem accusatory. Ramirez nodded, thankfully unoffended.

"He calls it a 'fortunate opportunity,'" Kumiko said with a wry grin.

"The Alliance was making a push to bury the hatchet with the Empire at the time, and I participated in the negotiations to end the embargo of Felyan tech trading. The Empress agreed, provided we seal the deal in the traditional Felyan way." He gently stroked the tiny tuft of hair atop the sleeping baby's head. "And that was how our little Ki'Lari Isabella came to be."

"So you had a baby out of both love and political convenience?" Xerx said.

"As I said, it was a fortunate opportunity," Ramirez answered.

"That was how the trouble began," Kumiko said, at last speaking up. "There were demands for his recall after the news reached Dorado, but there wasn't much they could really do if he refused."

"Of course, I did refuse," Ramirez said. "The government knew that it wouldn't look good for them to remove me by force. But assassination ..."

"You seriously think your own people would assassinate you?" Xerx said. Doradans were notoriously prejudicial against Felyans, with many parts of their society being deeply religious to the point of believing human-alien crossbreeding to be akin to bestiality. But outright assassination of a government official who had more or less "gone native" was beyond the pale even for them.

"Not me," Ramirez said. "Our daughter."

"And the worst part is that no one really knows if it's the government who is behind it," Kumiko said.

"The first incident was when we intercepted an attempt to poison her food," the Empress said. "With hybrids' nutritional requirements, we were using chemical monitors at the time. They detected a lethal dose of *gerisk*, a neurotoxin found in a type of seaweed in our oceans. It has no effect on humans and only makes full-blood Felyans mildly ill. But most hybrids suffer lethal allergic reactions." She held the baby more closely to her breast, giving a faint shudder.

"I was in the neighborhood at the time, and they put me into their employ," Kumiko said. "I interrogated the kitchen staff, but no one had a clue as to who had tainted the food. That was when the second attack came: a targeted variance in the island's gravity field. But it was set off a second too early and launched the nanny into the air. She was badly injured from her fall, but survived. I checked the systems with the maintenance crew ... and that was when I sensed her."

"Wait. Sense? When she's long gone?" Xerx gave Kumiko a shrewd look. "If you can do that, and even tell her sex, then that means—"

"It's most likely she's a tertiary too," Kumiko said, her voice grim.

"Wait, wait," Xerx said, gesticulating emphatically. "If that's the case—and I hope to God that it's not—then that's kind of out of my league." Without waiting for a comment, he turned back to face Kumiko. "You didn't tell me you brought me here to play exterminator to a tertiary. You know that's above my level of expertise. The last one I faced—"

"We don't want you to exterminate her." Kumiko's words paused Xerx in his tracks. "You'll be taking her off-planet."

"Off-planet?" Xerx blinked, his brain doing a hard reset. "Isn't that a bit … well … extreme?"

"Not when circumstances line up so well for a cover story," Ramirez said. "We're scheduled for a peregrination to Tophanavar, where the Alliance government will be finalizing relations with the Empire as a formal end to the tech embargo. Considering the growing danger of the Second Imperium, this will give tremendous advantages to the Alliance not given before."

"And put you in the Imperum's crosshairs," Xerx said.

"They've dealt with the Imperium before," Kumiko assured him. "Let's just say that they learned the severity of their error. The Alliance has more to fear from them than the Empire does."

"Our child will be present as a symbol of our unity," the Empress said. "And as the future administrator of the colony, once terraforming is finished, the people of Tophanavar deserve to meet their future leader."

"Don't you think that the fanfare for all this might attract even more unwanted attention?" Xerx said.

"Only if we announce it," the Empress said.

"I see," Xerx said.

"Still, it most likely won't be a secret to the assassin, being a tertiary," Ramirez warned. "But we're hoping for that. And Kumiko is our ace in the hole."

"Not that I don't have confidence in Kumiko," Xerx said, shaking his head, "but taking out a tertiary … then containing her instead of just blowing her out an air-lock? That's still a big gamble."

"One we'll have to take," Kumiko said.

"You'll meet with the interim administrator once you arrive," the Empress said. "And your mission will be complete." She then frowned deeply, seeming to become very old as her next words came out with some reluctance.

"And ... as much as I don't want to do this, you will have to remain radio silent with us. Outside of your ship, this mission will be top secret."

"You won't be doing it alone, as you can see," Ramirez said with a smile that attempted to be reassuring. "And besides, my *li-ah* tells me that you faced a tertiary and lived. Is this true?"

"Barely," Xerx said. Not even Kumiko had known this; he was surprised that the Empress would have been aware of it. His mind went back to the harrowing moment, recalling that time when a rival ordinance company in Pit Town hired a tertiary for a hit on the prefect. Xerx saved the man's life, but not before being given the rag doll treatment by her telekinesis. He'd managed to squeeze off several rounds that she froze in midair before throwing him into a nearby car, but the distraction had allowed enough time for the local militia to come in and chase her off. The ensuing fight and her audacious escape had left several policemen and soldiers in the hospital and him most likely on her respective shit list as she fled the planet, but he hadn't seen or heard from her since, and the company that put out the hit was blacklisted from Siberna spaceports afterward. He was more than a little surprised that the news of this kerfuffle had made it all the way out to An'Re'Hara. That fight hadn't made him cocky enough to want another go at her, or any other tertiary for that matter, but in the midst of his worried musings, he took one good look at the Empress and envoy's baby. The sight of her managed to spin up a desire to protect her stronger than he'd ever felt for anyone, even Neela.

"Still, I guess I can try," he said, giving in. "But I'll need to know everything I can about this person, and any information you might have about her powers."

Xerx knew that he was asking a great deal with this last request, as this meant going to the Vlissians, who took in any tertiary, and were more tight-lipped about their individual talents than they were about anything. And they spoke about very little. But he had little choice. After all, getting caught with one's pants down at the business end of a tertiary was a good way to prove you were just plain tired of breathing.

"That won't be a problem," Kumiko said, to his initial surprise. She presented a holographic image from an emitter fitted on her right ring finger.

It faced him like a recurring nightmare.

It was her.

Shit, Xerx thought.

"Captain, I think you meant 'in our care.'"

This time, Neela could understand the words spoken by the background officer.

"And it is customary to send a visual greeting," the officer continued.

"Coming in on visual," Mobola announced, holding back a snicker. Neela assented, and the image of a blue-furred *Re'Kya* Felyan with a prominently graying muzzle appeared in the holos before her. He was smartly dressed in the black vest and purple sash of a Felyan captain, with a series of silver links hanging prominently from his left earlobe.

"Neela Paraska, I presume?" he said. For a Felyan of his age, his smile was disarmingly handsome.

"Interim captain of the *Reckless*," she said, inclining her head to the captain.

"Captain Ar'Kesi, at your service," the captain said. "We're here to provide an escort to the homeworld. You've been summoned by her majesty on important business."

"The Empress?" Tyger whispered.

"Now I wish that I had brought something better to wear," Akiko said.

"It would be an honor," Neela said. "But we are in no need of assistance there."

"It's a courtesy," the captain replied, shaking his head. "You're royal guests, and the palace changes location. And as the location is kept classified, we are the only ones who can guide you. Also, it will take you a couple of days at maximum power to reach the homeworld, but we have a better way."

"A ... better way?" Neela glanced at Mobola, and then, as if it would do any good, Tyger and Akiko, who both shrugged. She supposed that even if Tyger knew, he probably would be reticent to say anything, if it involved Felyan tech at all, which the otherwise gregarious race was notoriously secretive about, ever since the Imperium Wars, before which records stated that they shared a much open technological exchange with humanity.

"You'll see, my dear." The captain gave a wink and nodded to someone off-screen.

"We received coordinates," Mobola said. "They're on the far side of Quandisa."

Mobola eyed the gas giant in the holos that still portrayed the conditions outside the ship, with the monstrous uninhabitable world dominating much of the sight before them.

"No doubt you have reservations, Mrs. Paraska," the captain said, in a softer, more sincere tone. "But trust us. Your presence is required at the palace as soon as possible. And this will be the quickest way to get there. All your questions will be answered when you follow us."

For a moment, Neela wrestled with doubt, but not quite understanding why. Perhaps it was because of the fact that in spite of most Felyans' overt friendliness with humans, their line of work bred a certain level of distrust when it came to newcomers, especially of the military variety, no matter what faction. But in all fairness, there truly was no need to not trust this eccentric captain Ar'Kesi. Even his openness didn't seem out of the norm as Felyans went. Plus, it would get Tyger to his destination faster. Today's events had already taken a toll on her nerves. Was being distrustful yet another strange symptom of it all?

She'd be damned if she let that happen.

"Lead the way," she said.

"With pleasure," the captain replied. "You're about to have the pleasure of a ride few humans are invited on."

"Whatever that means," Neela muttered as the holo switched off. "Mobola, you have the course put in?"

"Doing it now," Mobola said, and the images shifted to a view of the *And'Arra's Vengeance's* aft engines as the *Reckless* followed along, passing kilometers as it rounded the gas giant away from Tophanavar's line of sight.

"Now do you know what that's all about?" Neela asked Tyger, unable to curb her curiosity.

"Not really," Tyger said. "One thing I really didn't experience much was the military back on An'Re'Hara." He then tilted his head. "Unless you count that one ensign I had a fling with on an orbital once. But she didn't tell me much about her job."

Neela laughed. "Every one of your stories involves a girl, you know."

"It's my curse," Tyger said with a shrug.

"Is it true?" Akiko's question sounded curious rather than jealous, to Neela's initial surprise. But then she supposed that being a tank, her upbringing was most likely something where relationships were a nonissue.

"Mostly an exaggeration," Tyger said.

"I just hope you were careful," Neela said, casting a look on the hybrid that bordered on reproach. "If even half your stories are true, I wouldn't be surprised if you found other wild oats you've sown aside from Kumiko out there."

"Wouldn't surprise me either." Tyger's shoulders shook as he made a soundless chuckle. "In fact, it surprises me even more that I haven't been served papers from some girl from some backwater hippie fleet that claims I'm her baby's daddy."

"You sound almost like you're proud of that," Neela said, unsure of what to think about what he'd just said.

"Not proud," Tyger assured her. "I've just made peace with it, is all." He then sighed, slipping his hand into Akiko's, his tone becoming wistful. "I just hope that if I do have any other happy accidents out there, they don't hate me."

"Kumiko *doesn't* hate you." There was just as deep a reassurance in the tank's tone as Tyger had previously given. Neela supposed there was more history to that—perhaps something that she would want him to tell her later on.

"Um ... does anybody else see what I'm seeing?" Mobola asked, her voice breaking into the mild tension. Neela turned around and staggered back at the sight before her.

They had cleared Quandisa and were now above the northern hemisphere of its far side, which was shrouded from the system's main star. But in the darkness, several shapes could be seen, glinting like a circle of stars.

"What is that?" Neela asked.

"If the sensors are correct," Mobola said, "it's ... ships?"

"Ships?" Tyger stepped forward, his eyes fixated on the holos, along with Akiko's.

"Felyan ships, to be exact," Mobola said as a holo appeared in the center of the bridge. There were seven in all, streamlined as any Felyan vessel, and was the same shape as the *And'Arra's Vengeance*, but magnitudes larger in comparison. In fact, if the size specs were to be believed, these ships dwarfed both their escort and the *Reckless*, in the way a dinghy compared to an aircraft carrier.

"Okay, that's just weird," Mobola said aloud.

"*Now* it's weird?" Neela asked.

"Well, it looks like the hyperdrive rings on all the ships are ... disconnecting?" She looked over her console as if it needed psychiatric care before speaking again. "Yes, disconnecting. And they're forming ... something."

"Beautiful is it not?" Captain Ar'Kesi's voice chimed in on the comm, bursting with pride. "But in a moment, you'll see something even more beautiful!"

"They're making a ring," Mobola said as the hologram panned away, showing the circle of ships, fragments of their now disassembled hyperspace drive rings doing an elaborate dance in their midst, at last connecting together like pieces of a model, one after another. For several moments, the dance of interlocking played before the eyes of everyone present, ending at last when not only had the ring been fully formed, but the ships moved in, their bows touching their respective points on the composite ring.

"Now what happens?" Neela wondered aloud, forgetting that the comms were still open. The captain's response quickly reminded her.

"Now, the magic begins."

No sooner than he finished speaking, the bows of each ship connected to the ring lit into a brilliance that rivaled the system's sun. The holo display dimmed against the sudden intensity of light until it faded. The image clarified, revealing seven smaller points of light that traveled across the ring's circumference, funneling into a singular point at the center, their light like dazzling lasers flowing in perfect, concentric circles.

The light show suddenly exploded into a luminosity that caused the holos to go into a momentary white-out before again readjusting against the sudden brilliance. The sudden flash forced Neela, along with everyone else, to squeeze their eyes shut, then look away. A moment later, Neela opened one eye to the subsiding light, making sure she hadn't been truly blinded, then opened the other. She faced the holos once more, rubbing away the black blur that had been temporarily burned into her retina.

At the center of the ring was a spherical point that seemed to reflect the surrounding light, casting distorted mirror-like images of their surroundings, as if its circle were made of glass.

"I'm getting readings from that thing," Mobola said. "And I wouldn't believe it unless I saw it myself."

"Do you know what it is, *dada*?" Neela asked.

"Well, if it's true, then the Felyans were a lot more advanced than we thought," Mobola said. "If the sensors weren't damaged by that light show, then we're looking at a wormhole."

"Indeed, it is," the captain chimed in, as merrily as ever. "And through the belly of the beast lies our sacred home. We'll lead, and you follow!"

FIVE

Snow stared out the cockpit viewport and then spun around in the pilot's seat. Hyperspace was a beautiful swirl of blues and violets, high-powered streams of energy that, if harnessed correctly, could reduce interstellar journey times from centuries to mere days. Still, despite this fact, Snow found hyperspace travel extremely tedious.

She puffed out her cheeks in a long sigh and rose to her feet. Luckily, she had a ship full of distractions and she decided to head toward the hab section to fix a meal before refreshing her memory on the target.

The door slid open to reveal a roomy space with a large abstract painting in the form of a multicolored fractal mounted on the far wall. Curved steps led down to a 3-seat sofa and low glass coffee table, set on a thick cowhide-style rug. Viewports looked down on the hangar bay interior, each framed by thick red curtains.

Along the starboard side wall was a series of cupboards and cooking utilities and a sink. Snow stopped by the cupboards and reached inside, pulling out a bottle of dark liquor and a packet of pretzels before she made her way to the sofa. She reclined gently, placed the bottle on the table, then tore open the pretzels, tossing a handful in her mouth.

"Noo, pop the target file on the holo, would you please?" she said aloud, speaking around a mouthful of pretzels, seemingly to no one. "Subject: Frostbyte file 001."

Instantly, a series of holographic images and documents appeared in front of her.

"Thank you." Snow leaned forward and rearranged the images as if they were solid things floating in the air. She then began to pour over the data like she had done hundreds of times before. After a moment, she paused.

Yes, there, she thought, sitting back again and swallowing her latest mouthful of pretzels. *That would be a perfect opportunity!*

"Noomi, sweetheart, adjust course toward Alliance border world of Haven, please. Coordinates 128.2 by 95 and engage cloak."

Snow felt the light shudder as the ship began to adjust its course, moving between the streams and eddies of hyperspace energy flows. The lights then dimmed as power was shunted into the cloaking system, rendering the ship all but invisible. All the while, she continued to study the data regarding the world of Haven.

"Prep for a water landing near New St. Louis, please, Noo. We're going to have to park near the beach."

"Just for the record, you know I'm taking up this job under protest," Xerx said.

"Let's just be glad you didn't say that to the Empress after the ridiculous sum you requested," Kumiko said. "Fortunately, she didn't have a treasury representative present, or she'd think her ideas about pirates robbing you blind were true."

"That bad?" Xerx said.

Kumiko's expression remained neutral. "You'd have probably been dumped off the island's edge for insulting her."

"Ramirez didn't stop me," Xerx said. "He not much of a financier, either?"

"I just think he was amused."

They'd been dismissed from the audience chamber and were back outside in the palace gardens. And now Xerx was beginning to think that perhaps he was left out of something that no one had told him. The only one with him was Kumiko, and she had said nothing while he waited for the other proverbial shoe to drop. It was times like these that her penchant for silence was particularly annoying.

"So what now?" he said.

"What do you mean?" Kumiko asked, now looking as if she'd just appeared beside him.

"The plan's in place," Xerx said, "so I guess I'll be staying at the palace instead of at my cousin's, like I told him, right? Nothing's going to be ready until tomorrow, so should we be on patrol, or do I sleep outside on one of those benches?"

"Do you *want* to sleep on the bench?" Kumiko said.

"You know, it's not that you *don't* have a sense of humor," Xerx said. "It's just that it kinda sucks."

A faint, wordless smile appeared at the edge of Kumiko's mouth.

"Arrangements have been made here in the palace," she said, striding more purposefully away from the grand keep where they had their audience with the Empress. She gestured across from the garden to a manor whose distinctively human design stood out garishly from the grown-rather-than-built appearance of Felyan architecture. "You'll be staying there. And I was informed that your cousin will be visiting."

"Seems a bit far from the keep," Xerx said. "Shouldn't I be helping you protect them?"

"I thought you said you didn't want any encounters with a tertiary?"

Xerx found himself regretting his words, considering his reaction to the knowledge of what was hunting the Empress and Envoy's innocent child. His encounter with that particular tertiary had been brief, but it was more than enough to make him certain that any entanglements with their kind were out of his league. All human-Felyan hybrids, even his cousins, had some form of psionics, but something about "diluting" the bloodline by introducing more human parentage into the mix created something extraordinarily powerful. Because of this, tertiaries were feared just as much as they were revered in most places.

"You're thinking about your encounter with her, aren't you?" Kumiko said.

"Mind getting out of my mind?" Xerx said sourly.

"I wasn't *in* your mind to begin with," Kumiko replied and tapped him atop his head with an especially hard fingernail. "Things come up to the surface, remember? It can be really annoying, too."

"Indeed," Xerx quipped.

"And she has a name," Kumiko said. "Amira. Amira Ingles."

"You talk like you know her," Xerx said.

"I knew her once," Kumiko said. "We were students together on Lhirevlis."

The name of that planet piqued Xerx's attention even more than her knowledge of the rogue tertiary's name. He'd heard that Vlissians sought out tertiaries to train them, sometimes by force, bringing them to that enigmatic race's homeworld. But no one who had claimed to have been there ever spoke of it. Most thought it was all a fairy tale, and that the Vlissians, rarely seen by humans except in the company of Felyans of importance, were merely a transient, dying race. But he quickly curbed his enthusiasm. He knew that Kumiko would be just as tight-lipped as any other who had visited that legendary world.

"Yes, I've been to Lhirevlis," Kumiko said in a suddenly tired voice. "No, I won't tell you about it. Besides, I couldn't even if I wanted to."

"Why's that?" Xerx asked. This was new, and perhaps something no one else had been privy to.

"Vlissians fix it so that we can't say anything about it," Kumiko explained. "If we try to hold on to any detail ... well, you ever went into a room needing something, and suddenly forgot what you went in there for? It's a bit like that."

A slight chill ran through Xerx's innards at the realization of the power Vlissians could hold over the minds of even a tertiary to keep their world hidden.

"Anyway, Amira and I were students of Shezmi," Kumiko said, sounding almost relieved to change the subject. "He personally picked me; Amira was ... forced on him."

"Forced?" Xerx asked.

"She was what you'd call a 'problem student,'" Kumiko explained. "Too willful; endless questions; tested her boundaries beyond innocent curiosity. She was basically hardheaded."

"Ah, yes," Xerx said. "As Iriid would say, she was a 'Johnny.'"

"Johnny?"

Xerx chuckled. "In every class, you have good and not-so-good students. And then you have ... *Johnny*." He gave a special, foreboding emphasis on the name this time, and now saw that Kumiko understood.

"Yeah, she was a 'Johnny,' then, I guess," Kumiko said, more thoughtful than amused. "Well, as the saying goes, a hard head makes for a soft behind. And Amira got that in spades. But it had the opposite effect. She got in more trouble for her pranks, sass, and outright disobedience than I ever saw anyone get. But that never broke her. At least not in the way it was expected. She tried to get me to rebel, and for a little while, I did. But I couldn't stand to see Shezmi so disappointed, and fell back in line, leaving Amira alone."

It was the first time Xerx had ever seen the woman he'd considered the ultimate ice princess look truly regretful.

"She ... didn't take it well."

"She was kicked out, I gather?" Xerx said.

"It would have been so much easier if that were the case," Kumiko said, shaking her head. "But every tertiary knows that a renegade is especially dangerous. So she was arranged to be ... transferred."

"Transferred ... where?" Xerx asked.

"Someplace else," Kumiko said after a moment of what appeared to be some kind of futile attempt to remember—possibly the same memory block that the Vlissians had put on her memory of the homeworld? "They said that she would only sleep peacefully while she was repaired—whatever that meant. But she escaped. And left about a hundred humans dead in her wake."

"Why no Vlissians?" Xerx said.

"Ever known a human that could kill a Vlissian?" Kumiko replied.

"You did," Xerx said.

"He was a Seeker."

"Still a Vlissian."

"Trust me. Those monsters are Vlissian by species only." Kumiko's voice took on a foreboding tone before she made a small, but nonetheless menacing, grin. "But you're damn right I did. Still, has anyone else?"

Xerx had no need to say anything else. He knew the answer just as well as she did.

"She's managed to stay off the proverbial grid somehow ever since," Kumiko said. "Last I heard before An'Re'Hara, she was living as some kind of mercenary for the scummier individuals in the Colonies, doing what she can to survive, not caring what it is."

"Or how little of a conscience you have to have for it," Xerx said, thinking about her recent attempts to take out an infant. "I didn't realize she was *that* kind of a monster."

"You're lucky to be alive," Kumiko said.

"And you brought me right to where she is now," Xerx said, casting a narrow-eyed gaze at the silver-haired girl.

"If I had any inkling that you two had crossed paths before, I would've chosen someone else for this job," Kumiko said. "But to tell the truth, none of them would've been ideal."

"Why Madam Frostbyte," Zerx said, playfully using her *nom de guerre*, "If I didn't know better, I'd take that as you saying you actually like me!"

"Don't flatter yourself," Kumiko said, before giving a thoughtful pause. "Well, I don't *not* like you."

Following his guide, Xerx betrayed a shrewd grin as she led him over the bridge in the center of the garden and further on to the manor.

"Putting everything else aside," Kumiko said, once they'd reached the entrance awning of arched trees, "you'll be staying here until the Empress and the Ambassador are ready for departure. I don't think Amira knows of your presence here yet; she'd be crazy to hang around on the palace grounds with someone else hunting her, tertiary or not. And besides, you'll have other psionics to look out for you."

"What do you mean 'look out for me?'" Xerx said as they reached the large wooden front door. Kumiko touched its surface, and the sound of crystal chimes hummed from inside. It was not unlike a chorus of sopranos singing. Afterward, the door, which turned out to be a massive knot of flat vines, loosened and grew away from a central point, leaving a path open into the manor.

"You'll see," Kumiko said. "See you in the morning."

The door re-formed between them, cutting them off, and leaving Xerx alone …

… Or so he thought.

"Hey, mom! Were those the chime flowers for this place? I think someone's at the door!" The voice was that of a young-sounding female that he did not recognize. Xerx turned around, finding himself in a grand antechamber with fern-like fronds growing from the walls in neat rows, a glowing set of orb-like pods in the center of each, providing light to the room. On its opposite end, a grand staircase led to a balcony that opened up to two hallways on the second floor.

"Dira'Ni, I told you not to yell!" came an older voice that Xerx was much more familiar with, immediately before one of the large doors to the antechamber irised open like the entrance door. Through it stepped a tall *An'Kya* Felyan with blue-gray hair flecked with sparse streaks of silver. She wore a long, silken orange coat over a one-piece navy-blue dress, beneath which was a visibly pregnant stomach.

She turned away from the door and locked eyes with Xerx—after which her own golden eyes lit up like supernovas.

"Hi, Cala," he said as she ran up to him and threw her arms around his neck, pulling him into a hug that betrayed a much greater strength than her slender frame implied. She purred happily.

"*Li-ah*, was someone at the—Well, look what the storm blew in!" Even slightly choked and possibly losing consciousness, Xerx recognized the voice of his cousin Isibar. Over his wife's shoulder, he saw him step into the antechamber. With the exception of some lines around his mouth, he looked like he hadn't aged a day otherwise. He was followed by three smaller hybrids of varying ages, while he held one brown-haired toddler in his arms.

"Hey, Izz," Xerx said in a raspy voice. "Can you tell your wife to let me breathe now?"

The trip through the wormhole had been instantaneous. Not a vibration or any other sensation to be found. A part of Neela had been disappointed by this, but also thankful. But nothing could have prepared her for what the captain had informed them of moments later.

"What do you mean, we skipped a day?" Neela exclaimed to the Felyan captain in the holo, who now wore a repentant look on his face. Behind him, his *An'Kya* first officer stared daggers at him. They had just emerged from the wormhole, on the far side of Kilas, the last planet at the edge of the Felyan's home system. Another gas giant like Quandisa, it was green instead of purple, and much larger. They were now on a course for An'Re'Hara, and would arrive in synchronous orbit above the Imperial Palace within the hour.

"I apologize for not explaining earlier," Captain Ar'Kesi replied. "It's a side effect of wormhole travel. Some time dilation occurs due to space-time compression. That's the give and take of wormhole travel. But isn't one day better than three for a trip to the most distant inhabited world from your colonies? Consider that it would only skip a day, even if we made the jump from Hana IV, all the way on the other end. A day versus nearly two months, and you can see the advantages."

"You could still have warned us," Neela said, massaging the bridge of her nose. "Our ship has to synchronize its systems with the StellarNet to compensate, and that might affect some time-sensitive functions, you know."

"You are right, my dear," the captain said, his head bowing low. "That was a grievous oversight on my part. Again, I deeply apologize for my lack of foresight."

Neela exhaled, shaking off her frustration, and noted the curious look that Mobola was giving him. They both knew that there were no such functions aboard the ship, but as miffed as she had been at losing a day, she wanted to give this carefree captain something to feel ashamed about, and this was as good a reason as any.

"Well, all things considered, you did shave a great deal of time off of our journey, and for that we thank you," Neela said. "So we hope you won't spend the rest of the day in a bad mood for our sakes."

"I will endeavor to keep things positive," the captain replied, seeming to switch back to his jovial demeanor. "We'll escort you to the homeworld and once you're in stable orbit, we'll take our leave."

"Thank you again for your help," Neela said, and ended the transmission.

"Well, I didn't expect any of this to happen when I took passage here," Tyger said.

"You took the words right out of my mouth," Neela said. "I believe that we'll have to shave off some of your fare."

Tyger seemed quite pleased with his change of fortune. And considering the passage to Tophanavar had been all expenses paid by GI, it wasn't like the discount would hurt their crew.

"Probably the first time I've seen something turn out to be both an inconvenience and a convenience all at once," Tyger said to Akiko, "not counting that one time my ship broke down right in the path of a space gypsy fleet, that is."

"You are never without stories, are you?" Neela said. She tried to sound stern but was betrayed by her amused half-grin. Stories were, after all, the man's bread and butter.

"You have no idea how useful a thing they are to have," Tyger replied, and Akiko squeezed his side.

"It's one of the things I love about him," she said.

"Hey, guys," Pepper's voice broke in on the comm. "There's something wrong with the clocks. Why'd we skip a day? You seeing this, en-li? Can you run a diagnostic?"

Everyone, Mobola included, could not help but laugh.

SIX

HOLSTEIN DEEPS – UNNAMED RINGED GAS GIANT – WRAITH IN GEOSTATIONARY ORBIT

Alexa hated the deeps. They were a place of star formation, giving off ridiculous amounts of electromagnetic interference, making it a place where insurgents kept running off to hide.

No more, she had decided. She was pissed off with the malcontents' antics and their attempts to destabilize everything she and Iriid had built. Never before had the clans been so united under a single banner, working together toward a common purpose. The Pirate Worlds had prospered greatly under her husband's rule and she wasn't about to let these shits ruin it.

She surveyed the bridge of the *Wraith*: a large octagonal space with pods set into the walls. Within each sat a former Imperial tech: diminutive, cybernetically enhanced computational tanks, like Pip, which the Second Imperium utilized in large numbers as organic processors for their ships' computer systems. These were all defectors and, unlike their former stations in life, were piloting *Wraith* out of choice: a fact for which Alexa was thankful. Their combined abilities meant the ship could process and react to changing situations much more quickly than most other attack craft.

In the center was a dais with a large console and a lush captain's chair, upholstered in red leather—Alexa's personal touch. The walls were a shade of pale green, and dark green ornate support pillars separated each pod. Hidden lighting bathed the room in a soft white glow. But despite the ostentatious interior, this ship was built for war. Like her cousin-in-law's *Reckless*, it was a relic from wars long past. *Wraith*, however, was a lot smaller, inside and out.

Moreover, *Wraith* was clearly a predator. Similar in appearance to its much larger counterpart, *Belerophon*, her husband's mighty warship, *Wraith* featured the distinctive cross-headed bow but sported a narrow octagonal body with four V-shaped fins protruding from the top, bottom, and sides. The rear was a large sphere with four massive octagonal propulsion and maneuvering assemblies attached to it. Weapons were arrayed along its surface, giving it an almost sea urchin-like appearance. Nearby, two smaller vessels flanked the *Wraith*. Shaped like robotic sharks, aerials and weapons protruded from a number of points on the hull, each mounted on large engines at the rear.

Alexa stretched and yawned, then sat down in the captain's chair and placed her feet up on the console.

"You don't have to keep that bloody stealth mode active all the time, you know," she said, seemingly to no one.

From a position just behind the captain's chair, the form of a tall, muscular tank revealed itself, at first transparent, but rippling like heat haze before appearing in a ghostlike manner. She lowered her hood and undid a clasp near her neck as the diffraction cloth transitioned from transparent to a dull gray. In her right hand was a long, ornate spear that ended in a finely crafted MAG gun and blade. She was a ground type, engineered for planetary surface combat. Deep brown eyes sat within a fierce-looking visage, and long white hair cascaded from a tall top knot on her scalp bisected by a wide, black streak stretching from the hairline in the center of her scalp all the way to the tips.

The gray cloak fell open, revealing deep red armor plates, highly decorated in ornate, dragon-themed patterns, a style she chose to reflect her allegiance to the Draconid woman she served.

"Best way to keep an eye on you, your majesty," the tank said.

Alexa rolled her eyes and tilted her head. "Seriously Indira, you're not still upset about Tophanavar are you?"

Indira shifted uncomfortably as Alexa continued.

"I told you, it was my choice to go with Xerx. It was my order for you to remain with Tyger, and it was my fault I got shot."

Indira's eyes widened. "You did not tell me you got shot!"

"Oh, calm down Indy sweetheart." Alexa waved her hand nonchalantly. "Not like *shot* shot. I just meant when I got hit with that orgasm pellet."

"Regardless, your husband has ordered that we never leave your side again," the larger woman said, clearly unimpressed. "I will uphold that order."

"Yes, yes, I know. But even in my quarters? When I have company? It ought to be rather fun for you, then, standing there, all invisible, watching me fuck," Alexa said dryly but inwardly amused by the tank's reaction.

She watched as Indira, frozen for words for a moment, at last opened her mouth to respond, but she was cut off by a chime. Seeing that it was coming from her console, Alexa sat up straight and looked at the screens in front of her.

"Report."

The sound of several voices speaking as one came over the speakers.

"Contact confirmed. 60 degrees starboard, 43 degrees elevation. 3 ships, no FF confirmation received; modified Barracuda type craft, heavily armed."

Alexa stood and placed her hands on her hips. "Show me."

Around her, the bridge dissolved until it appeared as if Alexa were floating in space. The space ahead of her lit up with several red triangles marking the enemy vessels on approach, which would have otherwise been black against the brightness of the stars, nearly blending in with the void of space.

Feeling the distinctive thrill that could only come with impending combat, Alexa raised a claw to her lip and tapped it gently.

"Okay, then. Prep the drones and advise the other ships to get ready," she announced. "They clearly haven't seen them, or they wouldn't be steaming toward us so eagerly."

"The rings ma'am?" Indira asked as she stepped closer. She studied the steadily approaching ships.

"Yes, Indy my dear." Alexa snapped her fingers and pointed in the tank's direction as her expression broke into a vicious grin. "The rings!"

Alexa's smile widened. Paige's info had been right after all. They couldn't detect the rest of the fleet hiding below them.

They're in for a fucking shock, that's for sure, she thought, reaching out and drawing a square with her finger around the oncoming ships. Following her movements, a corresponding green square appeared on the hologram. She then spread her arms wide, and the image zoomed in on the highlighted section.

"Open the comms, all ships."

Alexa cleared her throat as the open comm chime chirped.

"Breaker nine-nine, this is Dragon Bitch; can I get a holler from Android Eater and Protective Pussy come on?"

Signals of acknowledgment returned, and Alexa nodded.

"Okay, brute force stun attack, YIPs and tricks, divide and conquer, I want prisoners from the lead ship; the others can rot."

From under the shadow of the planet's rings, two sizable vessels moved into the light. The familiar blunt arrowhead shape of the *Shadow Star* took the lead, followed by the sleek *Laughing Cat*, run by Iriid's head of security, the hybrid Arshosha.

Behind them, the *Wraith* began moving forward and with a bright flash, disappeared from view. The space between the ships lit up with cannon fire and beam lances. Doors on the underside of the *Shadow Star* swung open and rotary launchers descended. Tactical ion pulse missiles launched in quick succession, their trails diverging as they targeted the enemy vessels.

Lightning crept over the hulls of the insurgents' vessels as the TIP missiles hit and their weapons' fire faltered. A few moments later, their engines died. The *Shadow Star* and *Laughing Cat* moved in for the kill. Four large MAG cannons lit up on *Shadow Star*'s upper hull and tore one ship apart. *Laughing Cat* lit up the other with its beam lances and cut it apart like it was a loaf of bread.

The remaining ship fired its engines and tried to escape when it exploded in a bright flash of light. The *Wraith* appeared from the flash, its prow cleaving through the other ship's engine section like it was paper. It came to a stop halfway into the enemy vessel's length.

Alexa stood at her console as a concert of voices rattled off reports simultaneously. She raised her hands wide.

"One at a time, please!" she yelled.

A single high-pitched voice cut through the sudden silence.

"Prow ram successful, enemy ship disabled, *Shadow Star* waiting on confirmation to board."

"Thank you, Inori," said Alexa, a sigh escaping her lips. She would have to teach these techs to utilize more primitive communication methods for engaging with unenhanced people.

Alexa slapped the comm button.

"Dragon Bitch, here. Android Eater, you're free and clear. Good hunting."

Shadow Star moved toward the combined hulls of *Wraith* and the insurgents' ship and a small docking craft emerged from a hatch in the underside.

Paige acknowledged that they had access, and Alexa sat back in her chair. She returned her feet to the top of the console as she listened to Paige and her crew rampage through the enemy vessel's interior. When the commotion died down, she sat up as Paige's voice came over the comm.

"Lexy, sweetheart, I've got you a prisoner, but I think things just got a bit complicated."

Alexa rolled her eyes but leaned over the console screen as a data packet arrived from Paige. She studied its contents, ranging from surprisingly well-enhanced bodies to weapons clearly of better quality than the insurgents usually used.

She swiped across and frowned as a black double helix on a red background appeared alongside details of the Felyan Royal Palace with notes on other worlds the royal family was expected to visit.

"Paige, honey, I think we need to have a chat with Xerx, soon as."

They were all there.

On a particular level, Xerx did not find this all that surprising. Fourteen kids with a fifteenth one on the way would be a near-impossible request for nearly any one babysitter to take on, or family members to care for, even for the largest families on An'Re'Hara. And inter-species couples—those involving humans who mated with *An'Kya*, at least—normally had sizeable families, especially if they chose to live on the Felyan homeworld. Still, meeting them all here with Isibar and his lifemate Cala, all brought to the Imperial palace grounds as guests, had been a surprise even he had not expected.

"The kids kept you busy yesterday," Isibar said as he passed the plate of *kesi*, a Felyan breakfast pastry, Xerx's way. He sat on the veranda with his cousin and in-law, enjoying the morning breeze while the children ate in a separate room. Cala had run a tight ship among their children, charging the older ones to look after the younger ones, with Gran'Ninyurak, a dignified *Hara'Kya* Felyan, acting as nanny to the youngest.

"They never tire of questions," Xerx said. "You'd think it hadn't been so long since I'd last seen them."

"For some, it's the first time they've seen you outside of a holo," Cala said. "But *li-ah* has entertained them with stories about you."

"I hope it was good ones," Xerx said, casting an expectant look to the couple, who remained tell-ingly silent. Slowly, a mischievous grin erupted on Isibar's face.

"Izz ... what have you been telling them about me?" Xerx asked forebodingly.

"Nothing that wasn't true," his cousin answered, his tone incriminatingly evasive.

"You didn't tell them about the zoo incident, did you?"

"I ... didn't say names," Isibar said, shifting uncom-fortably in his seat.

Xerx frowned. "I swore you to secrecy about that."

"Like I said, I didn't mention any names."

"You never told me," Cala said, her tone slightly hurt.

"Sworn to secrecy, remember?" Isibar said. At this, Xerx's consternation faded into amusement, as he was now feeling the full effect of his cousin's cheekiness.

"Yet you told our children?" Cala said.

"Only the youngest."

"Why only them?" Xerx asked.

"Because they most likely won't remember."

Xerx was fairly sure that neither he nor Cala had the heart to tell him that it couldn't be guaranteed. Regardless, he let the whole thing go. That incident where Iriid had dared him to yell "Get 'em off me!" inside the Sepran arachnid exhibit at the Siberna Prime Zoo was an embarrassment he'd never fully lived down—a bit of childish mischief gone awry. Upon their discovery, both he and his cousin were banned from the zoo for life. Isibar, moving offworld only a few months later, got out of it easy, while he was forced to make ever more fanciful excuses to bow out of trips to the zoo that his family wanted to make.

"Well, all that aside," Xerx said, "It's been good seeing you again. I just wish Rati and Rinkya could have joined us."

"Are they doing all right?" Cala asked almost instantly after he brought the subject up.

"Seems like they were doing just fine, if a bit overworked," Xerx said. "And they were a big help in cracking the case with the Doctor."

"Slippery bitch," Isibar muttered under his breath. "All those years to catch her, and now it's going to take me another ten years to find her again."

"She can't run forever," Xerx assured him. "She was just lucky this time, is all, had an ace up her sleeve. But her luck will eventually run out."

"Speaking of important missions, you hear from your wife since yesterday?" Isibar asked.

"Or even your friend?" Cala added.

"If you're talking about Kumiko, she commed me shortly after I woke up," Xerx said. "She let me know that Neela should be arriving today. Something about a time rift effect from their method of travel? Sounds like a puzzle that Pepper would love to figure out, but it's a bit above my level of expertise. But after that, we put together a plan."

"Is it a good one?" Isibar asked, but Xerx could only reply with a shrug.

"That remains to be seen."

Just then, Gran'Ninyurak, a large, charcoal gray-furred *Hara'Kya* Felyan, ambled onto the veranda. Moving on all fours, she held a very fussy-sounding toddler hanging by the thick part of her onesie clamped securely in her elongated jaw. She held the little one aloft with the care of a mother wolf carrying a pup. Approaching Cala, she rose to two legs and took the child into her arms as she squirmed and reached out for her mother.

"Sorry, Lady Cala, but this one was a bit out of sorts," she explained as Cala rose from her chair and took the child in her arms. Immediately, she settled down but still appeared to sulk.

"Thank you," she said as the dark-furred Felyan bowed and took her leave. Cala then sat down, unclasping a silver brooch from the blue shawl she had wrapped about her shoulders, then lengthened the opposite end and tucked the child beneath as she re-pinned it, concealing her entire torso. She then shifted something with her free hand, and soon, the child's fussing calmed to muffled cooing. At the same time, the agitated twitching of her brown-colored tail calmed to a leisurely undulation.

"Sorry about that," Cala said, heaving a sigh, stroking the nursing child with a "what-can-you-do" expression. "You only met little Eria last night. She just found out that she won't be the youngest for much longer."

"And as you can see, she hasn't taken it very well," Isibar said.

"Indeed." Xerx grinned, sympathetic, though thankful that such drama was not something he needed to worry about—at least not yet. He and Neela had discussed children off and on every now and then, but thus far, she didn't seem to be fully serious about it. To tell the truth, he felt far from ready for that eventuality.

"But getting back to the subject," Cala said, her expression souring into a scowl, "of all things, sending you to take out a tertiary? What in the cerulean hells could that woman have been thinking? She's a tertiary herself, isn't she? Is she not up to the task?"

At this, Xerx stifled a laugh. Pregnant or not, Kumiko would have given Cala a piece of her mind if she'd heard that—and Cala would no doubt have served it back at her.

"I've never known her to not be up to a task," Xerx said, "but believe it or not, the Empress wants this woman alive."

"Alive?" Isibar raised an eyebrow. "You do know how much in love she and the ambassador are, right? This woman's going after what's possibly her favorite daughter."

"Oh, I have no doubt she'll be hung from the lowest part of the palace and dragged down through the ground below," Xerx said, "but they need to question her first. And the way Kumiko put it, she's not good at 'subtle.'"

"And you are?" Isibar cast him a shrewd look.

"Touché." His cousin knew him well. And Xerx could not help but laugh in spite of himself.

"Perhaps he's better at it than she is," Cala suggested.

"Touché," Isibar now said.

"But you said you have a plan?" Cala said.

"Of a sort," Xerx replied.

Isibar frowned, crossing his arms. "That doesn't sound like you're very confident. Weren't you the plans guy when we were kids?"

"Iriid was better at that," Xerx said.

"But you *did* make plans."

"Sometimes."

"And you were pretty enthusiastic about them, as I recall."

"Recent events have taught me to curb my enthusiasm when it comes to plans," Xerx admitted, recalling the events aboard the *Reckless* and the shitshow his first attempt at capturing the Doctor on Tophanavar had turned out to be. "Good thing for me I'm good at thinking on my feet."

"Better be doubly sure about that if you're going against a tertiary," Isibar warned him. "You did tell us she kicked your ass before."

"Yes, but my crew and I have resources I didn't have at the time," Xerx said.

"But ..."

"But she *is* a tertiary," Xerx admitted. "When is it ever safe to go after one of them? To be honest, a part of me wonders if I just should save her the effort and cut my own head off."

"Unusually morose of you," his cousin said, fixing him with a worried look. "If I didn't know better, I'd say you're worried that you don't have this one."

"Well, some might say I'm crazy for taking this on," Xerx said thoughtfully. "And maybe they're right. But as I said, we do have resources I didn't have the last time I crossed a tertiary. We're on a more even field. Fortunately for me—I think—it's Kumiko who will be doing the heavy lifting.

"Which means you'll be putting things in place for her?" Cala said. Xerx nodded.

"And I'll be doing a damn good job with that."

"Now that's the confident cousin I remember," Isibar said, pointing an uneaten pastry his way. He smiled with renewed pride before popping it into his mouth.

Xerx's comm signaled him, and he answered, transferring the call to the holoprojector at the table where Kumiko's image had appeared.

"They've arrived," she said.

"Oh, good," Xerx said. "Tell my crew to meet us here."

"That won't be possible," Kumiko replied. "We have a schedule to keep. The ambassador wants to be in space with his daughter within the hour."

"That soon?" Xerx's face fell in disappointment, but there was no leeway to be given in Kumiko's stony expression. Her words, however, were not unkind.

"I'm afraid so. Say your goodbyes. I'm on my way."

A singular sense of relief that Xerx had not realized he'd been holding onto coursed through his body. Neela could take care of herself, but Kumiko's sudden whisking him away from Tophanavar to An'Re'Hara had left him with little time to process their sudden separation, and he now found himself consumed with a need to be with his crew, and especially by his wife's side. But at the same time, he did not like the way that things were moving ahead a lot faster than he'd expected. He frowned as he looked at his cousin and his lifemate, whom he hadn't seen in years.

"Heading out?" Isibar said. Xerx nodded and glanced back toward the house.

"It sucks that I've only had so short a time to come back to you guys, and I have to leave so soon," he said. It really wasn't fair; he'd hoped to spend a few days at the least with them now that the exhibition tournament on Tophanavar was done, but this new adventure had chosen him, and he was the hobbit along for the ride with the dwarves and wizard.

"We'll meet up again before long," Isibar said, rising from the table to give Xerx a bear hug. "I'm sure of it. I got to meet my cousin again, and I'm sure you're not gonna be a stranger for quite so long next time, are you?"

"Not at all," Xerx said, and meant it. Somehow or another, he'd make time.

Cala came to his side and touched her nose to his with an affectionate purr. Just then, Kira, the oldest daughter, appeared in the doorway.

"There's a human girl in all black with pretty white hair and a face that looks like she bit into a sourberry at the front door, asking about cousin Xerx," she said.

Despite his disappointment at having to leave his family so soon, Xerx could not help but give a stifled snort at the blunt, but solidly honest way that the girl had described Kumiko. He sighed away the disappointment at learning just how little time he'd actually had with his family as Isibar stood with Cala. He hugged them both one last time and Cala licked his cheek with the tip of her tongue.

"That's my cue," Xerx said, at least looking forward to the welcome sight of his ship and wife returning safely.

A more welcome sight there never was.

Xerx watched with swelling relief as the *Reckless* made its landing at the spacedock on the tarmac at the palace grounds' edge.

And then his view was impeded by Kumiko's expressionless face, staring at him as if he were some new lifeform she'd found in a bush.

"You have a funny look," she said. "It's like you're in love with your own ship."

"Maybe I am," Xerx said with a cheeky grin, craning his head to the side in order to see around the white-haired girl's permanent resting bitch face.

"I don't think your wife would like that."

"It's really creepy when I can't tell if you're being serious or just deadpan," Xerx said, then returned his sights to the ship before walking back toward the observation tower's stairwell. "But as it stands, I could kiss both of them right now."

"You'd burn your lips," Kumiko said. "On the ship, that is."

"Now I know you're full of it," Xerx said.

Kumiko made a tiny, enigmatic grin as the ship's engines whined down. The automated airspace traffic control system signaled the landing's completion, and Xerx descended the observation tower, running across the tarmac. Its boarding ramp lowered as he picked up his pace.

He arrived as the steel surface of the ramp touched ground with a resonating metallic *clang*, and he saw his wife and crew waiting at the top. Xerx, though partly winded, still had enough breath left to run the remaining distance to Neela, which she closed to half as she hurried her way down to him. He picked her up in her arms and laughed, giving her a rain of kisses.

"I don't think I've been happier to see you," he said, at the end of one final, particularly lengthy kiss.

"You had me worried sick, you know," Neela said as Xerx set her back down. Despite the reproach, she was beaming.

"Blame that on Miss Emergency kidnapper," Xerx said, gesturing vaguely in Kumiko's direction.

"I heard that," she yelled back from the base of the ramp.

"And how was your first time in the pilot's seat?" Xerx asked.

"Different," Neela said. "Very ... different."

"Different indeed," Xerx said. He'd been wanting to break Neela in on the captain's dais for awhile, but between the comedy of errors that was their maiden voyage and the hours of training he'd put in during their trip to Tophanavar, he'd never had the time. It was a relief to see that she'd handled it well.

"Sorry to vanish on you like that," Xerx said, then again gestured Kumiko's way. "She can be ... insistent."

"And stubborn," Neela added, looking over his shoulder at the white-haired woman, who seemed oddly contrite.

"And reckless."

The final comment came from Akiko, who descended the ramp past Var, Salt, Pepper, and Mobola, all remaining inside the hangar bay. Xerx and Neela stepped back as both the statuesque tank and Tyger made their way down to their daughter. Tyger briefly bumped fists with Xerx as he passed him by, and Xerx smiled, looking forward to them sharing their respective adventures over a drink.

"You know how to contact us, dear," Neela said, crossing her arms like a disappointed mother as Kumiko approached her. "I'm sure you could've been more conscientious than that."

"She really couldn't," Xerx muttered under his breath as Kumiko, at first annoyed at Neela's words, seemed to at last notice her mother and father. A look of combined apprehension and annoyance flashed in her eyes before she turned away, muttering something that Xerx could not hear, but before he could wonder if she'd just insulted his wife, he understood.

Xerx didn't speak Jakartan, only he'd heard the language spoken enough between Paige's three tank sisters to recognize it as both mother and daughter conversed, Akiko using a decidedly reproachful tone.

"Seems she beat you to the ass-chewing," he said to Neela with a smirk that he hoped that Kumiko couldn't see. He wrapped his arm around his wife's waist, feeling like their separation had been for years, rather than only several hours. "Are we good for the preparations?"

"It's a risky plan," Neela said. "And the one we'll be flushing out is dangerous in a way that makes me wonder if you're not doing it under duress. Are you sure you agreed to this without them blackmailing you?"

"Since when do Felyans blackmail anyone?" Xerx said. "And unfortunately, I did agree to this."

"Do you trust our Frosty girl to make it work?"

"Her rep as a bounty hunter precedes her," Xerx assured his wife. "Even I know that she's never without a plan."

"Neither are you," Neela said, her superfluous comment understood between them. "But plans don't always go well for the bait."

"Don't remind me," Xerx remarked with a deep frown.

"Still, if we're doing this on the Empress' dime, then I guess you're right to trust her."

"You guys ready up there?" Xerx called out to the rest of his crewmates as he wrested attention from his wife.

"Always," Salt called down.

Immediately afterward, sound of another landing echoed across the palace tarmac, coming in fast. Judging from its combined volume and pitch, the craft was much smaller than the *Reckless*.

"Engine's still hot, sir," Pepper said. "We take off as soon as everyone's on board."

"Looks like our other guests are coming in, then," Xerx noted as the ship's incoming roar increased in volume.

"I spoke with Kumiko and Tyger," Neela said. "Since Kumiko will be coming with us, they want in on this plan. From what you described, we'll need the extra guns. The ball's in your court, though."

"Well, what the Empress is paying us ought to cover it," Xerx said, "so I can't say it won't be welcome."

The shimmering silver Felyan craft's engines switched to antigravs as it touched down and hovered across the tarmac until it came to a silent stop several hundred feet away.

"I'm sort of jealous for your nice rest at your cousin's," Neela said. "I didn't even get to say 'hi.' Though I am surprised that they were brought to the palace for that one night."

"You and me both," Xerx said. "Can't say that their red carpet welcome wasn't appreciated, though."

Before heading towards the Felyan craft, Xerx momentarily continued watching Akiko as she reprimanded Kumiko, then embraced her with a relieved smile. She even allowed Tyger to touch his nose to her hand affectionately, something he'd never seen her do before.

"I guess Kumiko has a sympathetic side after all," he remarked, more to himself than Neela, who noticed where his attention was.

"Stranger things have happened." His wife then nodded to the newly landed craft, "like escorting royalty."

"At least it's without fanfare," Xerx said before catching up with Ramirez and his daughter before they descended from the hatch of the ship. Kumiko had at last managed to break free from her mother's lecture and follow along. As expected, the Empress remained aboard, and the ambassador ducked out of the entrance. Across his chest was a sling, where his daughter slept soundly. Beside him, however, was the unexpected, yet unsurprising sight of two Felyans: one gray-furred *Re'Kya* and a shaggy blue-gray *Hara'Kya*. The first, with greenish-hued hair that was tied in a bun, was dressed more conservatively than any of her *kya* than Xerx had ever seen, in a way that reminded her of the lady of the manor in old Earth Victorian novels. The *Hara'Kya* possessed a mane of silvery hair and was protected by ceremonial body armor.

Kumiko, floating above the tarmac, glided ahead of them to meet with the ambassador, and, while still out of earshot, spoke with him. At first, Xerx thought that she had been gesturing toward himself and Neela, until he noticed Tyger and Akiko coming up from behind him, waving to their daughter.

"I've procured more protection," she at last announced, gesturing toward the two other Felyans. "They'll be useful in this mission."

"It's still my ship," Xerx said. "You need to run this by me."

"We don't have time for—"

"Captain Paraska right," Akiko said. "It's *his* ship." She faced Xerx intently. "Do you mind?"

"Not really," Xerx said. "It was just the principle. She's queen of the hill here—Empress notwithstanding—but my ship is *my* kingdom."

"They'll get paid for the work," the ambassador assured him.

"You sure you're okay with this?" Xerx asked.

"The Empress and I have grown to trust Lady Zero implicitly," Ramirez replied. To Xerx's surprise, it was the few times he'd heard anyone use Kumiko's last name.

"Then it's settled," Xerx said, then noticed Kumiko's reluctant but resigned expression. "So, who are our new passengers?"

Kumiko pointedly eyed the two other Felyans who had accompanied the ambassador.

"Ri'Kela and Biraknu," Kumiko said, as the two accompanying Felyans bowed. "They're the princess' official bodyguards."

"Think we're a bit underprepared for all this?" Xerx wryly observed. Ramirez chuckled, but he seemed to be the only one who found humor in his remark.

"Believe me, you'll be glad for the extra protection with what we have to go up against," Kumiko said, gesturing impatiently back toward the *Reckless*. "It's not safe out here, by the way. We ought to get going."

"No arguments there," Xerx said, and led the way back to his ship alongside Kumiko. The rest of the crew would certainly be interested in the much fuller house they would soon find.

As they boarded the ship, Xerx's comm signaled. He paused and answered it, hearing Var's voice. He spoke in a low, conspiratorial manner.

"Captain, she took the bait. The target's aboard."

"Game on," Xerx said, running back up ahead to lead the way beside his wife.

SEVEN

Xerx suppressed a laugh at the ambassador's expression of utter incredulity, wanting Kumiko to save face after mentioning, however erroneously, that the baby was live bait for this operation.

"Not like that," Kumiko said to Ramirez with her usual icy stoicism.

"Well, it's what you said," Ramirez said, unmollified. His tone made the words come out as every bit the accusation they were.

"You two are going to make the young mistress cry," Ri'Kela scolded in Felyan as she rocked the baby in her arms. A small, but nonetheless anxious-sounding gurgle disrupted the momentary silence, coming from the infant the governess had been holding in the sari-like harness she'd fashioned to her chest.

"Hey, *you're* the one with the ass-backward story here," Xerx quipped to Kumiko, attempting to defuse the situation. But the white-haired girl only proceeded to stare daggers at him. "I'm personally more concerned with the extra guests here." He then glanced the older Felyan woman up and down. "No offense, but she looks more like a nanny than any kind of protection."

"She's a former *Irekla* centurion," Ramirez said. At the mention of the elite force, Xerx almost spit out his soda.

"You're shitting me," he said, between coughs while Biraknu chuffed a throaty laugh in the background.

"Language, please," Ri'Kela said, frowning sternly.

"Sorry," Xerx mumbled before the ambassador spoke again.

"She's taken on rogue tertiaries before and survived," Ramirez explained, then grinned at what Xerx supposed had been a very amusing look on his face. "Now you know why I brought her along. And, well, Biraknu's armor pretty much speaks for itself."

Maybe I should have her take point, when the shit hits the fan, Xerx thought, redirecting his gaze to the holo-projector on the briefing room's central table, and the holographic map of the *Reckless'* interior that it displayed. They were well on their way back to Tophanavar, and with their prey on board, it was time to get to business as quickly as possible. "Mobola, you there?" he said as he switched on the comm.

"Yes, Captain," his resident techie replied in an unusually calm manner.

"Run the simulation."

The map shifted to where only the ship's interior showed, each deck glowing and semitransparent, then multiplying into reflections of itself, expanding into space that the ship could not have possibly had.

"Seems my brief visit with my cousin turned out to be a good thing," Xerx said as the image continued to shift. "I was able to plan this out last night with Izz and coordinate it with Kumiko. But it does start with some bad news for you, Ambassador."

Ramirez frowned. "Which is ...?"

"Your daughter already *is* the bait. She's been the bait since before you came aboard my ship. And as planned, the assassin has taken it."

"So she's on the ship?" Biraknu gave a soft growl, his eyes widening with incredulity. "When were you planning on telling us this? And how the hell did she get on without us noticing?"

"We planned to tell you right now," Xerx replied with a flat flippancy. He pointed to a red light that appeared on the grid. It began to move as the deck expanded, with the varying floors shifting in size and direction to lead her to a singular point. "And from what Kumiko told me, she has a talent for psionically cloaking herself from life sign detectors. That at least explains how she was able to crawl around the palace for so long unde-tected. Thankfully, our sensors are a cut above the rest."

"Where is she now?" Ramirez asked.

"In a storage cabinet near the cargo bay," Xerx said. "Thus far, she's been remaining in that spot."

"So you plan to use this garrison mode you men-tioned?" The ambassador said. "You'll trap her like the time you were trapped with that Second Imperium assassin?"

"Precisely. I've had firsthand experience of it in action. We can keep her going in circles forever if need be, once she starts moving."

"She's a tertiary," Ri'Kela said, sounding unsure of the entire plan. "Won't she just brute force her way to the target? I've dealt with their ilk before, but not while

I'm handling a baby. What's to keep her from breaking through walls to come after the young mistress?"

"Because we can keep generating corridors quicker than she can traverse them," Xerx explained. "She can bust all the walls she wants, but she'll just be getting further away."

"Having two tertiaries on a ship spoiling for a fight only makes me more worried."

The governess's expression showed how little she liked this plan.

"Firstly, I am not 'spoiling' for a fight," Kumiko assured her with a confidence that bordered on smugness. "Secondly, Amira is an inferior opponent. Any fight will be over in moments."

"Frosty here's got certain advantages," Xerx added.

"What kind of advantages?"

No sooner than Biraknu had asked his question, Kumiko blinked into existence behind him, holding a knife to his neck that Xerx had no idea that she'd had on her. The dark-furred *Hara'Kya* Felyan went stock still, his deep amber eyes wide as those on a stuffed toy.

Kumiko stepped back and removed the knife. She raised her opposite hand and the crushed velvet of her sleeve slid back, revealing a secret scabbard that was strapped about her forearm. She sheathed the blade.

"I can do things like that," she said, the rare grin on her face now making no effort to hide her own self-satisfaction.

"And other tertiaries can't?" the governess asked.

"No," Kumiko said, wryly pursing her lips.

Xerx covered his bemused expression in a way that made it look like he was scratching his nose. If only

Neela, who was currently holding down the bridge for captain's chair practice, had been here to see that little display.

"The look on their faces was worth the price of admission," he muttered to the silver-haired girl as she reappeared by his side. She cast him a glance that would have seemed bland had he not detected a distinctive twinkle in her eye.

"So, in simple terms, the plan is to trap her with garrison mode and then I head down and play smack-a-bitch?" Kumiko said.

"We'll, ah, have to guide you," Xerx replied, keeping his mind on the mission, as well as reminding himself that this Amira Ingles was now resting comfortably in the ship, waiting to strike.

"Why?" Kumiko asked, sounding irritated. At her response, Xerx smiled inwardly. She clearly assumed he was questioning her prodigious intellect. For some reason, vanity often wasn't something he considered where Kumiko was concerned.

That was where Mobola chimed in.

"Garrison mode is non-euclidean," she said, at first nervous as ever with someone whom she was less familiar with, but then her voice steadied and rose in volume. "That means unless you follow the path you're in, you might not end up where you intend. It'd be like breaking through a wall in the middle of a maze and finding yourself back at the beginning, or the end, or somewhere on the other side of it. Are you familiar with the hypercube concept?"

"I am," Kumiko replied. "So, it's 'follow your voice or risk fucking myself just as much as the target'; I understand."

"Language…" Ri'Kela growled. Xerx had to deliberately prevent himself from rolling his eyes.

"All right, all right," Kumiko said, making a fluttering, dismissive wave. "So, we engage as soon as she starts moving."

"Just give us the word," Xerx said. "We'll send Biraknu in with you."

"That would be pointless." Kumiko shook her head and eyed the somewhat miffed-looking Felyan. "No offense. To be honest, I think that Ramirez might actually *have* over-prepared for this mission after all."

"Don't insult the guests," Xerx said flatly. "If we get out of this, I'm sure they'll be just as useful protecting our precious cargo as they are back home. He shifted his gaze from the map as it reverted back to a standard plan of the ship's layout, then to the assembly. Nevertheless, with Tyger and Akiko on board, thinking at first that they would be needed for this adventure, he had to agree with the sour-faced girl. Or maybe Kumiko was being over-confident. She had a bigger arrogant streak than Radic on a hat in the tournaments.

"And so, with this little plan in motion," Xerx said, "we now play the waiting game."

Two hours later, no sooner than Ri'Kela had laid the baby down to sleep in the bassinet she'd fashioned in their quarters, Kumiko gave the word.

"She knows she's asleep," she said. "It's now or never."

I knew it'd be you.

Amira's mocking drawl echoed in Kumiko's mind as soon as she'd entered the decks that Xerx had arranged into the trap for her.

Whoring out your services to the catdog queen and her human pet, eh?

She'd been unusually chatty since Xerx had led her into this section of the *Reckless* and the blast doors slammed down behind her. Kumiko reined in her emotions at Amira's taunting voice as a memory came to mind—something from Lhirevlis, she knew, clouded with the fog of the partial mindwipe the Vlissians had imposed on all their acolytes. Shezmi had put them both through a challenge like this once before: a maze of shifting paths, created ... or perhaps grown? There had been something organic about it. Regardless, it was intended as a test of their abilities: avoid finding each other—a feat that required suppressing one's mental footprint. And it was one of the few skills that she could best her in.

"Shit," Kumiko murmured at this revelation.

"Language!" came Amira's mocking voice in an exaggerated facsimile of Ri'Kela's posh accent, followed by a peal of derisive laughter. Kumiko, grinding her teeth, cocked her fist back, ready to punch clear through the bulkhead to shorten her route to intercept.

"She's taunting you, isn't she? You're better than that, Kumi," came her mother's voice. She'd joined the group after the strategy meeting for moral support, for what it was worth.

"Your vitals are ratcheting up," Xerx said. "She really is communicating with you?"

"Really, now?" she replied in a sarcastic tone. "How'd you guess?"

"Remember, you're not the only one who's tangled with her," Xerx said. "She did that to me when we got in that scrape back on Dorado."

"Kumi, Sweetheart we're only trying to help you stay focused," Akiko added in an attempt to sound soothing. "You were hired for good reason. Show them they weren't wrong in that assumption."

Kumiko paused. Biting back any condescension toward her mother, she instead let out a sighing groan. She allowed the frustration to again bleed from her mind, despite the smug miasma of Amira's intruding thoughts. Though no match for her in a one-on-one fight, she'd always been the better one at mental intrusion. Kumiko had made her mind into a fortress before this mission, and Amira still could read what leaked to the surface and use connected thoughts and memories as a base to reach deep, dredging things left secret or forgotten. She'd sometimes been able to get the better of her this way, even back on Lhirevlis. Those times she could remember with perfect clarity. It started off as good-natured ribbing, but over time, as bitterness accrued, it devolved into insult. As much as she hated to admit it, her mother and Xerx were right. She had to grow past this vulnerability.

Kumiko held the home field advantage, in the form of a map encoded into the holo emitter fastened to her wrist. She'd close in on her and finish it. For now, she was allowing the arrogant bitch to wander and wallow in her overconfidence, circling her until she would begin to doubt herself, then move in for the coup de gras.

That's right, listen to mommy after all. We're a good girl now! Amira sneered. But this time, Kumiko decided to bite—not out of anger, but to bait her instead.

I was Shezmi's favorite for a reason, she replied, allowing her own arrogance to pour into their unwanted connection. *Maybe you should have listened to him more instead of attempting to sabotage his lessons.*

Amira's burning rage made her smile as Mobola spoke over the comm.

"Kumiko, I'm going to expand garrison mode. It'll get you closer to the target and save you some time."

"Understood," Kumiko replied.

"Brace yourself," Xerx said afterward. "This is going to feel a little weird."

It was indeed weird, but not the disorientation from the first time she teleported: a discomfort that she'd expected. Teleporting was a cacophony of fragmentation, flooded with the multitude of locales in the universe: being stuck in a wall, at the bottom of a pit deeper than the highest mountain was high, and at the same time existing in the burning core of a planet and in a star's blistering corona. This was completely different: a shifting of perspective that played a variety of tricks on her perception, and even her balance, as the dimensions and space about her expanded and contracted while she remained still. It was like watching a hallway camera trick in a horror vid come to life.

It also had another intended effect, judging from the flare of rage she felt through her connection to Amira.

She was indeed pissed.

When I find my way out of this funhouse from hell, both you and that captain with his shit-eating grin will wish I'd kept that mongrel baby as my only target! Her thoughts screamed, the words feeling like acid that burned through Kumiko's senses.

Aww, still not discouraged? Kumiko rounded several corridors and checked her map holo. She was close now. Much closer.

Why would I be? Amira seemed to have recovered quickly from her state of rage. *After all, you weren't discouraged with your boyfriend, right?*

I don't know what you're—

Amira's laugh was like the coldest ice. Kumiko tried to shove her out, but her mental push was stronger—not strong enough for her to attack, but purging her presence from her mind was like trying to remove grease with a trickle of tepid water. To everyone else, she was the ultimate ice queen. But Amira's talent could emotionally compromise her in a heartbeat.

She glanced at her holo. Only a couple of right turns away.

Don't insult us both, honey. Your memories about how many times you opened your legs for that little Felyan twink go way into the pathetic. And you even started to like him! Must've been heartbreaking when you ran into him playing hide-the-sausage with that half-breed house mother when you came to check on the kitten you left him. You're still doing that? Leaving stray kittens for people you like?

"I know she's still running her mouth—er, mind," Xerx said. "You can do this."

"Xerx, be a dear and shut up," Kumiko said as she checked her holo. Amira was right on the other side of the wall.

Are you still naming them all "Mr. Pickles" too?

Kumiko smiled. She grinned so hard that she felt the cords of her facial muscles strain near to cramping as she endured the woman's smug, mocking drone. Mobola's words of caution returned to mind, giving her fair warning about what she wanted so badly to do. She stared at the wall, her fists shaking, her barely contained thoughts causing stress fractures in the steel and carbon fiber plating about her, the sound of rupturing metal echoing in the background of Amira's voice.

Now that is just lame. But I guess that's to be expected from someone with the imagination of a brain-dead cumquat.

She focused her thoughts outward, toward the wall. Like the web of cracks in glass that had been struck by a projectile, fissures erupted in its surface, while pressure pushed the plating inward.

For a second, Kumiko's anger subsided just enough for some sense to process. She held back, hesitating on a momentary worry that breaking through this wall might indeed collapse the tesseract, as Mobola had warned. She hadn't had many interactions with the perpetually nervous girl, but she knew that she was smart—smarter than even her crewmates gave her credit for. And being shunted into some kind of pocket dimension would be a terrible inconvenience.

In for a penny, in for a pound.

Plus, the bitch had insulted her kitten-naming talent.

The wall imploded, and a scream on the other side gave her a sense of relief and renewed confidence. She leaped through the hole, creating a force that blew away the miasma of dust and particles, launching herself at the figure on the other side that all of her senses had locked onto.

"Frosty! What the hell just happened?" Xerx's voice cut in on the comm, but Kumiko was hardly in a position to respond. A counterforce slapped against her, sending her careening down the surprisingly long corridor. Fortunately, its length proved to be a blessing in disguise, as it gave her time to brace herself with yet another counterforce and steel her defenses.

"I see you've been practicing," Kumiko said, shaking off the blow like a Sunday morning hangover with some bemusement. "That riposte was better than I expected. But that won't help you."

"I've gotten better at a lot of things." Amira sneered. The still dust was clearing from the rubble of carbon fiber, thin steel paneling, PVC piping, and fiberoptics now strewn across the corridor, blowing away in an artificial wind generated by the figure who stepped forward.

Amira had not changed much from the last time Kumiko had seen her: same long, dark brown hair and swarthy oval face. She was somewhat fuller in the chest, but not as developed as Kumiko. She was also noticeably thinner, as if she'd been subsisting on a diet consisting of only reconstituted protein dinners. She wore an old jumpsuit with a ragged brown cloak about her, from which the breeze carried a slightly sour smell, as if she hadn't bathed in days. A deep purple radiance dripped from her eyes like tears as she approached, a smug grin plastered on her face.

"Time hasn't been kind to you," Kumiko observed, feeling the itch of the nanotubules' reactions to her psionics. She yearned to turn her into a cinder or freeze her into ice-encrusted fragments, but she unfortunately needed her alive.

"At least I didn't have a Seeker hounding my ass," Amira said. Kumiko had forgotten the Dorado accent she'd shared with the Ambassador. "Life hasn't been optimal for you, either, has it, *encanta*? Never thought I'd see you running from the Vlissians? Got disillusioned with Shezmi and his bullshit?"

"My reasons are my own," Kumiko said. "And don't lump Shezmi in with those fanatics."

"They're all Vlissians; who the fuck cares?" Amira said, scowling. Below her, a crack in the floor appeared and spread up the wall to her left. From it, Kumiko could hear a rush of air. If that one imploded, it would most assuredly not lead to another corridor.

"You can't beat me," Kumiko said. "You know this."

"There it is, that familiar Frosty arrogance," Amira snapped back. "You were never *that* strong, you know."

"Tell that to the two Seekers that got sent after me."
"*Two?*"

Kumiko laughed. "Looks like there are some things you couldn't pick out of my brain after all."

Amira's face contorted into a look that bled hatred as profusely as the purple light bled from her eyes.

"Then I'll just have to pick the brains out of your fucking corpse!" she hissed.

Kumiko felt a lance of pain strike her in the forehead. She recognized the psychic attack and steeled her will against the incursion, and the pain faded into a lingering ache. Still, Amira pushed back, undaunted. She stared at Kumiko, visibly straining, beads of sweat forming at her brow as Kumiko stepped forward, pushing further against the assault, the overlapping energies manifesting themselves as rippling heat waves against an ever-brightening lance of light. Soon, it would be like a welder's torch, and the heat was already becoming palpable.

The nanotubules in Kumiko's arm awakened. They began siphoning the heat energy, flash-cooling the air about her as she pressed against her former classmate, whom she felt begin to weaken against the strain. Like the integrity of the walls surrounding them, she was starting to buckle, losing control. The construct was in danger of collapsing about them, so she needed to finish this fight. Amira was no match for her, and she needed to prove it in no uncertain terms.

The nanotubules on her opposite arm flared to life—with emphasis on the flare. The overlapping energies destabilized into a combustion of superheated particles that splattered like lava throughout the corridor, while at the same time, a gout of flame licked outward from Kumiko's bare hand, half-engulfing Amira, who screamed in pain. The wall of psionic force collapsed, and Kumiko charged forward, striking her opponent full force across the lightly cauterized flesh of her jaw, and sending her reeling into a damaged section of the far wall.

The effect was an instant cascade of chaos. The corridor rippled out in both directions, then began to compress like a giant hand had grabbed it and closed its fist. Augmenting her strength with psionic force, Kumiko lunged forward, grasped Amira's unconscious form, and allowed her mind to fall into the nexus of locations for them to teleport. For a moment, she was everywhere at once ... and then, as the world about her bent inward to nothingness, it expanded into the briefing room.

She stood up, her senses attuning to Xerx, who was in the middle of a panicked conversation with Mobola, standing beside her mother, who had a look of utter horror plastered on her face, with Tyger staring blankly at the holo in front of them, glowing red spreading throughout the expanded section of the *Reckless*. Then, at the very next moment, they noticed her and froze.

Mustering her dignity, she stood up, laying the still-unconscious Amira at her feet.

"Well, that was, er, more eventful than I had planned," she said.

"**I** could throw water on her face," Xerx said.

"Then you'd give her a weapon."

"I was just joking," Xerx said. He gave a wry grin, despite Kumiko's reply making it sound like he'd said the stupidest thing imaginable. "I thought you could read minds."

Again, he felt the sourceless *thump* against the back of his head.

"Be nice, Kumi," Akiko chided from behind the two, observing the cell where Amira still lay motionless, slumped over unceremoniously on the bed platform. She then gestured to the roughhewn crystal that floated above her daughter's open right hand. "Are you sure that will contain her?"

"Yes," Kumiko said with noticeable irritation. From the looks on the others' faces, they were expecting her to elaborate further, but she wouldn't; the inscrutable workings of Vlissian technology would be beyond their understanding anyway, and she wasn't prepared to waste time trying to explain.

"Vitals are spiking, captain," Var's voice came in over the comm. "She's waking up." At the same time, Amira groaned, stirring in her cell.

"Moment of truth," Xerx said with a sigh. He glanced toward Kumiko, who nodded.

Xerx pressed the switch to open the cellblock door and Kumiko stepped inside. Quickly, he shut it behind her.

Behind him and Kumiko's mother, Tyger pushed himself away from his leaning position against the wall, joining them.

"She could tear this ship apart, couldn't she?" He asked.

"Like a laser on a sardine can," Xerx grimly replied as he watched Kumiko stand beside Amira's bed, unmoving, with the crystal-like object glowing a sickly yellow that reminded him of an untreated wound. "But knowing her, I doubt it'll come to that. Have a little faith, man."

"I do," Tyger said. "I just worry that someday, she'll find her limits and be too stubborn to ask for help."

Xerx couldn't help but agree. "She almost did that back on Siberna, if memory serves."

"That's why I'm glad she hasn't alienated everyone she's connected with."

For a moment, the blackness of space tore open like a gaping maw to reveal the blue energy realm of hyperspace, from which came nothing. Or so it appeared.

Aboard the cloaked ship, Snow studied the readouts on her cockpit display. Before them, the distant blue orb of Haven hung in the center of the viewport.

Snow brought up several topographical displays of its main continent and studied the coastal regions for a discreet place to land. She tapped her lip, then zoomed in on the coastal city of New St. Louis.

"Noo, check the files. I think this is the place our target tends to frequent, correct?"

The screen suddenly took on a life of its own, bringing up street views and surveillance footage of Kumiko Zero going about her business in the city. The footage was from several months ago, but Snow was confident that she would return here soon. Noomi's voice came through the console speakers, causing Snow to frown.

"Aye, this is the place. I'll scout for a sweet spot we can plonk our arses doon without being seen. Give me a sec."

The satellite view returned to the fore, and the image followed the coastline, stopping and zooming in on a small cove several miles to the northwest of the city.

"This wee cove looks like a good spot, Boss. There's no major access from above the cliffs and it's oot of the way enough for us not tae be noticed."

Snow shook her head.

"I will never understand why you chose such an outrageous accent to communicate with, Noo, but yes, this does look like a good spot: minimal chance of being spotted, I assume?"

"Ach, shove it up your arse, just cos I dinnae want to sound like some upper-class Iconan wench, but that's bye the bye, aye we can drop cloak there and save power."

Snow leaned forward and began typing some commands into the console and sat back, smiling.

"Looks like a water landing; that's good. I've been itching to try out the sea skimmer ever since they gave me it."

A warning chime sounded, and Snow sat up straight, her smile gone and her white eyes staring at the console as her focus returned like a shot.

"Hold up," Noomi said. "I'm picking up signals near the edge of the system."

The images hovering above the console switched from Haven to a view of Peridot, the green ice giant planet that marked the outer edge of the planetary system. Two faint dots could be seen moving past it.

"Ships?" asked Snow. "Can you identify them at this distance?"

"Oh aye, easy, just gimme a sec to break their IFF subspace transponder encryption. And ... done."

Immediately, two ident markers appeared in red above the dots. The names and ship class statistics began to appear. Snow rubbed her chin.

"The *Wild Wolf* and the *Saber of Montera*," she said. "Safe to say they're raiders, then. Oh, and what do you know? Running modified Barracudas! I'm sure they think the class name gives them some sort of street cred, but I've seen R18s perform better and they're literally flying bricks!"

"Looking at their course projections, it's highly likely they are headin' for Haven too," Noomi said.

"Shit, did they see our rift when we dropped out of hyperspace?"

"Och, naw, their sensors are nae that good; they piss all their money intae targeting systems and combat software. They cannae register much outside of 2 or 3 AU's, not clearly anyway."

"Enough to navigate and make the kill, huh? I wonder what they're doing here?" Snow rounded the chair to face the cockpit entrance and stood up. "Noo, take us in for the landing. I'll be prepping for the mission."

"Making love to your gun collection, you mean?" was Noomi's cheeky reply. "Aye, I got this covered. You go have fun."

Snow ignored her and continued toward the exit. She had few pleasures in life, and her proficiency with firearms was one of them. She wasn't about to let the cybernetic little gobshite take that away from her.

The ship continued toward Haven, invisible but for a faint shimmer as the sunlight pierced the gloom, the central star appearing from behind the planet's disk.

Amira flopped over, awakening like the life of last night's party the Sunday after, having cultivated a blood type of 50 proof.

"I'd say good morning, but ... you know," Kumiko sneered. "Now get up."

Kumiko winced, gritting her teeth as she felt Amira's spike of anger, fueled by the realization of her defeat and the crackle of pain that shot through her head. A moment later, the light of recognition switched on in her captive's eyes as she took full stock of her situation.

"Now, before you do something stupid—and believe me, it *will* be stupid—I just would like to give you fair warning." Kumiko gestured with the hand over which the sickly yellow crystal floated. It moved forward and to the left until it was caught between both their fields of vision.

"I'm sure you know what this is," she said, then paused, sensing Amira's wordless astonishment. "It would appear that you didn't believe me earlier."

"No, I didn't." Amira's voice came as a sour croak.

"Ever known me to lie?" Kumiko said, allowing herself a smug grin, and presented the crystal between them, twirling end over end as if in a slow cycle in the dryer. "So this'll be much easier. It's a little-known fact that when you off a Vlissian, unless you destroy this thing ... they're not really dead."

Amira blanched, her face a mask of utter horror.

"Good to see we're on the same page."

"You're fucking *crazy!*" Amira lunged, but Kumiko exerted her own counter force against inertia, throwing her back against the wall like a rag doll.

"Oh, if you're worried about him recovering, he can't," Kumiko stopped the crystal from spinning, making sure a particular part of its surface rested directly before Amira's wide eyes. The fracture stood out amidst its jaundiced facets, a glaring black void amidst its glow, through which exuding energies flowed like water falling down a cliff, but horizontally instead of vertically. "Not without the help of other Vlissians, at least."

"Is it … aware of us?" Amira asked, licking her lips as if they'd suddenly gone quite dry. Kumiko could see the distant shiver in her limbs, feel her restrained fear, edged with astonishment.

Kumiko shrugged. "I'm not really sure. But I sure hope so. What I *do* know, though, is that if I cause it pain, it'll scream. And other Vlissians—Seekers included—tend to hear that. So there's no telling who will answer." She then gave a fake squeal of delight and grinned. "Shall we find out?"

"No!" The pulse of unbridled terror was like a scream of its own, making Kumiko feel almost giddy with the residual epinephrine high. She almost laughed at how Amira cringed into the corner of the cell while the frame of the bed platform warped with her uncontrolled psionics.

"But Amira, dear, imagine the fun we'd have!" Kumiko said. "I've gotten stronger since my last go with a Seeker. And I've been wanting to see just how fast I could kick its ass this time around."

"You're psychotic!" Amira spat. As expected, Kumiko sensed that a great deal of the woman's fear was now ebbing away, replaced by just a bit of incredulity. "All that tech in your body has fried your brain!"

Kumiko kneeled directly in front of Amira, keeping the same unnerving smile on her face as she held the crystal directly in between them. She was surprised at how little psionic "pressure" it took: the equivalent of squeezing the trigger of a stick lighter, in fact. The cracks on the surface of the crystal began to spread. And from those new micro-fissures came a sound that thrummed across the gulf between both their minds, as disturbing as it had been the first day she did it. It was a scream, though faint, its pain and anguish bled out between them like droplets of agony. And the very walls felt as if they were reverberating with energy, creating a silent echo that threatened to tear across the universe.

"Okay, stop! Please!" Amira wailed, flailing her hands as if shooing the object away. "You crazy bitch, you made your point!"

With this, Kumiko let the full heat of her fury bear down on Amira's mind. Again, she scrambled into the corner, whimpering like a kicked puppy, unable to muster the psionic reserves to fight back like she had in the maze. The Seeker core crystal was doing its job splendidly. She could feel the woman's confusion and the impotent, seething fury beneath it all. She knew where this was going, and there would be little she could do about it.

"And what point was killing a *baby* going to make?" She snapped. "You've always been an asshole with little empathy, but I never thought you'd stoop *this* low. Was the money really that good? Fuck morals; just pop a kid for a big pay day?"

"You pampered little princess." Amira had lost her swagger, but the salt remained in spite of her fear. "With most people like us, we either become stooges for the Vlissians, or prey—and then slaves—to the Seekers, unless we can get together in big enough gangs, or we're hidden well enough. I saw through it all. Shezmi didn't want protégés; he wanted weapons. I tried to tell you, but you were too far up his ass to listen!"

"What sick fuck hired you to kill a baby?" Kumiko said, feeling about as much sympathy for her as she would a cockroach in her cereal.

"I wasn't ordered to kill her," Amira said.

"So says the woman who poisoned her food?"

"That was an accident."

"I'm going to 'accidentally' throw you to the Seekers," Kumiko hissed, practically shoving the core crystal in her face. Amira shrank away, pressing herself into the corner in such a way that it seemed that she was trying to pass through the very wall.

"No, I swear, it was an accidental overdose," Amira said, her voice straining with her state of near-panic. "The dosage was meant to make her sleepy while I took her away that night, so she wouldn't make any noise. I only realized my mistake after the fact."

Kumiko paused with some surprise, realizing the truth in her words and mind.

"So you fucked things up as usual?"

"They don't want her dead," Amira said. "I was ordered to kidnap her. That's all."

"Well, you've demonstrated admirable skill at that thus far." Kumiko let the sarcasm flow from her words like faucet water.

"You get off on rubbing it in, don't you?" Amira eyed Kumiko with naked disgust.

"It's a hobby," Kumiko said. "Something I've honed over the years, but that's not important right now." Again, she brought the crystal to her face. "Now, you said that *they* didn't want the princess dead. Tell me. Who, exactly, are 'they'? I want a name. Now. Or we'll play who's-going-to-answer-the-phone. What'll it be?"

Kumiko had been right. Amira sang like a bird. And though enlightening, her news was equally alarming—so alarming, in fact, that immediately after, Xerx went on the comm and called an all-hands meeting, including passengers. As everyone followed the captain out of the brig, Kumiko stayed behind, now standing outside the cell, the core crystal still in her hand.

"So you're on guard duty, watching over little ol' me?" Amira said, her voice low and sullen. "I guess that's some consolation, considering how much you 'love' being around me. I could turn this ship into swiss cheese with very little trouble otherwise. That crystal's the only thing keeping me from turning this ship into a derelict."

"Then where would you go?" Kumiko asked. "It's not like you'd know how to fly it, even if you managed to take out everyone here, me included."

"Distress beacon, duh," Amira drawled, rolling her eyes. "I'm pretty sure there's enough food in here to keep me going until somebody would come sniffing around. Then I'd just hijack their ship and be far away from here. But of course, there's the matter of your fucking core crystal suppressing my powers."

"Oh, this?" Kumiko inclined her head to the crystal, still glowing its dull, throbbing yellow, like a bug light on a sweltering Siberna night. "Yeah, newsflash. It's not suppressing you."

Amira narrowed her eyes, sitting up straighter and frowning. "What do you mean, it's not?"

Kumiko exerted her own power and created a fold in space, weaving a dimensional pocket, into which she slipped the core crystal. From Amira's point of view, it would look as if she'd flattened it into a 2-D image and slipped it away into nothingness.

"What I mean is exactly that. It wasn't suppressing your powers. Oh, but it could certainly have called for a Vlissian or a Seeker if I provoked it. But I don't need to do that, seeing how I already have one on speed dial."

As if it had been sheathed in diffraction cloth, a form rippled into existence beside Kumiko, easily two heads taller than she was and much broader. When it made its appearance, the reason for its size was obvious. Like a cone-headed centaur with a more compact rear body, the Vlissian stood before her, its shimmering black robe draped over its primary set of shoulders. In one of its four arms, it held a staff that held its core crystal in a spiral shaped cage, composed of the same material of the staff. It pulsed with its own inner light, but blue instead of yellow, and much brighter. Its small mouth below its nasal slits kept its eternal Mona Lisa-like smile.

It is good to see you together again, my students. The words reverberated in their minds with digital clarity, *though I wish it were under more amicable circumstances.*

"*Shezmi!*" Amira whispered the name with a combination of shock, fear, and utter hatred. Again, as before, during the events that led to her interrogation, she scrambled back, pressing herself into the corner at the end of the bed platform. "You bitch! I thought you weren't going to call them!"

Kumiko shrugged, shaking her head with a matter-of-fact expression. "I didn't say that I would *never* call them. Besides, do you think I want the captain looking over his shoulder during the whole trip? And I've got better things to do than stare at your ugly mug during that time. You gave us a lot of info, and he's not going to get far without me. You're just dead weight now. To be honest, I *could* have suppressed your powers with the crystal, and then spaced you when I was done."

I am glad you did not do that, Shezmi interjected. *I should like to think that I taught you to have some empathy.*

"That would've been preferable to what he's going to do to me!" Amira said, still panicking. "Do you have any idea what I went through to get away from those … *things*?"

"Now that's a hell of a way to treat our teacher," Kumiko said. "Besides, he thinks that his people can fix you. So, you're going with them."

"More like 'lobotomize' me," Amira spat. "I'd rather die than be like their lackeys … than be like *you*! I swear to God, one day you'll see that I was ri—"

The light from Shezmi's core crystal brightened into something like a flash, and Amira slumped over, unconscious once again. She toppled limply to the floor, but before she could hit the ground, an invisible force caught her. Shezmi glided forward, his form passing through the energized bars of the cell like a ghost. Amira rose higher, and glided over to Shezmi's back, coming to rest atop his centaur-like form like a sleeping rider slumped over a very small horse.

We will look after her, Shezmi said to Kumiko. *And we'll not make the same mistakes of the past.*

"I hope you don't," Kumiko said, and almost smiled at the warmth that came across their connection. Outside of her mother, and even her father's awkward, yet well-meaning attempts to form a bond with her, Shezmi was the only other person that she could call family. Despite her general loathing for Vlissians, she could never dislike him.

May you have good journeys and more adventures, Shezmi said as his form rippled away. *And thank your captain on my behalf for his cooperation.*

"I will."

NINE

Xerx took a sip from the Felyan brandy he'd held in his private stock, steadying his nerves after having watched the impossible happen. He'd already been through enough harrowing brushes with death since the incident on Siberna, and had been hoping for smoother sailing since Tophanavar, but of course, where tertiaries were involved, all bets were off.

He leaned forward over the bar, musing over how much action had just seemed to jump into his life like a fleet of ships off the far side of the moon. In fact, ever since Siberna, it seemed as if there hadn't been much in the way of peace. And they were once again in the middle of another big kerfuffle, not of his making. He longed for the days of accidental bar fights and crew-mates drinking down half a bar's supply being his only worry.

"It seems my saving grace here is that except for one baby, our passengers are all people who can hold their own in a scrape," he murmured aloud as the entrance door slid open.

"That's a lot of confidence in these people," Kumiko said, approaching his side, "especially when one is my father." The decanter of brandy moved of its own accord, sliding into her waiting hand as she joined him at the bar. It was joined soon after by a glass that seemed to flip backward from the cabinet and onto the countertop. "You know most of his 'war stories' are bullshit, right?"

"There's more truth to them than you think," Xerx replied as she poured herself a glass, much to his chagrin. "But he does like to embellish. I'm guessing our 'special guest' has been neutralized?"

"I forgot how draining dealing with her could be," Kumiko said. She took a sip of the drink, then tossed her silvery hair back with a sigh. "I've never seen such vitriol in a single soul. Still, she's gone now."

"Wait." Xerx froze in place, a distant feeling of dread beginning at the edge of his innards. "'Gone'? Please don't tell me you—"

"No, I didn't space her," Kumiko said, to Xerx's great relief. "Shezmi took her off my hands instead."

He'd met Shezmi before, back when he and the *Shadow Star* crew had to come to Kumiko's rescue in Siberna's badlands at the word of the surprisingly friendly Vlissian who had suddenly appeared to him and his Neela. The enigmatic race rarely showed themselves to others, especially not people like him, who were only StellarNet famous for pit-fighting giant antique robots. But perhaps it was just as well. It was said that meeting a Vlissian had a habit of meaning something big was going to happen in your life, and would either be very good or catastrophically bad.

"So he was here, aboard the ship?" Xerx said, trying to sound disappointed, and forgetting momentarily Kumiko's mind-reading. "Damn, I wish I'd been there.

Well, aside from the obvious, what's the deal with you and Vlissians, anyway?"

Kumiko frowned, not out of anger, but rather seemingly regret.

"It's—"

"—Personal, yes," Xerx said, finishing the sentence as she began the word.

"Well, at least I know you don't think I'm lying," Kumiko said, sounding almost as grateful as her phrasing of the statement. Xerx snorted.

"To quote your mother, you're as blunt as a sledge-hammer to the balls," he said. "You've never been someone who lies."

"I've always found dishonesty to be a stupid tactic," Kumiko said.

"Not when you're trying not to be rude," Xerx said.

"Ugh! Please, why is the truth always considered offensive?"

"Probably because most people can't dig around in other folks' heads," Xerx replied.

"Life would be easier if they could," Kumiko said. "You have no idea what it's like to stand there listening to people plead the truth while their mind is screaming all kinds of obscenities at you."

"Well, speaking of telling the truth, did you find anything else interesting from our guest before she got hauled away?" Xerx said.

"Seems like a Vlissian's visit was something good this time," Kumiko replied. "She really didn't talk much, in fact, until right before Shezmi put her to sleep. And it was kind of a jumble. Guess she had nothing left to lose when she knew the jig was up."

"So, you going to leave me in suspense?" Xerx said.

Kumiko swirled the brandy in her glass. "She was supposed to be the delivery girl."

"For who?"

"Helix," Kumiko said matter-of-factly.

"Shit."

"You know them?"

"Who doesn't?" Xerx said. A combination of frustration spiced with distant fear licked at the edges of Xerx's innards. He sighed and knocked back the remainder of the drink, letting its ghost-sweetness burn across his tongue and throat, imbuing him with that liquid courage he so often found himself in need of.

"Assume I'm the minority and enlighten me," Kumiko said.

"They're a dinosaur," Xerx said. "A human supremacist group dating back to the days of the Northwest Passage crossing." They fed off the chaos after the Imperium Wars and were the main cause of Felyans withdrawing most of their aid from the colonies. They made the dark age last longer, and because of them, there are still territories where Felyans and hybrids aren't welcome."

"That explains a lot," Kumiko said.

"About what?"

"Amira's vitriol against Felyans and hybrids," Kumiko explained. "I mean, she *hates* aliens of any kind, and especially half-breeds."

"Well, Helix was thought to have been wiped out after the colonial parliament was established," Xerx said, picking up where he'd left off. "They did a massive crackdown on cults like them. Felyans started dealing with humans again, and we wanted to make a good first impression."

"So they've been walking shadows since then?" Kumiko said.

"Of the worst kind," Xerx remarked grimly.

"You're surprised?" Kumiko said.

"No, but it's worrying," Xerx said. "They must've grown tired of being little more than boogeymen." He rubbed at the line of hairs on his chin. "I wonder what they'd want with Felyan royalty?"

"Whatever it is, it can't be good," Kumiko said

"Thank you, Captain Obvious," Xerx said, casting Kumiko a lopsided grin, and earning yet another invisible thump to the head.

"Well, we at least have something to start with," Xerx said, rubbing his scalp. Then, eyeing the renewed motion of the bottle back toward the silver-haired girl, he stopped it with one hand and placed the cap on it with the other.

"That first one was your reward for your help." Xerx nodded toward the glass in Kumiko's hand. "Earn your next one. This stuff isn't cheap, even on An'Re'Hara."

Just then, Neela's voice broke into the comm.

"*Kipenzi*, we're getting a priority comm from the *Wraith*. And Alexa says she'll only speak with you."

"The hell?" Xerx muttered. The Pirate Queen rarely made priority calls, even with him. "Okay ... put her in to my personal comm." He then stepped away from the bar and opened the channel, being greeted by Alexa's hologram floating before him.

"Xerx dear, you wouldn't believe a shit show I've just stumbled upon," the Pirate Queen announced, her face as deadly serious as he'd ever seen. "And it involves you and your merry band."

"Wouldn't happen to have anything to do with Helix, would it?" Xerx said on a hunch. At this, Alexa's expression went blank. She blinked twice, then seemed to accept his seeming clairvoyance.

"Well, now, this might make things easier," the Pirate Queen said. But her grin did not lighten the atmosphere.

"Wait, I was right?" Xerx said with a groan. "It was meant to be a joke!"

"Sorry, chicken," Alexa said. "No rest for the wicked and all that." She cleared her throat. "So I just cleaned house with a few raiders in the Holstein Deeps, and found some ... well ... weird shit."

"Weird shit, huh?" Xerx raised an eyebrow. "Care to elaborate?"

"Chiefly, these raiders seemed to have been equipped with far better armaments than they ought," Alexa replied. "We knew that they had a supplier ... but it was not who I suspected."

An image of a red flag with a double helix appeared in a separate image.

"Like looking at a fucking ghost," Xerx mumbled, as Kumiko came to his side.

"Indeed," Alexa said. "The raiders seem to have been serving as their middlemen. Worse yet, their ships' communications show that they're looking for you. Have you done something to piss them off?"

"Well, I did kill a fleet leader," Xerx said.

"We both know he was a small fry with big pipe dreams," Alexa said. "What I found was a raider equivalent to an APB. They're hunting for you. And I can't help you unless you help me." She eyed Kumiko briefly. "Probably something to do with her, from what it sounds like."

Xerx forced back a snicker at the silver-haired girl's reliable inability to stay out of trouble, certain that she would do something worse than just give him another psionic goose on the back of his head. He then gave Alexa an edited version of his latest adventure.

"So far, we've solved one problem," he said in conclusion, "but this'll be a problem of a different kind. Good thing they don't know where I am."

"No," Alexa said pensively. "But they know where you're going."

"How in the hell would they know that?"

Both women suddenly gave a synchronized grunt and rolled their eyes.

"Well, it's not exactly a secret that the royal family is visiting Tophanavar to announce closer ties between the Alliance and Felyan Empire, is it?" Alexa snapped.

"Still, there's no way they could know it's *me* taking the baby there," Xerx said.

"They most likely don't know it's you," Alexa said. "And they don't need to."

"Either way," Kumiko interjected. "This is a massive deal for both governments. It's been promoted for months, and we've already discovered they're not above hiring tertiaries and equipping insurgents to achieve their goals."

"This sure as hell complicates things, doesn't it?" Xerx said, pursing his lips. Space travel was never completely safe, but he was beginning to have severe regrets of dragging an infant into this whole fecal hurricane.

"Well, at least we'll be better prepared for them than we were the last time." He switched his attention back to Alexa. "Although an engagement in space above a major colony has 'bad idea' written all over it. How close are you?"

"Not close enough, I'm afraid," Alexa replied. "Sorry, sweetie. But the *Wraith* isn't *that* fast."

"So we avoid Tophanavar and move closer to your position," Kumiko said, attracting the attention of both captains.

She switched on one of the display holos set into the countertop, bringing up a system map, and zoomed it onto a system on the other end of Alliance territory.

"We could lay low on Haven," she said. "It's a planet that I've used to cool down in the past."

"That's the exact opposite of our current heading," Xerx said. "Not to mention twice as far. Odds are we'd run into raiders before we'd even get there. I know this is a warship, but that's pushing it, even for us."

"Not if I jump it," Kumiko said.

Xerx and Alexa both stared at her with narrowed eyes for several seconds.

"Jump, as in that instantaneous shit you do?" Alexa asked. "But a whole starship?"

Kumiko fixed her with a sullen glare. "You doubt my abilities?"

Alexa shook her head. "Sweetheart, I couldn't give a fuck about your abilities, but you're talking about risking the lives of my husband's cousin and those aboard his ship. Doubt doesn't come into it. The question is, can you *truly* do it?"

"I ... believe I can."

Even Xerx knew that her voice didn't portray much confidence here.

"I've never tried it before!" Kumiko snapped. "All I know is that I can teleport anything I believe I can, and for bigger things, it's best to aim for somewhere I've been before, as unfamiliar places will take more out of me."

"Didn't teleporting to Siberna from Haven wipe you out that one time?" Xerx asked.

"That was several years ago," Kumiko said. "I've gotten better. It doesn't affect me in the same way."

"It's still sixty thousand tons against what? Forty kilos? I'm just saying."

"Look, you want me to try it or not?" Kumiko said tersely. "This is the best and most logical choice, but by all means, crawl your way there and see how many pieces we arrive in."

Xerx glanced at Alexa for support.

"Ball's in your court, love," she said. "But I will tell you that I'm much closer to Haven."

"Guess we're going to have to try," Xerx said, hoping desperately that this wasn't going to be the bad idea that ended them all.

"Excellent!" Kumiko said brightly.

"I'll bring the crew and our guests to the meeting room," Xerx announced, then noticed Alexa's shrewd expression.

"Something's bothering you?" he asked.

"I still have the feeling you're still not telling me everything," Alexa said, casting him a piercing gaze from her ice-blue eyes.

"Yeah," Xerx admitted. "Truth is, there is more going on here."

"Out with it, then."

"Not now," Xerx said. "I'll have to speak with ... certain people. Plus, I'd rather keep the rest off the comms until we can talk person to person on Haven."

"I love it when you're all cryptic," Alexa said with a smile.

"Yeah, yeah. See you on Haven," Xerx said.

The waves in the cove shifted and broke in the breeze when a section seemed to flatten and spread out in a large rectangular shape and descend below the water line around it. In a shimmer of iridescence, the gray hammerhead form of the *Hammerfall II* appeared. From the underside of each wing, a triangular arm descended and at the base of each a large pontoon inflated as it reached the surface of the water.

Inside the hangar bay, Snow stood on the mezzanine floor dressed in her IR suit. The suit itself was made of black sheer material interspersed with several white hexagonal panels that interlocked and covered most of her body. Within each panel faint circuitry patterns could be seen. Snow's hair was tied back in a high ponytail and a series of aerials protruded from her upper cranial sockets. Above each ear socket were small disc-shaped comm units. She placed a hand to her right ear and 'spoke' using the nonverbal digital system that linked her with the *Hammerfall II*'s main processor.

"Ok, I'm linked in, prep for IR suit test."

"Way ahead you, I cannae pick you up on any of the infra-red sensors or life sign monitors. You're a ghost."

Snow rolled her eyes in irritation but remained silent on the connection. These uplinks tended to have a bad habit of transmitting unguarded thoughts.

"Excellent, then; let's proceed to the next step. Have you got some locations to check out?"

"Aye, a few, though some o' them are real bastards if ya ask me, I dinnae know how you make some of your shots sometimes."

"That's why you fly the ship and I do the shooting, Noomi. But then it's not like you're built for it anyway, now is it?"

"Ah suppose that's true, but this is what I was built for, so I make sure I'm damn good at it. I'm not sure I could do your job, anyway. Too much like hard work lookin' after all those guns o' yours."

Snow smiled at that comment. Not everyone maintained weapons to the same standard as she did, but a well-maintained rifle was a reliable rifle, and she wouldn't risk it for sake of a few extra minutes and a polishing cloth.

Snow opened the locker in front of her and pulled out a long black MAG rifle with a large scope on the top. She inspected it, checking every inch of the body and testing its mechanisms. She leaned it against the railing, reached into the locker again, and pulled out a large bulky-looking backpack. In several places were electrical warning markers. As she hefted it onto her back, she heard Noomi in her ear once again.

"Jeez, is that the battery pack for that wee bastard? You plan tae pop this gal through reactor plating or sommat?"

"We are dealing with the most powerful psionic currently known to exist, one whom it's not wise to get up close with if you plan to kill her, so I'll be needing the full 1.6 megawatts this pack can give me and running supersonic spin penetrators, she can't strike back if she's mist and that's exactly how I want it to be."

Snow snapped a tactical belt about her waist and began filling its numerous pouches with ammunition clips. She pulled out a final clip and loaded it into the rifle, then marched down the steps toward the waiting vehicle pen.

Moments later, the lower cargo door opened, and a small torpedo-shaped craft sped out, headed out to sea.

With the exception of Mobola, who was minding the ship from the bridge, the crew and guests were present in the rec room. Xerx had explained the situation, both from Kumiko's interrogation of Amira and their subsequent call from the Pirate Queen. All the while, he took note of the looks of concern on everyone's faces. Ramirez seemed especially nervous, as well as Ri'Kela, who held the infant closer, as if she were her mother.

"So much for a simple journey," she muttered.

Xerx replied tersely. "Yeah, it's a shit show I know—"

"Language."

"—However, this is where are right now and we're more than aware of our responsibilities," Xerx continued, ignoring her.

"A responsibility we share," Ramirez added, casting a reproachful gaze toward the governess, whose ears drooped like a puppy that had just been caught soiling the carpet. "I've made no secret of my reservations regarding the captain's methods, but Lady Zero has faith in him and he has delivered so far. I trust him as I do both of you."

"Thanks for the vote of confidence," Xerx said, secretly hoping that it would not be misplaced. "We know Tophanavar is a trap, so we're going to skip it for now, and lay low on Haven."

"Haven?" Salt said, speaking up. "That's on the other side of Alliance space. Even at full throttle, we'd never make it without being caught by some raider fleet looking to carve a reputation out of us."

"You're right, but this is where Kumi comes in," Xerx said, gesturing toward Kumiko, who stepped forward.

"Oh, yeah?" Pepper said, the doubt evident in his voice. "And just what can Snow White here do to help?"

He managed to surprise Xerx with the rare moment of agreement with his father.

Kumiko cleared her throat and glanced coolly at Pepper before turning her gaze to Xerx.

"Polite one, isn't he?" she sarcastically murmured as Pepper suddenly yelped and grabbed his tail as though someone had yanked on it. He cast a poisonous glare in Kumiko's direction but said nothing.

"It's no secret that I've killed Vlissian Seekers, but make no mistake. Neither encounter was an easy victory.

The last one ended up being fought across two worlds." She made sure to scan over everyone in the room before looking down. "The initial attack began on Haven and in order to escape, I jumped from there to the Badlands on Siberna."

"Shit..." Biraknu murmured.

"Language," Ri'Kela snapped with a sharp hiss.

"So you're saying you can teleport across worlds?" Var asked. "Like how the Felyan captain transported us to their homeworld?"

Kumiko wrinkled her nose. "Nothing so basic as that. I don't need a ship thanks to some Vlissian tech I ripped off the first Seeker."

"It's a part of her now," Tyger explained, then gave Kumiko a concerned look. "Hang on. Jumping from Haven to Siberna wrecked you afterward. And we're a lot farther away from Haven than Siberna is right now. You sure you can handle this?"

"As I told Xerx and Alexa ... and now you," Kumiko said with a tone that dripped a conflict of tolerance and irritation, "I've improved myself since then."

"To teleport a ship?" Akiko said.

"Yes, mother," Kumiko drawled.

"Look, it's not that I don't think that you can do it, but all this tech in your body ... it worries me. Sometimes I worry if you'll end up being more machine than a person."

"I'm still very much me," Kumiko replied. "And I can do this. So don't worry."

"Look, everybody, we don't have the time to debate the finer points of Kumi's cybernetics," Xerx said. "We're gonna do it. Alexa will meet us there as soon as she can.

She's also informed me that the *Shadow Star* is already on Haven as we speak. Paige was taking some down-time but she's put her crew at our disposal just in case."

"And what about Helix?" Var said.

To this, Xerx heaved a deep sigh, but Neela answered for him.

"From the evidence Paige and Alexa gathered, the Insurgents are being equipped and funded by Helix, so at least we'll be dealing with a single unified enemy."

"Haven might not be safe either," Tyger remarked. "Is this really going to be more beneficial than just hitting Tophanavar? This is a warship, after all."

"I'm pretty sure we could hold our own in a fight," Xerx replied. "But we'd be fighting in a comms box—shipping lanes, beacons, monitoring stations, not to mention all the big security ships. And remember, Tophanavar's an orbital colony. If something vital gets damaged in a space battle, well ... I don't want to be responsible for the fallout from that. So, long story short, it's all potential collateral. I'm not willing to risk it."

"I don't like this situation either," Ri'Kela said, "but I have means to protect the child." She gestured to Biraknu's hulking form by her side. "We both do."

"You won't be alone," Akiko said to the governess with confidence. "My furry fighter and I will fight to make sure no harm will come to her."

Tyger shifted uncomfortably at the use of the pet name Akiko had given him years before, as Xerx shared an amused look with Kumiko.

"Okay. Let's get to it, then." He glanced at Kumiko. "Will you need anything?"

"Just some silence and some space," Kumiko said after eyeing the room. "I'll let you know when I'm about to make the transfer. It can feel a bit weird if you're not prepared for it."

"'Weird' as in 'painful'?" Xerx asked.

"Don't be stupid." Kumiko snapped with sudden annoyance. "You'll understand when it happens."

Taking the hint, Xerx moved to usher everyone out of the room, leaving Kumiko by herself.

"Let's head for the bridge," he said to the crowd that had built up in the hallway. "I'd rather we not have everyone separated if weird things start to happen." He then followed the crowd at its tail end, walking beside Tyger.

"She's a condescending little toe rag sometimes, but I'd trust her with my life," Tyger said to Xerx confidentially.

"Truer words were never spoken," Xerx said with a soft laugh. "By the way, you don't seem all that nervous."

"Nervous?" Tyger stopped and gave him a blank stare. "Why's that?"

"Well, we're going to be working closely with Alexa again, and—"

"Oh, that." Tyger waved dismissively. "I'm thinking she'll still be satisfied from the last time. And besides, Aki is with me. She's never bothered me when that's the case. Even when she's in the mood, she looks for someone else."

"Basically, you're saying that Alexa respects boundaries," Xerx said.

"Believe me, I'm more thankful for that than you know," Tyger said. "Though she *is* persistent the rest of the time."

"Sorry you got dragged into this, by the way."

"Are you kidding? A grin broke out on Tyger's short muzzle as Akiko pulled up beside them. He wrapped his arm around the tank. "Aki and I live for this shit!"

"Language..." Ri'Kela called out from further ahead.

The two of them shared a laugh before Xerx announced that they would be headed for the bridge.

"Now this is impressive," Ramirez commented. "I've never seen an actual ship from before the Imperium Wars except in VR records and holos. They really were something to behold." He gestured about at the surrounding display, featuring nearby nebulae glowing in enhanced colors. "The sensors cover the environment in real time?"

"They give updates as well, as well as sitreps for StellarNet updates, ship IFF signals, planetary conditions, spatial phenomena, Lidar readouts ... the full monty," Neela said, pausing in her descent from the dais to meet her husband.

"And all that without any tech pods," Akiko added.

"So, when will we be getting this party started?" Tyger asked.

"Frosty said that she needs a few minutes of peace and quiet, so ... any minute now?" Xerx shrugged as he followed his wife back to the dais. He surreptitiously took her by the hand and gave it a squeeze.

"You did good," he said. "Getting the hang of it now?"

"I think I'll manage."

"You're looking for me to vanish without a trace again?" Xerx teased, affectionately bumping his hip against his wife's.

"Not if you can help it," Neela said with a laugh, then gestured toward the captain's chair. "The bridge is yours, *Kipenzi*."

At that exact moment, the plan-turning punch in the face happened. Var looked up from his console as Xerx ascended the dais, concern creasing his thick brows and large muzzle.

"Captain, we're nearing the jump point for Tophanavar, but..."

"I said that Tophanavar was a bust," Xerx said. "Why are we still headed there?"

"You didn't say to change course."

"Shit."

Xerx stood quietly for a moment, letting the feeling of being an absolute fool wash off him before speaking again.

"What have we got?" he asked.

"I'm reading some sharks in the pipeline swimming upstream, four thousand klicks and closing."

"Dammit," Xerx said. The ambassador, who stood sans the baby with Neela, moved aside as he stepped forward gripped at the railing on the dais' edge. He watched as the surrounding holograms highlighted several contact points with bright red circles.

"Pipeline upstream?" Ramirez said. It was a rare moment where he was not with the sleeping baby. "The hell's that?"

"He means the hyperspace corridor we're traveling in, sir," Mobola replied, her voice coming through the ship's PA. "Enemy vessels are closing, Captain, but they're traveling against the flow of the energy streams."

"That should buy us enough time to get Kumi's plan into action, then," Xerx said. His posture was relaxed despite the situation, perhaps because by now he'd grown to accept the fact that his life was occasionally governed by Murphy's Law—this recent hairball being yet another result of its sublime influence. "Frosty, you there?"

"Obviously," Kumiko's voice crackled over the comm. "I sense tension; what's happening?"

"We've got company," Xerx replied. "A *lot* of company. Intercept course; I'm afraid time is no longer on our side."

"I'm assuming that the clock is ticking and it's nearly midnight?"

"We can hold out for a bit," Xerx replied, "but there's quite a few of them. Even the *Reckless* can't take them all on."

"Even against the flow, they'll be at weapons range in three minutes, captain," Var warned.

Mobola brought up a countdown clock on the holo, numbering down the time to fleet contact. If there was any time to do anything, it would be now.

"Don't mean to hurry you," Xerx said to Kumiko, "but—"

"Yes, yes, tick tock tick tock; I know!" Kumiko snapped. "I'll tell you when I'm ready."

Until that moment, Xerx was at least glad that he had a plan for the time being.

"Var, weapons hot," Xerx said. "Let's go spear fishing!"

"That's dangerous in hyperspace," Var said.

"Kinetic kill weapons only," Xerx replied. "Less risk of disturbing the flows."

"Yes sir," Var said. "Weapons free. Popping hull blisters now; auto tracking engaged."

The holos switched to ordinance tracking toward the approaching ships, and Xerx held his breath.

Contact.

Red flashes scattered along the hyperspace corridor as one exploding ship rammed into the others nearby, creating a hellish chain effect. The hyperspace currents would atomize the remaining debris.

"Got 'em," Neela said beside him, breathing a sigh of relief.

"That's just the vanguard Captain," Var said. "More are coming behind those. The wreckage has caused eddies to form in the flow and the pipe stability is fluctuating. We could be about to lose this stream."

"Drop out of hyperspace," Xerx said.

"I don't think that's a good idea," Neela warned.

"We should be okay," Xerx assured his wife after seeing the look of concern on her face. Just then, Kumiko's voice came back on the comm.

"I'm ready."

"Do it," Xerx said.

Snow strolled through the narrow streets of the city. She'd stashed the wave runner under a pier near the more decrepit end of the local dockyards. It was unlikely to be discovered. The sun was low on the horizon, casting an orange pall over the city itself and the sea shone gold with its reflection. Despite the golden glow across the water, dark clouds that had blown in from inland hovered directly overhead, and it was raining.

Snow didn't mind the rain; its touch reminded her that she got to experience such things in a different way from most of her kind. No dirty trenches or siege actions for her. But, for all the freedoms she enjoyed, she was still very much a slave to the Imperial war machine.

Snow raised her hood on the dark gray poncho she wore over her IR suit and adjusted the rifle on her shoulder. It clattered loudly against the battery pack on her back, and a couple of people looked up from their huddle in a nearby doorway. Seeing her, they turned back to their conversations.

In this part of town, heavily armed individuals were not an uncommon sight and Snow just assumed they'd taken her for another gun-toting mercenary heading for the Hub to check out the latest wanted lists. This was fine by her—no need to keep to the back streets and alleyways to avoid being seen.

She looked down at the small comm unit in her hand and pulled up the map screen, this was the final location she'd worked out with Noomi, the other three had been unsuitable in the end mostly because they didn't fit with the target's habits when visiting the area. But here, there was a nearby pleasure house where she would often visit and request the same male to service her. From her records, Snow noted that the target had also kept a property not far from the pleasure house.

The location she'd selected was a tower situated between the two sites that gave an almost unobstructed view of the multiple routes that could be taken. She approached the entrance to the tower and checked around. No one was visible and the local CCTV units were focused on the pleasure house and drinking dens. The main crimes on this backwater world usually consisted of disorderly drunk visitors, so the focus was primarily on those hot spots.

Still, that was no excuse for a lack of discretion. Snow slipped a small device from her belt and pushed it into the lock of the door. There was a click, and the door swung inward.

As she reached the top, Snow paused to survey the city below; the sun was starting to disappear below the horizon and its last red rays created a brief rainbow. Slowly, the darkened streets began to turn orange with the glow of sodium lamps. Shapes moved in the shadows, people moving back and forth, running whatever errands were required in the late evening.

Snow set down the battery pack and leaned her rifle against the parapet. She pulled out her music player and headphones and sat down next to her equipment. Her chosen location was surprisingly sheltered, and she made herself comfortable. This, at least, was a better location than her last foray into Alliance territory many years ago. At that time, she'd been hiding out in a forest full of giant spiders nursing an infected head wound after her original ship, the *Hammerfall II,* had been shot down. Placing the headphones over her ears, she selected some music and leaned her head back. Closing her eyes, she let the music take her away. There was plenty of time to kill before she had to focus on the task at hand.

This tune was a new one recommended by Agent Four, an Old Earth band called Genesis this time. She let the drum beat wash over her and allowed herself to drift off to sleep. Although she was unsure just who this 'Mama' the man was singing about so passionately, she wasn't concerned about being discovered. Noomi would wake her long before anyone came close to the tower or her position. Perhaps she would ask the eccentric processor unit what they thought of the song also, well maybe later.

"Xerx, turn the engines off," Kumiko said. "We won't be needing them."

"You heard the lady." Xerx leaned over the railing that encircled the dais above Mobola's console. "Throttle back; kill the drive units."

"Thrust at zero," Mobola said as Xerx settled into his seat. "Drive units disengaged." After a moment, the faint vibration of the ship's engines thrummed to a lower register throughout the bridge.

While everyone waited patiently down below, the comm gave off its signal. Seeing Alexa's code, he opened it on his personal console.

"Something you forgot?" Xerx said.

"Yes, actually," the Pirate Queen replied. "I just needed to tell you something important. Because of the raiders, you'll need to try to get innnnnnnnnn aaaaaaaaaaat thhhhhhhhheeeeeeeeeeeeeeeeeeeeeeee..."

Her voice slowed, then deepened in an odd, digitized crescendo, and into incomprehensibility. Before Xerx could say anything, Alexa's image shattered into static and vanished, leaving the words, SIGNAL LOST on the holo.

"Did you see that?" he said, believing Neela to be still beside him, but when he switched off the comm, he noticed she was gone. He launched to his feet and located his wife halfway down the ramp from the dais, staring outward, mouth agape. In fact, everyone was frozen in this position, staring in complete, wordless, transfixed wonder at the surrounding holos. And as if to add extra strangeness, their bodies were wreathed in a bluish glow that Xerx slowly came to realize was more than just a reflection of the ambient light from the holos' enhanced images.

In fact, everything was alight with the blue glow, from the consoles below the dais to the dais itself: the captain's chair and consoles as well. Xerx looked in the direction that the entire assembly was fixed upon, and froze in the bluish halo that was illuminating from the images of space, which were beginning to blur, like a movie image that was being altered by a prismatic future, giving things a stretched appearance.

Xerx tried to reach Kumiko on the comm, but a flood of what could only be described as pure, indistinct white noise drowned out his question.

Next came the sensation.

And it truly was odd.

The wall of noise ended with a deafening abruptness ... then he heard the voices of his assembled guests and crew that faded, shifting to an eternity away, coupled with a sudden sensation of being a rubber band stretched into that eternity.

Then the exclamations returned: a cacophony of its own, followed by the snap, as if someone had let go of that rubber band that he had become, letting it fling across impossible distances. The halo of light flared into a blinding instant—

—Then all was silent ... and altogether alarmingly normal.

The blue glow had vanished, leaving the bridge feeling strangely dark. The holos were now showing different surroundings, but not what Xerx had expected. Rather than the predominant vast oceans of Haven, a massive pale sphere of a different kind dominated their view, mostly obscured by a shadow with a halo of icy green revealed about its edges where the sunlit side was mostly obscured. A beautiful sequence of rings formed a band that appeared fragmented in the stark shadows.

"The fuck just happened?" Salt said. And for once, the governess did not admonish anyone's use of language.

"Did we make it?" Ramirez said.

"*Dada*," Neela projected her voice toward Mobola. "Do you have a fix on our location?"

"Almost ... got it..." Mobola drawled. "Ah, here it is. Starcharts are a match for the Haven system. We're just hanging out at its edge. The big green thing out there with the pretty rings is Peridot, its last outer planet."

Tyger gave a whistle. "Guess it was kind of a stretch for her after all, if she couldn't quite get us all the way there." He then gave a worried look to Akiko, whose expression fell into the same demeanor ... right before an alarm sounded.

But this noise, shrill and plaintive, did not come from the consoles. From the end of the line, Var growled, glancing at a device on his wrist.

"Medical alert on the obs deck," he said.

"Kumi!" Akiko breathed, moving with a swiftness borne of sudden terror. She beat the large *Hara'Kya* Felyan to the bridge's exit, followed by Tyger.

"I'm going too," Xerx said, wracked with a sudden spike of guilty fear. Immediately, he followed after the three who had just left. "Mobola, set a course for Haven. Neela, you have the bridge again."

A couple of corridors and a lift later, they arrived back where they'd started, and to the sight of Kumiko lying prone in the middle of the floor, with Var settled on his haunches beside her, sweeping her over with bioscanners. Xerx's stomach dropped as he noticed a small rivulet of blood trailing from one eye and her nose.

Var gently opened one of her eyes. Blood vessels had burst all over her sclera, creating a vision of a blue iris bathed in a viscous red sea.

"Medkit's beside the dishwasher," Var said. "There's a collapsible stretcher there."

Xerx leaped over the bar and located what Var had described, then brought it their way. He pressed a button at its side, and the entire thing unfolded into one piece with a loud *snap*. Var then nodded toward Kumiko's feet. "On three, you grab the bottom half, and I'll lift the top. Be gentle."

Xerx nodded and followed the directions. In moments, he activated the stretcher's antigravs and Var was sliding her to sickbay.

Tyger, Akiko, and Xerx stood at the edge of the room, Akiko looking paler than normal, and biting her lower lip while Tyger's arm and tail went around her shoulder and waist. Var used the servo arms of the medical bed to lift Kumiko from the stretcher and place her on its mattress. He then hooked her up to a set of health monitors before switching to four legs and loping over to several cabinets. Standing upright, he grabbed multiple vials as a series of alarms went off from the machinery. Several tubes snaked out from the servo arms and hooked into Kumiko's arms as Var returned with the vials and slipped them into a line of receptacles alongside the machine's arms.

"Nanos injected," Var said, frantically typing on a datasheet. It was hard to read a *Hara'Kya* Felyan's expression sometimes, as subtleties were lost on their more animal-like features, but the worry was clear in his eyes. "Electro-stim types in position ... clear."

Kumiko's body spasmed, and some of the alarms died down while several others remained.

"She's stabilized, but the repair nanos are still working," Var said, transferring the datasheet's info to a screen beside the bed. "It's not working; she's losing too much blood." He took a second vial into his hand. "I'll give a second dose. If that doesn't help, then I'll have to try to manually remove pressure..."

His words softened into nothing as the remaining alarms quieted down. He paused, walking slowly back toward the screen beside the bed, jaw hanging wider with every step.

"Well, I'll be damned," he murmured.

"What?" Tyger asked. "What's going—"

Var gestured for silence, then began frantically typing on his datasheet, switching from it back to the screen, as if he were in the middle of some intense video game.

"I'm not sure what I'm looking at here," Var said, frowning at the datasheet, then switching the display on the screen to a cross-section of Kumiko's head, showing a digital readout of her brain and spinal cord. A red mass was slowly turning green. "But I wouldn't have believed it if I hadn't seen it with my own eyes."

"Are the nanites working after all?" Akiko said.

"By all rights, these readings say she should be dead," Var answered. "There's a massive hemorrhagic aneurysm in her brain..." His voice then trailed off into astonished silence. "Well, there *was*." He then began tapping the device on the side vigorously.

"So the nanos worked?" Xerx said, approaching the shaggy Felyan's side. Var shook his head.

"They don't work that fast."

"So, you gonna keep us in suspense or what?"

"See for yourself," Var grunted and handed the data-sheet to Xerx, who squinted at the screen, not exactly familiar with medical tech. But after a few moments, even he could make out what Var was looking at.

"It's healing?" Xerx sounded just as incredulous as Var. "Shit ... she just blew her own brains open and is now reversing the damage."

"*Without* the help of nanos," Var added, looking up at Akiko, who had approached her daughter. She took her hand and clasped it in hers.

"Guess she inherited your tank super healing?" The utter astonishment in the shaggy Felyan's voice made it sound like both a statement and a question.

"So you're saying she'll be all right?" Tyger asked, coming to his daughter's opposite side.

"I ... suppose?" Var said, nodding at the readouts from yet another on-screen bioscan. "I'm kinda out of my league here; normally I'd hit her up with a second injection of nanos and pray, but if this is all correct, I don't think she needs it." Nodding to Xerx, he then gestured toward the bar. "I think she's stable."

Xerx stood there wondering if Kumiko had taken a bigger risk than she knew. Being stable was a good thing, but he knew that she was not out of the woods yet. And though both Tyger and Akiko seemed to be more at ease, he knew that they would not be fully relieved until Kumiko was sitting up and conscious.

"We should have stopped her," Tyger said, "or at least tried to."

Akiko snorted, the ghost of a smile at the side of her face as she shook her head.

"Always so willful, that one." She then settled her gaze upon Tyger. "She wouldn't have listened to either of us, and you know it."

There's no lasting damage, as far as I can see," Var said after performing a double-check on the holos beside him, then for the first time, seeming to relax. "I can't guarantee I know exactly how she'll be when she wakes up, but if she pulls through—which is what it looks like—she's gonna feel it for a while. No matter how fast you heal, you don't just get up from your lumps after giving a beatdown to a biker gang in a bar fight."

"Something you're familiar with," Xerx quipped.

"Hey, I never started it!" Var protested, then gave a sly grin. "But I did finish it."

Though they made no sound, Xerx could feel the virtual sigh of relief from Kumiko's parents as they thanked Var and went to the bed's side, assuring Xerx that they would be fine here. Exhaling with greatly reduced stress, he smiled and headed back to the bridge, leaving Var to keep his vigil over the patient.

You sure as hell earned that second drink, he thought, eyeing Kumiko, who still lay unconscious as her mother wiped away the blood from her nose with a strip of gauze. As he witnessed this, his comm signaled another incoming communique from Alexa.

He switched open the channel to the Pirate Queen's holo.

"The fuck happened?" she said.

"Kumiko did," Xerx said. "She jumped the whole ship."

"Ah, so that was it," Alexa said. "Good to see you're all in one piece."

"Wish I could say the same for Kumi."

Alexa's blue eyes widened with alarm. "Is she all right?"

"Var says she will be," Xerx replied, scratching the back of his head. "So, what were you trying to tell me before she did her thing?"

"Ah yes," Alexa said. "Contact Paige once you hit orbit. She'll have a team ready to take over duties for a few hours and allow some time to rest and recover."

"I'll have to run it by the Empress and Ramirez," Xerx said.

"Oh, no need for that. I arranged it all with them just before you jumped." She reclined to the side, resting her cheek in her hand. "Royal contacts, honey; you're welcome by the way."

"Yeah ... uh, thanks," Xerx said, bemused. Suddenly, he went wide-eyed. "Wait, you spoke to them *directly*?"

"As I quite vehemently reminded you not too long ago," Alexa said in a tone that carried a slight edge of condescension, "I *am* actual royalty."

"Duly noted," Xerx said.

"Get yourselves some rest, now," Alexa said before ending the transmission. "I'll see you soon."

ELEVEN

The instant Kumiko woke up, she realized that something was different. And she didn't like it.

It was quiet, too quiet. Normally, there was a constant buzz in her mind, a byproduct of her psychic abilities. Like background comm static, the thoughts of millions constantly permeated her consciousness. Now it was missing, and instead of being a relief, it was disturbing, like being the only person on an empty library floor.

"Shit..." she groaned.

"Kumi?"

It was like she was underwater, and her mother was trying to speak to her from the surface.

A blinding light flashed in front of her eyes. This was followed by the scent of the powder that most Felyans dusted themselves with. The scent ignited a fleeting memory of one of her many nights with Remli at the pleasure house back on Haven.

"Get that light out of my face, or you'll be coughing up whatever's making it," she warned, squinting against the bright blur that had formed in her retina. There was the whirr of machinery as the light moved away from her eyes with inhuman precision. The voices became clearer.

"You okay, kiddo?"

Kumiko's vision began to clear up from both the retinal blur and prior blurriness of before, focusing on her father's face, gazing at her with concern. Her mother soon came into view, her look of worry quickly melting into relief. Her concern deepened. Kumiko shared an especially strong connection with her parents, usually sensing her mother's overbearing worry for her from several light years away. Even the earnestness of Tyger's inept attempts to earn her affection were usually pretty strong. But this time, there was nothing.

Kumiko sighed as she let them argue over whether her father's question was relevant, Var having told them she'd be fine before he left. She always found her mother's literal interpretations of certain things endearing. Again, she tried to sense them, and again, it was a blank. She hated this. How did non-telepaths stand the silence?

"I can't hear you, either of you," Kumiko said, and watched the worry return to their expressions.

"Hear ...?" Tyger gave a blank stare. "Ohhh, I see; 'hear.'" He tapped his forehead. "Is it permanent?"

Kumiko rolled her eyes. "It only happened once before, so how should I know?"

"That's enough!" Akiko snapped, casting her a sharp look. "I don't care what you think of Tyger. He is still your father, and he cares about you. You *will* show him some respect."

Kumiko rolled her eyes. She didn't need to hear her mother's thoughts to know how she felt about the hybrid on the other side of her bed. Still, she felt exhausted and didn't have the energy for another family dispute.

"Yes mother," she said.

Akiko raised an eyebrow, still not liking the slightly sardonic tone in Kumiko's voice, but brushed it off with a brusque nod. Finally, after several moments of silence that was more awkward than she could tolerate, Kumiko looked at her hands, the nanotubules she'd altered herself with during her time on Lhirevlis now at rest beneath the skin.

"Stand back," she said to her parents and held her arms out. Knowing what she was about to do, Tyger and Akiko gave her a wide berth. Kumiko concentrated ...

It was like flipping a switch. All she needed to do was find it ...

And there it was.

Ice crystals formed on her right hand as the air around her left hand began to glow with ripples of intense heat as the nanotubules erupted from her skin, siphoning ambient potential energy and transforming it into heat energy. Then, as quickly as it happened, she stopped, not wishing to set off the medbay's fire suppression system. The heat and cold from both hands transitioned back to room temperature nearly instantaneously.

"Well, that still works," Tyger said.

Kumiko gave a vague nod, choosing not to mention that it had taken a ridiculous amount of effort to achieve, as her parents were fussing enough as it was.

"You think Shezmi could fix you?"

Kumiko nodded. "Probably so. But I have no idea how to contact him outside of mental contact." Choosing to change the subject, she then asked, "Where are we now? I should have gotten us pretty close to Haven."

"Well, the outer edge of the system is pretty close in relative terms," Akiko said with a wry grin. "But we're just about halfway across the system now."

"I guess I'll have to try harder next time," Kumiko said, and was met with a pair of aghast stares from her parents.

"You can't be serious," Akiko said. "Doing those jumps can't be safe."

"You don't know what this last one did to you, do you?" Tyger asked.

"Well, it clearly didn't do me any favors," Kumiko said, and suppressed a twinge of annoyance at her parents' frightened expressions. Were they always so dramatic? "I'm alive, aren't I?"

"You were dead," Akiko said in a brittle tone.

"Dead?" Kumiko just stared at her mother. "What do you mean, dead?"

"Well, actually, Var said that you should've been dead," Tyger replied. "You were bleeding from your mouth, eyes, and brain. Then your vitals ... well, just restarted."

"Huh," Kumiko said. "Not too bad, then."

"Is that all you can say?" Akiko said, reaching out to take her hands. Her ice blue eyes were wide, perhaps suppressing terror. "Your father and I searched for you for years before we found you. Yes, we know you were doing fine on your own, but you really need to understand how much you mean to us. If we lost you again, I'd..."

Tyger wrapped his tail around Akiko's waist as she grasped the edges of the bed, shaking.

"Just ... just stop it," Kumiko said at last, leaning forward and cradling her head in her hands. She found herself momentarily grateful that this jump had overloaded her telepathy. Regardless, seeing her mother so distraught gave her a particular sense of disquiet.

"Look, I can admit that I bit off a little more than I could chew trying to jump a whole ship," she said, "but if we don't try, we achieve nothing. By attempting the jump, I've brought us to a point just a few hours away from a safe place to recharge and strategize. I'm an adult; I know myself and my abilities, and I'm still here talking to you. Let's be thankful for that and move on, okay?"

"I am still not comfortable with the risks you take, Kumi dear." Akiko took her daughter's hand gently, the look of worry slowly fading from her face as she gave a hesitant but distinct nod. "But I will accept that you are old enough to make your own choices. Do you agree, furry fighter?"

"She's old enough to take care of herself," Tyger said. "I'm pretty sure we're gonna have to."

"Excellent." Kumiko slipped out of the bed, pulled off the medical sensors adhered to her body, and buttoned up her pinafore. She searched the ground for her shoes and found them neatly placed under the bed. She bent down to retrieve them.

"Wait, Var wants to give you a checkup before you leave," Tyger said, glancing at the instruments surrounding the bed that had set off small alarms after their disconnection.

"Where is he?" Kumiko asked, searching the medbay only to find it empty.

"On the bridge."

"Then I'll meet him there," Kumiko said, slipping into her black boots and tightening the steel clasps that ran up the length of their front.

Paige shielded her eyes against the sunlight as she strode through the market: a strange blend of archaic and arcane, with wooden tables and canvas shades protecting the traders from the heat, whilst all around were digital screens advertising wares and announcing the latest bounties for various villains in the region. Up ahead, Pip zipped between the stalls, and she was having a hard time keeping track of the tiny woman. She puffed out her cheeks and sighed. This was meant to be some quality time spent together, trying to repair their relationship after the events on Tophanavar. In truth, she didn't know why she'd even bothered. Fortunately, Pip seemed none the worse for wear, considering everything she'd been through. Her arm and shoulder were fully healed, and the diminutive tank seemed just as cheeky as she ever was.

Paige did, however, appreciate the chance to wear something other than a flight suit or combat gear for a change. Dressed in a loose Hawaiian-style shirt with the traditional flower print in purple with a white background and a pair of long khaki cargo shorts, she finally relented and pulled the pair of mirrored aviators from her shirt pocket and put them on. Her prosthetics were painted in a matching negative pattern to her shirt.

Suddenly she felt her internal comm buzz in the side of her neck and the name "Xerxes Paraska" appeared in her corneal display. She touched her right ear to accept the call.

"Hey there Chook, I take it you've arrived?"

"In one piece, thankfully," Xerx replied. "Alexa said to contact you once we made planetfall so here we are."

"Yes, I've got Maria and the boys on standby. I'll signal them to head over to you. I can imagine a few of you could do with some rest with all that pressure you're under. I heard the announcement postponing the royal visit to Tophanavar. I can tell you that went down like a shit in a lift."

At that moment, Pip reappeared from around a corner, waving a particularly garish hoodie with some retro metal band logo printed on it. Paige simply nodded and gave her a thumbs up, signaling she was on a call. Pip nodded and then, with a grin, disappeared back around the corner.

"Couldn't be avoided," said Xerx "Thanks to the efforts of Alexa and yourself we got word that Montera's Raiders are on the prowl, brazenly too, like they don't care about facing off against Alliance patrols or even Felyan security."

"More like stupid," Paige said. She nodded, rubbing her chin thoughtfully. "They're being equipped with some serious tech. Whoever resurrected Helix, they've got money, and resources, and contacts. This goes deep, chicken, and it's got me very worried. We'll need to watch our collective arses 'cos I think they're just getting started."

Pip skipped back over toward her, now dressed in her new hoodie. Underneath, the tiny woman was wearing a short-sleeved, black playsuit and a simple pair of trainers. The colors on her tattoo-covered legs were a rainbow of blue and orange hues among a tribal-style tiger stripe pattern. Paige allowed herself a proud smile, glad that Pip was not afraid to be herself, even if it meant she could be invasively nosey and woefully arrogant at times.

"Listen, Chook," she said, "I'm out with Pip at the moment. I've signaled Maria as promised, so take it easy for a few hours and I'll most likely see you in the morning, okay? We can catch up properly then."

"Understood. Glad you two are getting along better. How's her shoulder?"

Paige snorted. "Ugh, please, you'd never know she was injured. Thick hide that one."

"She needs it with you, P." The sound of Xerx's laughter came over the comm.

"And just what is that supposed to mean?" Paige scowled, and looked over at Pip, who had wandered over to a nearby candy stall and was busy sampling their various offerings. "If she wasn't so fucking nosey, I wouldn't need to tell her off, would I?"

"I'll catch you tomorrow," Xerx said, unperturbed. "Stay bad."

Paige ended the call and shook her head with a thin smile. As she made her way over to Pip, she was barged into by a large, bearded man.

"Excuse you," she said, unimpressed by the man's lack of spatial awareness. It wasn't like the market was overly crowded, after all. The man eyed her up and down and grunted before moving on. Paige stared after him briefly, noting several tattoos on his arms.

She cleared her mind of the incident and made after the pint-sized tank, who had now moved on toward the hot dog stand at the end of the row. Pip could eat her body weight in food within minutes left unchecked, plus she had temporary access to Paige's credit account. She'd be damned if that girl was going to spend her entire holiday allowance on junk food and clothing.

"Take a little rest," Xerx had said right before they'd homed in on the *Shadow Star*'s signal and started their descent to the Haven's surface. "We don't need you dying on us again."

"I wasn't planning on making ship jumps a regular activity."

"Good Lord, not if I can help it!" Xerx laughed, ignoring the passive-aggressive undertone in Kumiko's otherwise bland response. "We're all going to be lying low for a bit and making plans. I'd prefer you to stay aboard the ship, but I won't stop you if you want to get out and stretch your legs. Just be discreet."

"I should be telling *you* that," Kumiko said.

"Probably," Xerx replied, staying in good spirits. "Trouble does tend to find me. Maybe we're just more alike than you'd like to admit."

Kumiko scowled, both irritated by her still-muffled senses and her inability to protest Xerx's observation, which was sadly spot-on. Worse yet, like her father, she preferred the dangerous life.

"I'll try not to ruffle feathers," she said dryly. "*You* try not to get yourself killed."

"No promises," had been Xerx's flippant reply. How apropos.

But he had been right. It hadn't even been a day since she'd jumped the *Reckless* across known space to Haven—and damn near died for doing it. Despite this, she needed to take a trip of her own. They were landing in New St. Louis, where she'd made her home three years ago, and there was someone she wanted to see.

She waited for the exact moment when her mother and father would take advantage of the mostly empty ship and abscond to their quarters. Free from their unwanted, awkward questions, she took her leave. It was bad enough that Tyger had known about Remli. And of course, Amira had gleaned those memories from her mind.

"It's time to put it all to an end," she murmured to no one in particular as she descended the ramp and left the spaceport, then hailed a taxi to her old neighborhood.

The driver prattled on about the changes to the city in the last ten years: expansion of the offshore farming arcologies and local law enforcement cleaning up the old places. She'd been surprised to hear that her old neighborhood and haunts had been part of that list. She wondered exactly how much this so-called cleanup had changed clientele at the pleasure house. Back when she'd rented a loft next door to it and had taken up a profitable stint as a bounty hunter in the area, Mama Gold, the house caretaker, would have to bar some asshole from entering at least once a night. If they returned and got violent, she was called to handle it, usually with profuse apologies for interrupting her sessions with Remli and handsome pay along with discounts for her trouble. Remli, the excessively cuddly *An'Kya* Felyan, had grown to be her favorite of all the pleasure boys among the house's staff. They'd become almost exclusive by the time she was forced to leave, though she left him a tortoiseshell kitten she'd found in an alley as a parting gift, insisting that he be named Mr. Pickles, the same name she gave any stray cat she would pick up.

She returned only once to check on him after that, finding the cat healthy and sleeping on the front porch of the pleasure house. Surprisingly, he recognized her, and jumped into her arms before she teleported into Remli's room—and immediately regretted it, having forgotten to scan first to see if Remli was preoccupied.

He was.

Remli and Mama Gold, well into an off-the-clock session together, had frozen like deer in headlights at the sight of her. At this, Kumiko found herself managing to crack a weak joke about how both Mr. Pickles and Remli's "pickle" seemed to be doing just fine before quickly leaving.

Though she rarely contemplated the memory, the whole thing hadn't come as any big surprise in hindsight; Remli and Mama Gold had always been close, but so were she and Remli, in a way. Despite how much she tried to keep him at arm's length, they got along better than she wanted. His affection for her was annoyingly

easy to read, and the night she had announced her decision to leave for greener pastures, he had offered her a
chance for employment at the pleasure house to stay
with him. She was indeed tempted, but her wander-
lust was a stronger drive. When she left for good, it only
made sense for him to go with what was there.

It shouldn't still hurt, but it did.

The cab dropped her off near the familiar alleyway
that led to her old home and the pleasure house where
she'd spent so much of her money on that stupid man
to whom she'd grown inexplicably attached. The place
looked a fair sight nicer than it used to. The pleasure
house staff had always done their best to keep the
grounds clean in the small courtyard where it was
located and had added vines and potted greenery to
give it that Felyan touch to make the path to their business attractive, but their efforts could only do so much,
surrounded by run-down buildings, graffiti, and back
alley dumpsters as the area had been.

Now, however, it seemed as though the city had truly
put an effort into making the courtyard look attractive
to more than just drifters or kids looking for a low-rent
area where they wouldn't be robbed by the first punk
with a gun and something to prove. The dumpsters
were removed, and the walls had been nano-scrubbed
free of graffiti. Even anti-defacement nodes had been
placed on the corners of the now immaculate-looking
buildings' brick and stucco facades.

It was then that a second sight surprised her.

She supposed that if her telepathy had still been
at a hundred percent, she would have been able to
sense the lack of minds, but she realized that she'd

been caught up in her memories to the point where she hadn't even noticed the lack of the scent of *riss*. The pungent Felyan aphrodisiac had been a constant background in the air, even inside her old apartment, whose second story balcony door she could see across the narrow, adjacent alley.

The pleasure house was closed. And it looked as if it had been for a very long time. There were no potted plants, no vines, no holos advertising their various pleasure boys and girls. Even the desk at the foyer was gone, replaced by a small icon of Trisii, the Felyan saint.

A happy, high-pitched sound startled her—damn her muted powers. This was coupled by a familiar sensation rubbing against her ankles. Kumiko looked down to see a familiar face looking up at her. None other than Mr. Pickles was here to greet her, fat and healthy, the pattern of his tortoiseshell fur brilliant and glossy as he rubbed affectionately against her.

"So you're still here," she said, squatting down to her haunches to give the needy feline a scratch between his ears. "They're still taking good care of you, I see."

She then stole a glance at the door and noticed a nameplate on the posts. She frowned as she read the two names written in brilliant yellow Felyan calligraphy painted beneath a sheen of varnish on the wooden plate: Remli and Gold. More importantly, she noticed how the symbols of the names entwined as it was customary for lifemates.

Giving Mr. Pickles one last pat, she stepped up to the door of the former pleasure house that she was now certain Remli and Mama Gold had converted into a home for themselves, pausing as she stepped on something that squeaked under her foot. She stepped back and noticed a small toy plushie next to a set of magnetic building blocks.

"I really have been gone too long," Kumiko said, suddenly overwhelmed with a deep sadness as she looked back down at the cat, who gazed at her quizzically. "What the hell am I even doing here, Mr. Pickles?"

The cat had little to give her other than another meow.

She stepped up to the door yet again. She raised her fist up to the post ... then sighed.

"You're happy," she said, as if her words could reach Remli, "both you and Goldie. And you know, I think I can live with that."

She turned and walked away from the door and back into the open courtyard. What more could she say to him, anyway? Even a "congratulations" wasn't needed. Not after all these years.

"Make sure he stays happy," she said to Mr. Pickles as she made her way back toward the alley to the main road.

She'd reached the alley's entrance when footsteps caused her to pause in her tracks. These were coupled with the sight of someone dropping into view, blocking her path out of the alley. The light from the opposite end obscuring the form, combined with the light-bending effects of diffraction cloth caused the hairs on the back of her neck to stand on end.

Other footsteps came from the adjoining alleys that led to the courtyard. Kumiko glanced about, taking note of their numbers. Four by her count; diffraction cloth was easy to spot if you knew what to look for. They were also big bruisers, judging by their size.

She scowled. Xerx could be an idiot, but his instincts had been irritatingly on point this time. Trouble had indeed been looking for her, it seemed. But what kind?

"Get out of here," she said to Mr. Pickles, who seemed to understand the danger and sped off, climbing a nearby set of vines to a balcony above. Adrenaline flowed into every limb, putting her on a scintillating high. Kumiko then sized up her challengers. Being unable to sense them, she wondered just how much they knew about her.

She was about to find out.

TWELVE

Snow woke with a snort and rubbed her eyes. A subtle signal from Noomi had triggered her into rousing. Shafts of sunlight pierced the gloom through the slats in the shutters and Snow gently rose to her knees, reaching to swing one of them open. She pulled several small drones from her belt pouches and threw them out of the window, watching as their rotors quickly powered up and arrested their fall and they spread out high over the city. In her retinal display, Snow watched each drone's various video feeds and data. Outside, the bright morning saw people milling around a market that had been set up in the square below. It was hot out, but not oppressively so, like most places on Mandela I, or Siberna.

Snow scooted back and brought her rifle into position, extending the bipod and placing the barrel tip in line with the opening. She dragged the large battery pack alongside the weapon and plugged in the various cables along its length. There was a faint hum as the systems ran their boot cycle and the rifle began its charge sequence. Snow then pulled her headphones from her ears and threw them aside, her concentration now fully focused on calibrating the scope and preparing for her chance to fire.

She watched as the white-haired woman hesitated outside the door of what appeared to be a former Felyan pleasure house, then turned and walked away. Snow could have taken the shot at any time, but wanted to see what her target was up to first. Sometimes it was prudent to ensure they weren't about to die in front of a gaggle of witnesses.

Snow saw her quarry pass into a series of narrow back alleys devoid of people: the perfect place to take her down. She drew back the slide handle and loaded the round into the breach. Snow exhaled and rested her finger on the trigger ... then paused.

There was movement in the alleyways, shadowy, blurred-looking figures stalking towards Kumiko, and moving quickly at that.

Snow suddenly realized why the figures were hard to see. Diffraction cloth! At a junction that connected three alleys, the figures abandoned their invisibility and readied themselves to strike.

Snow watched, enthralled by what she witnessed, and more than a little apprehensive. This was precisely why she worked at a distance when it came to tertiaries. The raiders struck at Kumiko with batons and knives, which the white-haired woman parried with ease. Her sleeves began to smoke and slough off her arms as her deadly nanotubules began to assert themselves through her skin. They generated a visible, rippling heat haze as they drew energy from the surrounding air, their nano-structures resembling strange, spiked gauntlets that moved across her hands and over her fingers.

Snow watched on as Kumiko grabbed a blade from one of her assailants, who stared aghast as the weapon glowed red, then yellow, and then ran in molten drops onto the floor. She then flicked the remaining drops from her hand into his eyes. His screams of agony didn't last long as she then proceeded to set the world aflame around him.

Snow took her eyes away from the scope and then returned to it, not quite believing what she was seeing. She gasped as she watched Kumiko grab another man's face and freeze his entire head, then tear it off and use it to crush his comrade's skull, the skull shattering into countless pieces of bone and solidified brain matter. But in the course of this slaughter, Snow realized something. Kumiko was showing clear signs of exhaustion. This was both unusual and wholly unexpected. Given how powerful Kumiko Zero was known to be, this little skirmish should have been nothing short of a warmup act.

Down the alley, Snow spotted more assailants approaching, these carrying shields and stun batons. As she watched, Snow recognized the design.

"Null shields!" she whispered.

Null shields were an experimental technology being tested by ISID, the secret black ops department of the Second Imperium. They were designed to project a null psychic field, in an attempt to suppress a tertiaries' abilities ... at least in theory. They'd had little field testing, and Snow had no idea how they would work on an individual as strong as Kumiko. But that was the least of her concerns. Somehow, the raiders had gained access to classified Imperial technology. Something both very wrong and very disturbing was going on here.

They poured into the opening, surrounding the woman, and waited, as if weighing up whether to strike together or in turns.

One of them made the decision to try and was met with a punch to the face. Kumiko then raked a red-hot hand down the face of the shield. The shield, against all logic, remained intact. Kumiko paused, appearing nonplussed at her turn of fortune; then the others, seeing that they now actually stood a chance against the weakened tertiary, closed in.

Snow gritted her teeth; this was a wrinkle in the plan. She didn't like wrinkles. They meant that achieving the objective just got complicated. She decided to change the plan. If someone was supplying insurgent raiders with Imperial tech, then it was highly likely that a powerful psionic would be a great asset in uncovering whom that might be. She would need to have a discussion with Miss Zero, and this meant a change of plans.

Adjusting her sights, Snow targeted the assailants and pulled the trigger, turning each one's upper torso into mist. The mulched remains dropped to the floor around Kumiko, who stood stock still as Snow, unseen, made short work of the remaining crowd.

In the ensuing silence, Kumiko reached down and picked up a pistol from a dead man's belt and looked up. She stared straight at Snow through the lens of the scope. Snow gasped and leaned back from the scope. She stiffened as, in the next heartbeat, she felt the muzzle of a gun at the back of her head.

"I don't need to be psychic to know those bullets were originally intended for me," Kumiko said, keeping the pistol held, unmoving, to the back of her head. "So, would you mind explaining what changed your mind?"

Snow snorted. "I don't tend to respond too well with a gun to my head. It affects my recall somewhat."

There was a long pause. Then Snow at last felt the pressure of the gun barrel remove itself.

"Very well, then," Kumiko said as Snow eased herself into a sitting position. "Start talking. What's your name?"

Not robbed of salt, Snow tilted her head to one side and sneered. "Why don't you just pull that from my head like everything else?"

"I'm arrogant, but I'm not rude," Kumiko said as she stepped around to face Snow, who saw that she was still holding the gun. "So, please. Your name."

"It's Snow. Snow Lake. I have no further designation, as I'm not supposed to exist." As she shifted to a more comfortable position, she circled a finger around her face, drawing attention to her white irises and eyelashes. "As you can probably guess, this isn't normal for a tank. I'm what they call a Blank."

Kumiko dropped to her haunches, placing the gun on the floor. "Like an albino?"

"Kind of, but not quite. I'm the result of the random sequencer somehow landing on this combination."

"We're getting off-topic," Kumikio said. "Let's return to the situation at hand. You were supposed to shoot me, but you shot those raiders instead. Why?"

"Because they're carrying tech that they shouldn't even know about, let alone be using," Snow said, then glanced about nervously. "Look, could we discuss this somewhere more private? The authorities will no doubt discover those bodies soon and start looking for where the shots came from."

"Of course," Kumiko said, holding out her hand. She pulled Snow to her feet, and Snow suddenly realized that they were back aboard the *Hammerfall II*, the lounge to be more precise.

"Shit!" Snow exclaimed. "How did you—?"

"I can teleport," Kumiko said. "To be honest, I'm surprised it worked."

"Why?"

"Let's just say I haven't been feeling well," Kumiko said. "And it's far easier to jump to places I've been."

"Been having a hard time reading minds, I gather?" Snow asked. "I saw you having an equally hard time with those goons a moment ago."

A scowl briefly crossed Kumiko's face but quickly vanished as she gave a sigh.

"I overreached trying to reach this world. I have a device that assists me with traveling, but it takes energy and when you cross between hyperspace and realspace, dragging a ship with you it kind of takes its toll. "

Snow gave a slight grin. "From what I've read, you admitting a mistake is a rare thing indeed."

"Well, you're not wrong." Kumiko's reply came without an ounce of false modesty.

"How exactly did we end up here then?" Snow said, somewhat awkwardly.

"Well now, that's all you. I just took your hand and let you think of somewhere."

The conversation being finished for the moment, Kumiko walked unsteadily towards the seating area.

"I don't think we'll get much more private than this, wouldn't you say?" she said before sitting down heavily on the sofa nearby. She looked exhausted, and her nose had begun to bleed.

Snow walked over to the kitchen area and grabbed some paper towels from a roll near the sink. She opened the cupboard and pulled out her box of pretzels and the whiskey. She walked over and sat handing the paper towels to Kumiko, then placed the bottle on the table whilst digging pretzels out of the box and tossing them into her mouth.

"Agreed. Now we can talk."

Paige sat up in the bed in her oversized Siberna G1 t-shirt and a pair of shorts and returned to the page of the book she was reading. Beside her on the other bed, Pip perched on the edge in her orange tiger-striped pajamas, mashing buttons on a video game controller. She whooped, then cursed as she played some kind of racing game on the screen mounted to the wall.

The room itself wasn't much—just a double in a cheap motel near the spaceport. The walls were an uninspiring shade of magnolia and the whole thing had a bit of a worn, shabby feel. Even the small desk and chair seemed to hail from a time before the arks left Old Earth. There was a single large window next to the door with dirty old blinds covering it, which the orange of the streetlamps outside still penetrated. However, it felt nice to be somewhere other than the interior of a starship for once. Clearly, Pip was enjoying herself.

You can take the girl out of cyberspace... Paige thought ruefully and smiled to herself. It had been a long day, all things considered, and yet somehow the diminutive woman next to her still maintained a ridiculous amount of energy. Paige winced and reached under the covers to scratch at the mounting points for her prosthetic legs at her knee joints. The legs themselves were detached and sat side by side at the end of her bed like a pair of high-tech boots. Paige continued to read, suppressing a giggle as Pip told someone on the game-link to "suck it" and proceeded to describe them as a Doradan cat whore. Clearly, Paige needed to pay more attention to what she was saying around Pip. The traditional insult of her home world being spoken by a tank just didn't seem right.

At that moment, something caught Paige's eye. It was a shadow through the blinds: vague shapes. *Human* shapes! She snapped her fingers at Pip to get her attention. The tiny tank was about to protest when Paige signaled in battle sign that someone was clearly lurking outside. Pip, still perturbed but understanding, nodded, put down the controller, and stood up. She took on a ready stance based on her MMA training as Paige discreetly slid herself toward the end of her bed.

But before she could reach her prosthetics, the door exploded inward, and two men charged into the rain of wooden shrapnel, both dressed in combat armor and brandishing firearms. Paige, in one fluid motion, ducked the pieces of flying debris, then immediately spun and dropped to the floor at the side of the bed, pulling a MAG pistol from under the pillow. One of the men lunged at her, but she emptied several rounds into his chest armor before he could get a grip. He stumbled backward clutching at the point of impact, stunned by the high-velocity rounds, but the armor had clearly dulled their full effect.

To her left, the other man charged at Pip. He was a clear head taller than the small tank, but that clearly had no impact on her resolve as she dodged aside, grabbing his arm and forcing it into a triangle hold behind his back. With a cry of surprise and pain, he dropped the weapon. Pip then raised her foot and kicked him forward, tutting at him as he stumbled and fell through the door to the tiny bathroom, hitting his head on the rim of the toilet.

"Pip, window, now!" She yelled, noticing more armored bodies appearing in the doorway, drawn by the commotion. Pip nodded and grabbed the chair from in front of the desk. She pirouetted and launched it through the window. The window shattered, and the blinds fell from their moorings, dragged through the opening along with the furniture piece. Paige then dragged herself through the broken frame, wincing as some of the remaining shards grazed her abdomen. She tumbled to the floor and immediately turned to see Pip leaping across the beds, avoiding the grasp of their would-be assailants who piled into the room, and performing a surprisingly graceful forward roll through the window and into the street. Pip sprang to her feet and grabbed Paige's hand, helping her to move on her knee joints toward a nearby alley. They rounded the corner and Paige leaned back against the wall, pistol raised, and panting with the adrenaline high.

Pip clenched her fists and readied herself. Paige waved her back. "No, honey; save your strength. There's too many of them."

Pip opened her mouth to argue, but Paige raised her hand and opened her palm, revealing a blinking red light in the center of the prosthetic limb. She winked at the tank.

"Besides, backup is inbound."

Just then, one of the armored goons rounded the corner and pointed his weapon at them. Paige raised her pistol with lightning speed and prepared to fire, but the man suddenly flew backward, as if abruptly grabbed by the force of a black hole. Paige heard his scream fade and then stopped as a faint metallic impact cut off the noise. Paige leaned forward and craned to see what had taken him. In the orange twilight of the streetlamps stood the silhouette of a large, tall woman. Behind her, in the distance, was a dumpster, heavily dented—a limp body at its base.

Pip gasped and grinned broadly. "Hey Maz! Are we glad to see you!"

Before the tall woman could answer, she turned and clotheslined another raider, the sheer force of the blow letting out a resounding crack as his neck snapped. Four more charged her all at once, and Paige watched in awe as Maria dispatched each one in turn. Being a ground tank, she was stronger than these men by several magnitudes and had the combat skills to implement that prodigious strength to its full potential. The now-dead raiders had been foolishly optimistic at best if they thought they could prevail against her.

Maria intercepted yet another one by punching him in the chest and collapsing his entire rib cage. His death rattle was a sound Paige would rather not hear again. Another she grabbed in a headlock and casually popped his neck, dropping his corpse like a sack of garbage. She then swept the legs out from underneath the final assailant, then dropped her knee onto his chest. He vomited blood and tried to gurgle an insult as his life faded. Finally done with her grisly work, Maria stood up and wiped her bloodied gloves on her legs.

"You okay, Boss?" she said, as if she hadn't just finished killing an entire team of men with mechanical efficiency.

"All the better for seeing you, my dear," Paige replied. "I thought you were on the *Reckless*?"

"Ah, yes," Maria said after clearing her throat. "Well, the boys could handle that assignment." She then shifted nervously. "And Miranda has the dock covered from her perch, so I, erm, made plans."

"You two are terrible," Paige said with a smile, knowing what kind of "plans," specifically with Artemis, the tall woman had meant. That smile quickly became a suppressed chuckle while Pip openly giggled.

Suddenly, there was a click, and another raider stepped out of the shadows. Paige recognized him as the bearded man from the market. The bastards; they'd been waiting for them the whole time!

"Don't move," the raider said, his voice a mix of a gravel pit and a wheeze. "You killed a lot of my boys and for that, you're gonna pay. I'm sure I'll be compensated handsomely for delivering your heads to the Father."

He moved to pull the trigger when a blade penetrated his neck. A gurgle escaped the raider's shocked face, along with a stream of blood as his head slid off his shoulders and dropped to the floor with a sickening *smack*. It was followed quickly by his body.

Two pale feet stepped gently over the corpse and Paige immediately recognized the pink-haired form of Artemis.

Speak of the devil ...

She stood in a matching set of black lace lingerie and held a blooded tanto knife in her left hand. This was the first time she'd seen Artemis in her underwear. God, she'd never realized just how many tattoos the woman had, or how short she was without those massive gothic platform boots. Now barefoot, she was only about an inch taller than Pip.

"Sorry," said Artemis. "My piercings got caught on the bra."

Maria laughed. "Well, that's what you get for wearing the nipple spikes in bed, little one."

Paige rolled her eyes and then saw Pip making a grimace. Funny how the tiny woman could face just about anything from pain to gore, but listening to Maria and Artemis discuss their love life made her uncomfortable.

"Maria, if you wouldn't mind grabbing my legs and some clothes," Paige said, focusing her mind back on the important issues, "I have a horrible feeling we weren't the only ones targeted tonight."

With a nod, Maria headed off to retrieve the items. Artemis remained looking around the dark street, unblinking and, it seemed, completely uncaring about her attire or lack of it.

"Ah, Arty," Paige said, "Don't you want to go get some clothes on?"

"Not until you're safe," she replied.

Paige said no more. Despite her appearance, the pink-haired woman exuded confidence. She had no doubt any would-be attacker would regret their decision very quickly. She then put a finger to her ear and brought up the retinal display for her implanted comms unit. She selected Xerx and began the call sequence.

"That wasn't a very long walk," Neela observed over Xerx's comm.

"There's only so much sea air a man can take," Xerx said as he jumped off the stacks of empty crates that formed a series of geometric hills at the edge of the seawall and jogged back toward the hulking sight of the *Reckless* at the other end of the spaceport dock. "'Sides, I'm just following Paige's advice and not wandering too far from the ship."

"You listen to that woman's advice more than mine," Neela said. "I should ask what her secret is."

"Very funny."

"Shame Kumiko doesn't follow it," Neela said.

"Does she seem like the type to be told what to do if she doesn't want to?"

"No arguments there. She's worse than you, *kipenzi*."

"Hey, that's not fair," Xerx protested. "I'm not an arrogant, super-intelligent psychic, but in all fairness, she can take care of herself even with a fried brain."

Still, a frown remained plastered on Xerx's face as he made his way back to the ship, reaching the opening that led back toward the inner berths. For the better part of the day, he kept patrol with Ike and Brogan around the docks, far less curious about this planet than he would have been on a normal day, but from what he'd read, he knew that Haven was a quiet world, little more than a strategic trade port between the outer worlds and the Alliance proper, far away from the contested border skirmishes with the Second Imperium.

He guessed it hadn't been a busy day with how few ships were currently in dock. Currently, aside from the tankers and freighters on the ocean docks, there was only the *Shadow Star* and *Reckless* beneath their respective canopies. Here, the docks held cargo freighters lined up like rows of low, flat buildings. His stroll had taken him further out this way, watching dock workers driving their load lifters and cranes, bringing in freight from the colonies: seafood from Columbus, timber and dilkin silk from Sepra, and electronics from Siberna and Dorado. He paused and watched another canopy roll up about a newly landed freighter, connecting at the top and encasing the ship in something resembling a massive, blue-black steel burrito. The canopies aboard his ship and Paige's, respectively, had rolled up in a similar manner when they'd landed, with an interior fully equipped with diagnostic sensors, as well as servo arms with nano-applicators for cleaning and fuel servicing. The entire setup was a newer configuration being phased into stations and ship docks both planetside and orbital across the Alliance, replacing teams of workers that used to perform often dangerous work.

New St. Louis, it seemed, despite its paucity of entertainment venues, had certainly earned its stripes in the modernization and automation department.

Plus, the girders of the whole structure's canopy gave Miranda a good lookout perch.

"You haven't seen anything weird going on, have you?" Xerx asked his wife.

"You mean outside the usual almost-flirting between Pepper and Mobola when she's supposed to be on the lookout?" Neela gave a sweet-sounding giggle. "Well, if the *Shadow Star* crew didn't see it, I doubt I'd have seen it, either."

"You doubting our expertise?" Ike's jocular voice crackled in on the channel. "Captain Paraska, I am insulted."

"That makes two of us," Brogan added in Ike's tone of feigned offense. "And after we all hung out at that sauna on Dorado."

"Yeah, you've seen us naked," Ike said, adding to the mirth. "No loyalty, man."

Xerx cradled his face in his hand as he heard his wife having a positive conniption fit in the background at the conversation. Miranda might have been listening in, but thankfully, she had nothing resembling a normal sense of humor, or, as he imagined, even an ego. Thank God neither Paige nor the rest of his own crew had heard any of this.

The moment when everything went tits up happened when Miranda's voice broke into the comm.

"Bogies."

"Shit," Ike said. "Where?"

"Paraska. Run."

Out of the corner of his eye, Xerx saw movements done in unison. He quickened his pace, turning his head only slightly to see several of the dock workers surrounding him putting out their cigarettes, then reaching into their coats and pants.

There was a resounding *bang* and the one closest to him suddenly crumpled and collapsed to the ground, his head erupting into a spray of blood that the wind thankfully took in the other direction. Everything seemed to freeze in an infinite moment, right before Xerx's mind rebooted. With no other encouragement, he bolted, weaving around the field of crates and barrels that led back to his ship.

A cacophony of gunshots followed, instantly thinning out as Miranda's sniper shots returned fire. Xerx, in turn, dived over a metal crate, drawing his pistols on the downward curve and rolling onto the ground, bouncing into a crouched position behind the hard cover, his senses alert to screaming precision, assessing his surroundings as he drew his pistols ... then almost dropped them as he stood.

He'd fled too late, he realized, finding himself in the unenviable position of standing at the business end of several drawn pistols. The dock workers were all fixing him with smug grins bearing teeth that ranged from tobacco yellow to pearlescent white, and even steel implants. One had a set filed down to something that resembled Alexa's shark-like mouth.

One stepped forward, a quintessential "brick shithouse" of a man, with a pistol in hand and a particularly murderous look in his dull brown eyes.

"Back off, boys. He's mine," he growled, his graying beard opening up into a toothy grin.

With yet another shower of red, he fell, headless, onto the pavement. Unlike the last time, the crowd shattered, stumbling over themselves, wailing incomprehensibly as they took their own cover. It seemed that though the first of their company being turned into hamburger meat hadn't been enough to convince them, this second demonstration seemed to get the point across.

The bedlam ensued as more of the crowd found themselves unlucky enough to find themselves in Miranda's crosshairs. Like a sudden fireworks display of gore, limbs and heads began to explode into showers of viscera.

"*Sniper!*" someone screamed. The guns, previously aimed at Xerx, were now firing blindly, while Miranda's deadeye shots found their targets one by one.

"Cover fire," Miranda said with her usual eerie, deathly calm. "Paraska, RTB."

Xerx scrambled away from his hiding place, keeping low as the rain of death kept the raiders at bay. Bobbing and weaving, clearing the maze of crates, Xerx met with several close calls as the occupied raiders tried to take potshots at him.

His chest and throat were burning as he neared the ships, adrenaline and borderline fear being the only things giving him the strength to keep moving.

"Little help, guys..." Xerx wheezed over the comm.

"Ask and you shall receive!" Brogan's boisterous tone bellowed.

"Xerx tumbled onto the ground as he heard the staccato thunderclap of a pair of auto-rifles erupt into the semi-silence, laying out the remainder of his pursuers.

"We got 'em," Brogan said. "Get your ass back here."

Cautiously, and nowhere near relieved, Xerx stood up, looking tentatively back the way he'd come and seeing nothing but the chaos and carnage still being meted out by Miranda, still about her business with her usual machine-like efficiency.

"Guess I didn't have anything to worry about?" Xerx said, nearing the *Reckless* with knees that had gone slightly wobbly.

"I swear you have the worst luck," Neela said.

"You saw all that?" Xerx asked.

"I've been keeping my eye on you since you went on your walk," his wife replied. He heard her inhale a shuddering sigh. "I swear some cosmic force wants me to have a heart attack before we have any children."

Xerx felt himself flush at the sound of Ike and Brogan's laughter. And he began to feel somewhat better for at least a moment.

"Well, it looks like this place is a bust for safe harbor," he said. "Let's get on the horn with Paige and let her know—"

His words were drowned out by the engine roar of a craft that sounded like it was close by. Xerx paused in mild consternation as he waited for it to pass, but the sound only grew louder, as if whatever was in the sky were approaching.

"The hell is that?" he murmured as he shifted his gaze upward. As he thought, the chemtrail of a low-flying craft had streaked the otherwise clear sky. It grew larger and closer. He followed it until he was looking directly above the *Reckless*.

A Corax dropship, about the size of the *Reckless'* *Grasshopper*, he guessed, was coming in hot, as if about to open fire. He bolted the rest of the way toward his ship, then paused as the craft began an upward arc from a point that was a couple of hundred feet in the air. From its rear, however, several small dots scattered, as if it were a giant bird relieving its bowels over them.

Then he realized what they were.

"Grav chutes..." he groaned, then closed the final distance back to the *Reckless*. "Guys, we're about to have company!"

THIRTEEN

They wanted this ship badly.

"Seal the entry," Xerx commed to Neela as he took out the first raider of the pack to land, and Miranda turned another into fertilizer. He ducked behind a coolant storage tank as three others landed and began to open fire. Behind him, Brogan and Ike were taking out their fair share, with more efficiency than his own pistols, while Miranda continued evening the odds.

He'd just begun to hope that this gang of would-be paratroopers had jumped to their deaths when his hearing picked up the sound of another low-flying craft passing above, causing his heart to sink.

"We've got a lot of incoming," he said. "Neela, we got that entry sealed?"

"That would leave you stuck out there," his wife replied, hesitancy evident in her voice.

"Do it, *kidege*," Xerx said. "Better that than they get to the baby." He fired around his cover at two other raiders who had chuted in, but two others landed behind him immediately after, armed with MAG rifles; they opened fire before the bodies of the first two had fully hit the ground, pinning him down. Worse yet, his peripheral vision had picked up three more just descending below the concertina-style ridges of the awning.

"Shit, they're coming like rain," Ike said.

"We're probably gonna need backup," Xerx said. "You guys get through to Paige?"

"I think outside transmissions are being jammed," Brogan said after a moment.

"Figures," Xerx said as Miranda took out two more raiders on the descent. With how the bodies were piling up, port authorities would have a huge mess to deal with tomorrow. "Mobola, you heard Brogan?"

"Yes, sir," Mobola replied. "Working on it."

"I'm sealing the entry," Neela at last announced. Her tone was anything but enthusiastic.

"Oh, that's a big one!" Brogan exclaimed, just as Xerx noticed what he was talking about. The man was about the size of the ringleader of the raiders who'd boarded his ship back when they were stuck at the pulsar. Thankfully, this one wasn't armed with a rotary MAG, but the heavy cannon didn't look much friendlier.

"Paraska, you might wanna try a new cover if you don't want to get iced in both senses of the word," Ike warned. Realizing his position and the firepower the bruiser was packing, he scanned his surroundings, eyeing a concrete partition. It was lower to the ground and didn't provide as much cover, but it would have to do.

He leaped toward the partition—

—then slipped, tumbling onto his stomach.

The familiar sound of a MAG's accelerator charging came to his ears. Xerx turned his head and became a deer in headlights, unable to do much else but watch as the bruiser towering above him trained his weapon directly on him. He barely had a second left. No time to scramble to safety, or to get Miranda's attention, busy as she was with the steady stream of incoming raiders.

Helluva way to die, he thought.

A black blur suddenly leaped in front of him, just as the shot fired. The form silhouetted in the light beyond the awning emitted a low growl, not unlike Var on a bender about to start another bar fight.

But he didn't own a Felyan glaive.

The echoing *thump* of the MAG cannon sounded, and the towering form shuddered as steam rose around him, partly concealed by a blur that he hadn't noticed before.

No. Definitely not Var. He didn't own a personal shield.

"Biraknu?" Xerx said, rising to his hands and knees.

"Are you all right, Captain Paraska?" The voice, even more erudite than even Var's, was definitely the bodyguard's.

"Wounded pride, but otherwise good," Xerx replied as another *thump* sounded, and Biraknu shuddered yet again as his shield ate the blast, followed by the gunfire from several other raiders who chuted in. He stood up with renewed confidence, safely behind the Felyan's protection.

"Want to get in close and personal?" Biraknu said with impish delight.

"Your shield gonna protect me all around?" Xerx said.

"No, but this will," Biraknu said, as his clawed hand slipped him a starfish-shaped device.

"I need to save up and buy one of these myself," Xerx said, recognizing the duplicate personal shield device, as rare as it was expensive.

"I meant it for the ambassador," Biraknu said, "but he's safe enough at the moment. It should handle the smaller caliber fire, but it's not military-grade like mine."

"Guess I'll need to play dodgeball with anyone packing something more powerful than a pea shooter?" Xerx said.

"That would be advisable."

To his left, Xerx realized that the others had now joined the fray: Tyger and Akiko rushing in with their respective rifles, both wearing Sepran spidersilk armor, while Ri'Kela stood behind the ramp leading from the now-sealed door, aiming her own sniper rifle at the incoming storm.

"Do me a favor then, and take down that asshole with the cannon, would you?" Xerx said to Biraknu as he holstered one pistol and exchanged it for his knife. He slapped the shield onto his breast and pressed the activation sigil. "I'm about to relieve some stress."

Biraknu nodded and rushed out into the fray on all fours, claws extended. Xerx followed, taking a hard right just as another Corax flew in low, dropping a fresh cargo of meat.

"Miranda, help out Ike and Brogan on my six," Xerx commed to Miranda. "We got it on this side now."

"Acknowledged," Miranda replied.

"Mobola, any luck?" Xerx asked, reaching the awning's edge, the MAG rounds now disintegrating against his shield. He dashed up to one of the newly landed raiders and planted a MAG round into his chest.

Hearing another one approach directly from behind, he turned and slashed his knife across his chest, then shot twice to end his suffering.

"It's ... multiple signals," Mobola said. "The incoming ships are broadcasting a jamming signal one by one, overlapping their signals to keep us comm silent."

"Can you do anything about it?" Xerx used the momentum of another raider who attempted to rush him in order to throw him to the ground. His rounds were eaten by his shield as he placed two shots in him, sending him permanently to the ground.

Several seconds passed, and Xerx made short work of three more raiders while Biraknu tore into his own like an enraged bear. Meanwhile, Tyger, Akiko, and Ri'Kela provided suppression fire, making their own kills.

"I ... have an idea," Mobola said. "I'm going to attempt to punch through the jamming signal-ah, signals. It'll have the added effect of overloading the receivers' antennas."

It'll at least be interesting to see how they handle that, Xerx thought as he wrestled one raider who decided to grapple with him. It was a raider who, being built like a beanpole, seemed to have an over-inflated opinion of his own abilities. He went down with a solid punch to the gut and lay still.

"Do it," he said, just as he caught a swift motion at the edge of his vision, then felt a sharp sensation across his right arm. He yanked it back, aiming his gun at the source of the movement and firing. The raider collapsed and Xerx noticed the massive rip in the sleeve of his jacket. A quick glance at the fresh corpse revealed the knife it still held.

"Shield doesn't block blades?" he commed to Biraknu, who had grabbed an incoming raider mid-fall. He broke his legs before slashing his head clean off.

"Sorry. I forgot to tell you," Biraknu said.

"Don't worry about it," Xerx replied. "Not my first rodeo with one of these; I just forgot."

"Initializing!" Mobola's shout cut through the comms as the *Reckless* emitted a low-pitch hum. Xerx gritted his teeth at the accompanying odd sensation that he could feel in his spleen.

In a near instant, a sound like a distant thunderclap overshadowed the entry of yet another Corax as the ship rocked from an explosion that erupted on its hull. Immediately, the ship pulled out of its parabola and flew away, even as more raiders clumsily deployed from its rear. Xerx, the *Reckless's* passengers, and the *Shadow Star* crew made short work of these, and Ri'Kela and Miranda managed to take out those who had missed the landing zone due to the ship's abrupt change.

A second Corax came in, followed by yet another explosion. It flew off before it could release its payload, giving everyone some much-needed breathing space. The remaining raiders were easy pickings after this, but once the last one fell, Xerx knew that more would be coming. They clearly had tons of expendable troops, and had been recruiting them from somewhere to have kept them on a slow drip.

The faint sound of yet another incoming Corax confirmed his fears.

"Signal's restored, Captain," Mobola said, and Xerx breathed a sigh of relief.

"Good work, Mobola," he said. "Neela, see if you can get through to Paige. Ike, Brogan, how are you guys and Miranda doing?"

"Cleaned up on our end," Ike replied. "For now."

"Tyger, Aki, Ri'Kela, any more targets?" Xerx said.

"Clear here as well, Captain Paraska," Ri'Kela replied.

"Good job, then," Xerx said, turning and nodding to the governess. "Ri'Kela, you're almost as good as Miranda with those sniper rifles. Believe me; that's a helluva compliment."

"'Nother one's coming in," Brogan said. "Look alive."

"I've got her," Neela said triumphantly. "Patching Captain Paige to you, *kipenzi*."

"Paige?" Xerx said, at the same time rearing up to fight yet another incoming round of raiders.

"Here."

"It's damn good to hear your voice," Xerx said. "We got problems here."

"On our end as well," Paige said.

"Ambush?"

"Unfortunately. Caught us with our knickers down. We're inbound. ETA about six or seven minutes. What about you?"

"Still in the middle of a hairball here," Xerx said. "It's raining mooks, and it doesn't seem to be stopping. These guys want our asses bad."

"Then bug out," Paige said. "Don't be sitting ducks. Tell my crew to get aboard the *Shadow Star* and fire it up. I can make it to our shuttle; I'll meet you when we hit orbit."

"Sounds like a plan," Xerx said. "But first … question. Any idea how they found us so quick in the first place?"

"Your guess is as good as mine," was Paige's upsetting reply, not that he expected her to know, but it was worth a shot. "Wish I had known; it would've been nice to head them off at the pass, or avoid them altogether. Meet you on the other side."

Xerx wasted little time as he relayed the instructions and had Neela unseal the entrance as Salt and Pepper brought the *Reckless'* engines to life. He watched Ike and Brogan disengage as they headed with Maria toward the *Shadow Star*'s docking, Ri'Kela by his side, keeping aim with her sniper rifle in case some more raiders tried to make their descent on them. When all seemed clear for the moment, he headed inside where the others waited, sans the ambassador, whom Ri'Kela said had remained in his quarters, looking after his daughter.

"Let's fly," Xerx said, heading to the bridge. "Honey, get Frosty on the comm and let her know about our situation."

"I tried already, but she's not responding," Neela said.

Shit, Xerx thought. "Then leave a message. Let her know we'll be in orbit. We can send the *Grasshopper* her way by remote if we have to."

"She won't like that," Neela said.

"She'll understand," Akiko said, coming up beside him.

"Heard that, *kidege*?" Xerx said.

"What choice do we have?" Neela replied.

"Life's a bitch," Xerx said. "Let's get outta here now."

"Captain, we're picking up a squadron of Coraxes on our six," Mobola said. "Nine in all."

"Nine?" Xerx mouthed the word without a sound.

"That *is* desperate," Tyger said as Xerx handed the personal shield back to Biraknu.

"Fun place you have here," Akiko added. "And here I was thinking that this trip would be boring."

"Glad one of us is having fun," Xerx said.

"You want me to what?" came the anxious voice of Mobola over Xerx's comm.

"Bounce, take her up, get us airborne like, now!" Xerx responded breathlessly. He hadn't stopped running since Paige told them to get aboard and get the hell out of Dodge.

"I ... I don't if I can do that, Captain. The systems have been powered down for several hours, there's a warmup cycle, if we don't follow it, we could—"

"Just find a way, dammit!" Xerx said impatiently.

He immediately regretted his tone as the permanently on-edge girl began to stutter.

"I'll speak with her," Neela said. She had been about to rise from the captain's chair when suddenly Pepper's voice cut in.

"*En'li*, listen. It's okay, it's known as a cold jump and *Reckless* is more than capable of handling it. In fact, I've got us a consultant on the line with experience in this sorta thing. She's gonna talk you through it okay?"

Talk her through it quickly, thought Xerx as he reached the elevator and commanded it to head for the bridge deck. He jumped as a familiar high-pitched voice cut through the comm system like a shrill knife.

"Hey, Mobo! I hear you need some tech support!" Pip chirped. "So, you're going to need to dump power into the antigravs, and make sure everyone is braced cos the compensators aren't gonna be able to hold on for a few seconds. Oh, and you'll likely get a bill from the New St. Louis Municipal Docking Authority for the mess you're about to make of their berth."

"I'm on hand with the power distribution, Pip," Pepper added. "What do you need me to do?"

"Get the antigravs running, honey. Mobo, you got this, babe. Once the ship is in the air, all you gotta do is punch it skyward, okay?"

The unshakable confidence in Pip's voice seemed to empower Mobola as she set to work. "O-okay, diverting power n-now," she stammered, and Xerx could feel the dull vibrations as the antigravs started to build charge. He felt a tinge of pride at Pepper's quick thinking, getting Pip to guide her through the process. The two women had struck quite the bond since Tophanavar, and it had saved them precious moments.

"Mobo, honey, I'd stay on the line, but I'm busy remote starting the *Shadow Star*'s own systems, so I'm gonna have to go. But call if you need me, okay?"

Xerx heard the line cut and Pepper yell for everyone to grab onto something. Suddenly the elevator lurched and Xerx felt like his last meal was going to make a reappearance on the deck. Outside, the *Reckless* seemingly jumped off the ground, causing spiderweb patterns of cracking concrete to form beneath it. The resulting gravity pulse turned the remaining raiders into a bloody pulp and tossed crates and loading vehicles in all direc-tions as though they were mere toys. The landing gear retracted, and the ship reversed out from the hangar, turned, and launched skyward as its rocket motors lit. The enemy Corax units gave immediate chase, firing their myriad weapons at the *Reckless*.

Xerx walked onto the bridge, still feeling a little woozy from the sudden takeoff, his vertigo further exac-erbated by the surrounding holo image of the receding surface of Haven and the numerous craft in pursuit.

"Are we going to fire back or what?" He asked Var somewhat sarcastically, as the orange *Hara'Kya* Felyan took his place at tactical.

"No need, Captain. The ship is already computing targeting solutions and about to return fire," Var replied. "It's impressive, really. I think it learned from our last major engagement and has prepared itself for future attacks. Thing is gonna put me out of a job."

"Our bar bill would certainly be smaller," joked Neela as she vacated the captain's chair and gestured for Xerx to sit.

Turning the chair to face the rear of the bridge, Xerx watched as red targeting markers lit up around the chasing craft. Small doors opened along the hull and the surface erupted in a series of tiny blisters, each with a series of three holes that moved as though with a will of their own before they came alive with red flashes. Xerx couldn't help but smile as the Coraxes exploded into tiny fragments, pulses of red energy tearing through them like paper.

"We're about to hit orbit, Captain," Mobola said, her voice now coming over the speakers from her hard link with the ship's systems. Xerx nodded, relieved to see the black of space ahead of them—only to have yet another wave of anxiety rise as the proximity alarm trilled.

"Hostile vessels inbound!" shouted Var. "Modified Barracudas, three of 'em; looks like your salty friends are still looking to fight with us. Also, I'm reading heavily upgraded shield systems and some major firepower."

What the hell didn't *they fucking modify?* Xerx thought, rubbing his chin. He then toggled the comm for engineering. "Pepper, bring the ion pulse emitter online, then ready the rail cannon. It's time we showed them this ship's got teeth as well." He then turned back towards Var's station. "Open up with everything we've got. I've had it with these assholes."

"One weapon salad coming up," replied Var with a hungry grin. "*Reckless* has heard you and is responding, Captain. Spinal missiles are deploying, and the ventral plasma cannons are coming online. Blister pods are already in position and ready to fire."

Along the raised upper spine of the *Reckless,* rows of doors receded into the hull, revealing racks of missiles. The sloping forward panels began to ship and swing open like a flower and the dish of the ion pulse cannon began to glow a laser-bright yellow. In the center of the dish, a long hexagonal barrel extended forward. Underneath, six parallel doors opened and large cannons extended on pivoting mounts.

The ship exploded with light and smoke as the weapons began firing toward their opponents, missiles leaving white trails as they shot toward their targets. The enemy vessels retaliated, and the explosions were joined by blue flashes as ordnance impacted on shields.

The ion pulse cannon flashed, and the raider vessel directly ahead was engulfed in lightning. Less than a second after the pulse was launched the rail cannon fired a bolt at near-light speed. It arrived at exactly the moment the ion pulse disrupted the Barracuda's systems to maximum effect, removing all resistance. It vaporized in a flash of superheated hull plating and uncontrolled reactor explosions.

Xerx squinted as the scene played out before him. One of the raider ships suddenly jumped into hyperspace, seemingly unwilling to continue the engagement against such overwhelming firepower. The remaining ship, however, had other ideas and began closing the distance between them, firing as it came.

"How long on the ion pulse?" he asked.

"Five minutes at least. It's a power hog, I'm afraid," Pepper replied over the comm.

"Understood," said Xerx through gritted teeth. "Is it me or are they accelerating?"

"It's not you, *Kipenzi*," Neela replied. "It seems they're positioning to ram us."

"Shit. I was afraid you'd say that. Death or glory for them, it seems. We'll survive the impact, though. Right?"

"We will," Var answered. "But we'll be a mess, looking at weeks in drydock. Self-repair systems can only do so much."

"Damn," Xerx growled. "Hit them with whatever is left. Maybe we can break her up before impact."

"Captain!" Mobola called over the speakers. "I'm getting a jump signature, extreme close range, brace for bow shock!"

The *Reckless* rocked as a bright flash lit up the space before them and the *Wraith* materialized at speed, its cross-headed bow plowing into the side of the enemy Barracuda, nearly cleaving it in two. Debris and vented atmosphere spewed out in all directions as the momentum of the *Wraith* shoved it aside and out of the *Reckless*' path.

The comm immediately lit up, showing the callsign, DRAGON BITCH. Xerx gave the command to connect, and Alexa's image filled the holo before them.

"Sorry I'm late, sweetie. Got delayed decrypting the last of the Helix data we retrieved. We need to get together and discuss this face-to-face. I'll be heading over momentarily."

The comm cut and Xerx turned to face his crew. "Damage mitigation and repairs as necessary. You all know the drill; I'd better go and greet our royal guest."

Kumiko woke with a start and sat up straight. Quickly, she took stock of her surroundings and relaxed a little. She was clearly still aboard Snow's vessel, the *Hammerfall II*.

"Good, you're awake," Snow said. She was standing near the kitchen area preparing what looked like soup in a cup. "I'm just making some soup; you want some?"

Kumiko shook her head, then winced. It still hurt, but she could feel things returning like someone gently turning the volume up on a stereo. She fixed her gaze on Snow.

"What's happened?" she asked.

"Your friends have caused quite a commotion," Snow replied, leaning against the counter. She took a sip from the cup. "They were attacked by a large force of insurgents. 'Warriors of the True King Montera the First,' they call themselves."

"Raiders," Kumiko said, with a derisive grimace.

"Yes, that too. Your friends made a mess of the spaceport and an even bigger mess of the raiders, all things considered. The *Shadow Star* recently took off in a much more sedate fashion, it has to be said. There's been some fighting in orbit with quite the impressive display of firepower."

Kumiko stood up and joined Snow near the counter.

"I was attacked by the same people," she admitted, "but there's much more to this than meets the eye. Have you heard of Helix?"

Snow nodded. "Oh yes, they've been hiding in the shadows around the Imperial border worlds for a while now. We've been doing our best to try and uproot them, but their main base of operations has eluded us so far."

"I'm certain they're behind this, but I'm struggling to understand what they would want with the child of the Felyan royal family."

Snow shrugged. "Their plans are convoluted and deliberately masked in subterfuge and confusion; their motives are concealed beneath many layers of misdirection and lies. Even with the resources at my disposal, I'm at a loss as to why they act the way they do."

Kumiko suddenly tilted her head and looked around as if someone else were in the room.

"We're not alone, are we?" she asked.

"Well, kind of yes and kind of no..." Snow gave her a hand-waving motion. "I think an introduction is in order. Come with me."

Snow led Kumiko toward a door in the center of the rear bulkhead and keyed the code into the pad nearby. The door opened with a hiss, revealing a dark room filled with cables and blinking lights, and cold enough to hang meat inside of. In its center stood a large rect-angular unit that the cables fed into.

"Noomi, you awake?" Snow said.

"Aye, when am I not?" Noomi replied.

"You up for a personal greeting?"

"Sure, why not? Mah fluid could do wi' a rinse, anyhoo."

"In that case," Snow gestured toward the unit, "Madam Frostbyte, meet the central processing unit of the *Hammerfall II*."

Snow reached out and turned a large radial handle on the unit. There was a hiss, and warm, clear fluid drained into channels around it. The top section then raised upward, revealing a small, pale woman covered in connector cables and wearing a breathing appa-ratus. Her hair was white like that of Snow's. Circuit-like patterns covered her skin around the areas where the cables intersected.

"Kumiko Zero." Snow gently raised the woman in the unit to a sitting position, delicately removing the breathing apparatus. "This is Naomi Brabham, or as you've no doubt guessed, Noomi."

As Snow set about disconnecting the cables, the tech tank blinked and opened her eyes, revealing white corneas. She coughed and then spoke.

"Hey, are you's gonna stare at me like that all day or what?"

Kumiko blinked and shook her head. "You can see me?" she asked.

"Och no, Ah'm blind as fuck, but I've been linked up to the ship's systems, so I've seen you on the cameras. We're like the white hair gang, aren't we?" Noomi gave a slight chuckle.

"Snow, is there a chance I can get some clothes? I'm fookin' freezin' here, an' I'm pretty sure Kumi here does nae wanna stare at mah tits for too much longer."

Kumiko suppressed a chuckle; she hadn't expected the diminutive woman to actually sound like she did over the speakers. Though there was a slight slur to her speech, and she could see Noomi's limbs seemed to move with a mind of their own.

Snow noticed her looking.

"Noo, like me, shouldn't exist, not in terms of what is expected of a tank. She's blind and suffers a condition called cerebral palsy. They would have rendered her down as protein mush for the rank and file if it hadn't been for Agent Four."

"Aye, ahm a wobbly bobblehead and mah limbs don't do as they're told sometimes," Noomi said, "but I can link with machines as good as the best of 'em. Basically mah body's shite, but mah mind is sharp as a razor."

Kumiko frowned. This was intriguing, but she had priorities.

"Not to be rude, but I really need to get back to the *Reckless*," she said, and flashed a rare pleasant smile at the blind tank. "It's still nice to meet you, though, Noomi."

Noomi winked and gave Kumiko a smirk.

"Gee us five minutes, an' I'll have mah wireless head plugged in," Noomi said. "We'll be airborne 'fore ya know it."

Moments later, the *Hammerfall II* was in the air and its four massive drive units lit up, punching the ship skyward. As it reached the upper atmosphere, the engines cut and then the entire vessel faded from view as the cloak engaged.

In the cockpit, Snow sat at the controls while Noomi sat beside her in an oversized dark blue arran knit sweater. Underneath, she wore a gray compression suit. Across her cranial implants was a crown of aerials and small spherical cameras, small wires fed into a pair of glasses that carried various even smaller camera units. Kumi stood at the back of the cabin observing the two pale women silently going about their business. She looked ahead through the viewport and observed the carnage of the recent battle that had taken place. The remains of two insurgent vessels drifted around the other ships like oversized glitter in the sunlight.

The *Reckless* floated with the *Shadow Star* docked belly-to-belly like two giant spacefaring creatures in some bizarre mating ritual. But what struck Kumi the most profoundly was the *Wraith*, the vessel of the Pirate Queen, sitting further out, its cross-headed prow bearing the scars of its signature ramming move and the remaining raider vessel split in half, the rubble strewn across its middle, with both halves turning slowly in the void. Fires and sparks spat occasionally from the bisected ends.

"Would it be possible to patch me through to Xerx aboard the *Reckless*?" she asked Snow, as their approach began to slow.

"Frequency?" Snow asked, keeping her focus on the instrument panel in front of her.

"Ach, you dinnae need that. I'm already on their band. I scanned as soon as she asked," chirped Noomi, shooting a little smirk toward Kumi.

"Show off." Snow looked at Noomi with a nonplussed expression while the tank just grinned.

"Channel's open when you're ready, hen," Noomi said to Kumiko after a moment.

Kumi nodded and cleared her throat.

"Zee, you there? It's Kumi. I'm safe, and I'm okay, so don't bother asking, but I'd appreciate an update on the situation. What the hell happened here?"

There was a click of static, and then Xer's voice came over the comm.

"Frosty, it's good to hear your voice! Good to see someone knows your travel habits, eh? We had ourselves a little skirmish with these guys, but *Reckless* was up to the fight. Alexa arrived to put the finisher on the final ship, though."

Kumi crossed her arms and frowned. "So it would seem. Well, I'm aboard a cloaked Imperial vessel, of all things. However, they're to be considered friendlies for now. Our missions would appear to converge for the time being. Anything we can do to assist?"

There was a palpable hesitation and Kumi could hear faint whispering in the background before Xerx returned to the comm.

"Well, that's a curveball, but Paige said if it's who she thinks it is, then the Imperials are welcome to join the fight for now. Alexa sent some of her guard over the remaining raider ship's hull where the bridge is located, hoping we could get some information out of the bridge crew, but they've locked themselves down tighter than Salt's wallet when it's his round. Reckon you could help us smoke them out?"

Kumi suppressed a laugh at the sudden indignant, gruff-sounding "Hey!" that erupted in the background.

"I'll see what I can do, Zee." With that, she cut the comm.

"Can you get us closer?" she asked Snow. "I think I can bypass the bridge doors, if you know what I mean."

"Really?" Snow looked at her quizzically. "You think a nap and a cup of soup and you're ready to throw yourself across the void and back?"

Kumi pursed her lips, then cast her a faint grin. "Watch me."

She closed her eyes and then opened them again as a trickle of blood ran down her nose. Clearly, it hadn't worked. She felt the strain though, and a wave of dizziness washed over her.

"Fine," she said, putting a hand against the wall for balance. "What do you suggest?"

Snow snapped her fingers. "You're half-tank, aren't you? I think I have something that will help!"

She stood up and opened a panel near where Kumiko was standing. Inside was a series of medical supplies and what looked like a nano-injector. Snow pulled the injector out and clicked the dial on the top.

"Combat stims?" Kumiko said.

"They're to keep us going until we can seek medical attention for injuries that won't heal on their own, but they're way too strong for a normal human," Snow explained. "Given your mother, though, I think just maybe, you might be able to handle it."

Noomi giggled. "If nothin' else, you'll kick some arse 'fore your heed explodes at least."

"Your concern is appreciated," replied Kumiko.

She rolled up the sleeve on her left forearm. "Hit me."

Snow inclined her head and jabbed the injector into Kumiko's exposed forearm.

For Kumiko, the world suddenly coalesced into sharp focus. Her blue eyes grew wide as she drew in a sharp breath through her nostrils. In a ripple of reality, she was gone.

Aboard the raider bridge, the crew took positions behind their consoles, weapons pointed at the door, which had begun to glow orange as cutting torches began to make headway. The captain stood proudly in the center of the room, a large knife in one hand and an ornate pistol in the other. He grinned through a wiry orange beard in anticipation of the coming fight.

A pop and a smell of ozone came out of nowhere, followed by the sight of his men suddenly raising their weapons in his direction. Before he could ask what the hell was going on, he felt a forearm across his throat. Kumi held him close like a shield and stared down the other raiders on the bridge.

"Hold your breath," she whispered in his ear.

The other raiders opened fire, but their shots hit nothing but air as Kumi jumped out with her prize.

Xerx, standing alongside Paige in hologram form, both of them glad to have escaped Haven with their heads still on, watched the wreck rolling in space before them. It had been a few minutes since Kumiko had made contact, and nothing seemed to be happening. He reached for his personal comm when suddenly Kumiko appeared on the bridge and strolled toward him. Her eyes were inhumanly alive with a strange level of focus he'd never seen from her before.

God, she looks wired! he thought with a sense of foreboding.

"Did I just see what I think I saw?" Paige asked.

"With Frosty, I've learned to expect anything," Xerx said, stepping over to the young woman with a modicum of caution. "And yes."

"Zynj," Kumiko said, her voice came as a croak at first, then began to gain strength. "They're on Zynj, and someone in the council has been helping them. We need to go there—now."

"Uhm, good to see you too," replied Xerx. He nodded toward the wreckage of the raider ship in the holo. "I'm guessing you've already been over there then, huh?"

"Might I ask how you came by this information?" Ramirez asked, approaching them both.

As soon as he finished speaking, a body seemed to hit the holographic display and drift past them. The raider captain's head looked like it had been burned up from the inside out.

"He was most forthcoming," said Kumiko.

"Jeez, Kumi," Xerx said, the look of shock on his face contrasting her look of determination. "That's cold, even for you."

The rest of the bridge just stared at her, dumbfounded. Kumiko swayed slightly and then steadied herself. The combat stims had begun to wear off already—no surprise, considering the jump to the raiders' ship had been more or less blind. It clearly used more energy than she'd expected.

"I don't have time for your disapproval. Helix is on Zynj; the captain's brain burned out before I could get much more.

"Kumi, I don't think anyone doubts you're telling the truth," Xerx said, stepping forward. "But look at it from our point of view for a change. You look like shit. Are you on something?"

"It's the stims I took," Kumiko said, then glanced at her mother, whose look of concern was even deeper than the rest of the crew. "I had no choice at the time. But it got the job done."

"This isn't gonna be a problem, is it?" Xerx said.

"I only did it once!" she snapped, spinning back towards the captain.

"Don't yell at him," Akiko said. "He's the captain and he's concerned, like we all are."

"I know," Kumiko said, cradling her head against a sudden splitting headache—no doubt a symptom of her crashing from the stims. "I *always* know, dammit. Trust me, all of you; it was a one-time thing. It gave me the boost I needed to do what I had to do, and we got significant intel. I think the phrase is 'thank you, Kumiko,' Now if you'll excuse me, I'm going to listen to my body and pass out."

With that, she tumbled to the vacant captain's chair and slumped into it, eyes closed and cutting herself off from the emotions that pelted at her mind.

If only everyone could read each other's minds, she thought before slipping into the bliss of unconsciousness. *Things would be so much easier.*

FOURTEEN

"**I**f you ask me, I think this mission has gone far off the rails," Ramirez said. His hologram floated before Xerx, arms crossed, while Ri'Kela stood behind him. The governess held the baby to her breast while she chewed on a lock of her hair.

"But..." Xerx prompted.

Ramirez frowned, capitulating. "But ... for good reason, it seems."

"Look if there were any other way..." Xerx began, but Ramirez cut him off with a sternly held hand.

"Save your apologies, Captain Paraska. They're not needed. Trust me, if I felt that we would be safer on an orbital colony or space hippie fleet, I would've had you leave us there. But it seems we're in the safest place we can be, even going into the lion's mouth."

"Then we're on the same page, you and I," Xerx said with some relief. Ramirez himself let out a sigh that he'd seemed to be holding for a long time.

"For better or for worse," the ambassador said. "Despite my reservations, Miss Zero chose you for a reason. Her judgment has yet to prove ill so far, so continue with your plan, Captain." He spoke around his daughter's tiny hands, which pawed at his face as he held her.

Xerx suppressed a laugh at the sight as the transmission ended, then leaned back in his chair, feeling a bit better, but vaguely apprehensive over past discussions with Neela that the conversation had brought to mind.

Why you would think that I'd be a good dad is beyond me, Kipenzi, he thought, hearing his wife snickering beside him along with Akiko on the other side. Refusing to make his thoughts known, he recalled Alexa's brief visit after the battle in Haven's orbit.

"Zynj? Dear Lord, not that fucking dump," she said, somewhat louder than Xerx would have liked. "I mean, have you actually ever been there? The place literally runs on racism, xenophobia, and prune juice."

Xerx looked at her quizzically. "Prune juice?"

Alexa nodded, her expression as serious as it could be. "Their diet, mostly reconstituted protein chains, can leave people backed up for days. They literally import the stuff by the ton."

Xerx shook his head. "They can't be operating there alone," he said, trying to steer things back to the business at hand. "A place that tightly controlled would have surely been on to them within days."

"Oh, they had help. I'm fucking certain of it." Alexa put her hands on her hips and looked Xerx in the eye. "I'll arrange for you to have an audience with the council. There's something I want you to do..."

Hellbent on making use of the relative peace they'd found for a bit of research, Xerx pulled up a document on Zynj society and social structure that Alexa had recommended to him. The insular world was not a place to visit blind; one wrong move could see you in jail, or worse. The *Reckless*, *Shadow Star*, *Hammerfall II*, and *Wraith* were well on their way, though their destination was still a good five hours away, giving Kumiko time to heal. Akiko gave her a bit of a scolding when she learned that she took those combat stims, but she'd seemed to recover enough from their effects, and her powers were returning to what passed for normal in Kumiko's case.

"At least the ambassador's calmer than I expected he would be," Xerx finally said, knowing that both women were waiting for him to say something.

"Ambassadors' jobs aren't quite as cushy as you'd think," Akiko said. "Well, depending on how dirty they want to get their hands, of course."

"This one seems to be made of sterner stuff than most," Xerx said before wrapping up his brief read. He went silent again after digesting what he'd just read.

"You know, it all makes sense now," he said at last.

"What does?" Akiko asked as Neela leaned up against the captain's chair. Xerx had summoned the tank to the bridge to discuss strategy, but before they could decide what to do, the pieces to a grander puzzle had fallen together in the back of his mind, leading him to his research before Ramirez had commed him.

"The fact that Helix would've dug its heels in at Zynj, of all places." Xerx then transferred the information on his datasheet to the chair's holoprojector. "Exactly how much do you know about Zynj?"

"Not much," Akiko said. "It's one of the few Alliance worlds I haven't been to. Once, Tyger and I were afraid that Kumiko might have been taken there, so I got some info about the city layouts from a former citizen who I met on An'Re'Hara: a scrap hauler who married a Felyan and was exiled for it."

"You never got the chance to use the info?" Xerx asked. Akiko shook her head.

"We found Kumi before I could put it to use," she said. "Maybe it was for the best, though. Place has potential landmines all over its society. You would have probably ended up in hot water one way or another."

"I see," Akiko replied. "Please continue."

Xerx flipped through the holographic slides, stopping on a bright symbol of the original First Imperium.

"Zynj used to be the capital of the original Imperium, before it imploded. Its status meant that separatists and seditionists decided that it should be bombarded to dust. They nuked almost the entire surface. They were too proud to surrender and paid the price." Xerx adjusted the holo once more, showing a video recording of the Zynj natives digging out tunnels and building huge underground cities capped with gigantic metal domes. "This vid makes it look like they did it all themselves, but the truth is they were helped by the Felyans, who installed the ventilation and life support systems using their technology. Despite that fact, though, Zynj is very much a homo sapiens-only club."

"They seriously relied on Felyan charity?" Neela's incredulous words shook with a laugh.

"For nigh on a century," Xerx replied matter-of-factly. "Until about five years ago when the pirate clans bought them out."

"Fucking hypocrites as well as racists," Akiko said, shaking her head.

"No arguments there," Xerx said, still reading. Again, he paused, raising an eyebrow at a piece from the file he'd overlooked. "Damn ... they even use DNA scanners."

"Why?" Neela asked.

"I have a pretty good idea why," Akiko said. "Felyans leave a genetic fingerprint on anyone they've been intimate with. It leaves a scent for a time. Kind of a 'keep out' marker for any other potential paramours. For humans—even tanks—the marker integrates into our genome. It's pretty easy to detect."

"You'd be right," Xerx said with a nod. "If they pick you up, it's seven grand and jail time."

"Shit."

Xerx's eyes went wide, then he snickered, being treated to one of his wife's rare expletives.

"God only knows why they still have the things, though," he said a moment later. "After the environmental systems switched hands, Felyans and hybrids without diplomatic credentials were basically banned from the planet."

"Paranoid clowns," Neela remarked.

"And this gives us a bit of a problem," Xerx said. "We'll have to leave most of our crew aboard for this adventure, especially the guests." He glanced at Akiko, who appeared to know what this meant, judging by her look of disappointment. "Even you and Tyger, it seems. Sorry."

"What about tertiaries?" Neela asked.

"I'd like to see them try to round Kumiko up." Xerx gave a loud snort. "I'd make popcorn just to watch that ass-kicking."

As all three laughed at that mental image, Mobola spoke up from her sole active station below the dais.

"Captain, the *Wraith* is hailing us. It's Queen Alexa."

Xerx closed the file he'd been studying, then stood and moved up to the railing with Neela beside him.

"Put her on the holo," he said, deciding not to tell his most self-conscious techie yet again that she didn't need to be so formal with his sister-in-law. Akiko hung back, watching as the Pirate Queen's face materialized.

"Your conversation with Paige took longer than I thought it would," Xerx said with a playful grin.

"Dealing with Zynj requires a level of ... finesse," Alexa said. "And making plans to deal with it takes time."

"Kumiko's not going to like that," Neela said, her shoulders shaking with a silent laugh.

"I'm sure she'd like to huff and puff and blow the doors down," Alexa said flippantly. "But I digress. We're going to have to do this in a way that at least has the appearance of diplomacy if we're to get anywhere." Her expression then transformed into a very rare look of utter sincerity. "Therefore, I'm giving you strict instructions not to attempt any landings when we arrive, until I deem we're all fully ready."

"Okay then," Xerx said, slipping out of his more casual mode. He knew a royal command when he heard it. Alexa gave very few of those to him, and despite how close he was to his sister-in-law, she was still the Queen. "Look, you know I'd trust you with anything short of keeping a good poker face, but are you able to tell me why?"

"Leverage," Alexa said with a curious grin.

"Leverage?"

"You'll see." There was a twinkle in the Pirate Queen's blue eyes.

"Sounds like you have a plan," Xerx said, more hoping than asking.

"That I do. Now first, there's a blind spot in the planet's sensor grid. Clans used to use it for smuggling scrap right under their noses. I'll send you the info. I'll need everyone to meet up there so I can let everyone in on the plan."

"Well, that's a load off my mind." Xerx smiled a wide, genuine smile at the news. "So why wait to tell us?"

"Two reasons," Alexa said. "Because, as I implied, once we get there and put things into motion, time will be of the essence. The Council on Zynj has a finger in every pot, and word moves fast."

"And the second?"

"Second ... and quite frankly..." Alexa's expression softened into an apologetic one, "you look like fresh shit. Seriously, when's the last time you slept?"

Xerx, at first taken aback, reflected on the events of the day, suddenly realizing how haggard he must have looked. It had only been about half a day since he'd left An'Re'Hara, and they'd traveled over half of Alliance space, then fought for their lives twice on Haven.

"We've all been through a lot today," Neela said on his behalf.

"It ... has been stressful," Xerx added, sighing as his wife laced her fingers with his. "I guess it couldn't hurt to take some down time before getting into another hairball."

"Damn right," Alexa said before ending the transmission. "I sent you the coordinates for the rendezvous point, by the way. We'll speak again at Zynj."

Now that they were relatively alone, Neela leaned into his side: an act that brought out a flare of warmth through his body. Out of the corner of his eye, Xerx noticed Akiko quietly taking her leave, descending the dais ramp and exiting the bridge.

"I know a lot of ways to relieve stress," his wife said, whispering in his ear,

"I know you do," Xerx murmured back, smiling.

"Why don't we go try them out?"

"Mobola, put my girl into autopilot," Xerx said, leaning over the railing before he and Neela descended the dais ramp to the dais and made their way to the exit door. "Stay hooked to the sensors if you're going to get any shuteye, and alert me if anything changes."

"Yes, sir," Mobola replied, and Xerx caught a glimpse of her leaning back in her chair as the threads from the *msaidizi* in her hand shunted into the console in front of her.

He paused, looking back at the bridge before exiting, and smiled.

"I know you're a bit miffed at my popping up just about anywhere here," Kumiko remarked as Xerx reappeared with Neela on the bridge, feeling both tired and refreshed at the same time. Kumiko tapped Mobola's console, where she still lay reclined and inert, her mind

still linked with the ship's computer systems, and probably conversing with Pip aboard the *Shadow Star*.

"You've been like a housecat, to be sure," Xerx said with a bemused expression. "But I'm used to it."

"But ..." Kumiko prompted.

Xerx sighed at her telepathy.

"*But* ... don't just pass out in my chair on the bridge again."

"I'll try not to make a habit of it."

"You slept off that crash?"

Kumiko made a side-to-side teetering gesture with her hand. "I'm not at a hundred percent, but I do feel better—certainly not 'hearing colors' like I was before. Mobola and I were just talking about how she handles all the calculations." She inclined her head further out to the next console over, where Pepper shot up like a flustered dog that had been roused from a deep sleep.

"Oh, captain!" he said, a bit more loudly than he perhaps expected, from the way he jumped at his own voice. "You're back."

"He was just keeping me company," Mobola's voice said through the intercom.

"As you said he would," Neela whispered cheekily to her husband.

"How far out are we?" Xerx asked, suppressing a smile.

"We've reached the system's outer edge," Mobola replied, and Xerx hurried up the dais.

"Looks like this is it. Let's get on the comm with everyone. Message the *Wraith*, *Shadow Star*, and *Hammerfall II*. Let them know we're ready."

"Yes, Captain."

In a moment, Alexa, Paige, and the new face of Snow appeared in the holos surrounding the dais. Two he trusted with his life, but all he knew about Snow was what Kumiko had relayed. She was yet another Second Imperium bounty hunter: one who had orders to round up his resident tertiary—God only knew how she would manage that—and had now decided to forego those orders to help them out ... at least according to Kumiko. If it hadn't been for her telepathy, Xerx would have told the strange pale woman to go suck stardust.

"So, let's hear it," Xerx said to Alexa. "What's this plan of yours?"

Alexa gesticulated flying in a certain path. "There's a massive debris field surrounding the extreme outer orbit of the planet—leftovers from the war. There are routes through—tricky, but not impossible for ships of our size to navigate." She then arranged her hands, one in front of the other. "We'll need to travel line astern, but it's fairly straightforward, to be honest. Once we hit orbit, I'll make the call and work my magic. *Hammerfall II* will get you down to the surface."

"I'll be coming along, bringing Maria and Miranda with me," Paige said. "They'll be the most useful in what I think will be coming."

"I'll have someone with the appropriate skills joining in," Alexa said, then pointed at Xerx. "Keep a low profile in case I'm not successful on my end. Wouldn't want to start a firefight with a registered Alliance member, even if they are a bunch of wankers."

"You're the queen," Xerx said, nodding to Mobola, who announced their change in course to a pursuit vector behind the *Wraith*.

He had selected his team: only himself and Kumiko. Neela would stay behind and handle the *Reckless* as they boarded the *Hammerfall II*. She, in turn, would be keeping the ship warm for his return and keeping the Ambassador and princess safe. Still, he left orders for her to bug out if things went sideways. Bringing Kumiko raised concerns in the back of his mind, as he knew it would. This would be a gamble, to be sure. The game was discretion, and he wasn't sure how tertiaries, whose genome was an amalgamation of their human and Felyan lineages, would affect the cities' gene scanners. Kumi's powers were extensive, but her patience was not. He hoped she wouldn't nuke the council out of spite.

When the dusty brown orb of Zynj became visible on the surrounding screens, he knew it was time. And as if she could read his thoughts as clearly as Kumiko, Mobola spoke up.

"*Hammerfall II* on a parallel trajectory," she announced. "Docking rings aligned; extending umbilical."

Xerx patted his holstered pistols and knife, then kissed Neela goodbye.

"Moment of truth," he said, smiling into her almond-shaped eyes. As always, he hoped it wouldn't be the last time. "Keep it all together here."

Neela gave a slight nod. "Come back to me," she whispered.

"I will."

FIFTEEN

Once Xerx finished boarding the *Hammerfall II* with Kumiko, they found themselves in a long corridor with benches that stretched the length of the wall across from the airlock door, from which a series of harnesses hung. They sat down and waited for the next ship to dock. It turned out to be the *Shadow Star*, as Paige stepped through, accompanied by Maria and Miranda.

"I'm surprised your shadow's not coming with you," Xerx remarked, genuinely surprised at seeing Maria without Artemis. If it was one thing the pink-haired angel of death would go for, it was a good fight.

"And she was *not* happy about it, believe me," Maria said.

"If you love them, let them go," Miranda said, seeming to stare into space. "If they return, they're yours."

"No one's letting anyone go, honey," Maria said to her sister with a patient smile.

"Can't argue that she'd have been a big help, though," Xerx said.

"She has an ... affinity for small, tight spaces," Paige said, shaking her head. "She'll crawl into air ducts and access tubes just for fun. And Zynj cities have miles upon miles of them, last I heard."

"You're worried about her getting lost?" Kumiko asked.

"Oh, she could never get lost," Maria said, waving off the question with a titter. "She'd be able to sniff me out from the bottom levels of Xiao."

"But she'd crawl through every tunnel doing it," Paige explained. "She's..."

"Not conventional," Maria said, finishing the sentence.

"Just like her GI tactics," Xerx said, giving a rueful grin.

Within a few minutes, they docked with the *Wraith*. But instead of Alexa, Xerx was surprised to see the airlock door closing immediately after another tank stepped through. He had never formally met Alexa's entire entourage, but he knew that the Pirate Queen, by Iriid's orders, had a cadre of tanks as her bodyguards—one of the most superfluous jobs he believed anyone could have—but they were usually invisible, hidden with diffraction cloth suits. From the way this particular tank carried herself, she seemed as stoic as Miranda, and just as battle-scarred as Maria, perhaps even more so, with deep claw marks raked across her face. Like Paige's crew, she was impressively armed, carrying an extended vajra with a detailed likeness of a Tantagel dragon's head at one end, along with multiple swords and knives across her back and in scabbards at her hips.

"Looks like our laddies and lassies are properly nestled in like a bunch of wee birds, Cap'n!"

The woman's voice over the ship's PA spoke with an accent so peculiar that Xerx at first could only barely understand what she was saying. He believed it was Neo Caledonian—something he hadn't heard in ages. God only knew how she had managed to pick it up.

"That's Noomi," Kumiko said.

"The tech tank you mentioned earlier?" Xerx said. "That's the weirdest sounding tech tank I ever heard."

"Well, Captain Gobshite, ye can just kiss the crack o'me moonlight-colored arse," the voice snapped back. "That sound weird enough?"

Xerx opened his mouth, unsure if he would retort or apologize, but the door at the end of the corridor opened, ending the potential confrontation.

"Noo, manners," Snow chided as she stepped through. Her skin was even whiter than the holos suggested. The sight of her, in fact, took Xerx immediately aback. Not a speck of black showed on her body. Tanks usually had at least some monochromatic complementation in their hair. His shock, however, shifted quickly to amusement as, inwardly, he chuckled, figuring that "Ghost" would have been a more appropriate moniker for the pale tank.

In her hand, Snow held a holoprojector with the image of Alexa standing cross-armed, a shrewd grin on her face.

"Small force, eh?" Snow said, giving the assembly a once-over. "Good; less of a chance of being found out. But if the plan goes right, that'll be a moot point."

"Lex, I thought you were coming with," Xerx said to the Pirate Queen, who gave him a playful grin.

"Oh, I know you miss seeing this sexy arse of mine," was Alexa's cheeky reply, "but I'll be able to handle things better where I am on my end. So, my Indira will be keeping you company for this sortie. Besides, if things go well, you won't have any problems getting to Helix."

The statuesque tank beside him snorted, grimacing as if she'd had her favorite toy taken from her. Alexa only laughed. "Yes, love. I know you'd be disappointed with that."

"Exactly how long has it been since any clans have checked in on these guys?" Xerx asked.

"Longer than I think I ought to have let it go," Alexa said, now speaking with somewhat less confidence.

"That might not work out well for us," Xerx said, crossing his arms against the sense of foreboding that formed in the back of his mind. "Let's hope the Council is the bunch of craven cowards you say they are."

Alexa pursed her lips, raising an eyebrow. "Well, let's not be too optimistic now."

Xerx shrugged. "Realism is an unfortunate part of my intrusive thoughts sometimes. But don't worry; I'm ready. Everyone's ready, I'm sure." He removed his gun from its holster and primed it. He then turned to Snow. "Just one question, though. Why are you helping us out? What's in it for you? It doesn't look like you have any skin in this fight."

"The fact that raiders have weapons that they shouldn't," Snow said.

"Come again?"

"You think raiders are only a pain in the Alliance or pirates' asses?" Snow gave a sardonic grin. "I got a glimpse of their capabilities back on Haven. And because of that, the mission has changed. This upgrade in arms is a point of interest for the Imperium as well."

"Makes just as much sense as anything," Xerx said. "Well, then, Let's get this party started."

"They're all yours, then," Alexa said to Snow. "Do bring them back in one piece."

"All right, everybody, sit tight, and grab a rebreather mask from the equipment lockers," Snow said as Alexa's image vanished. A door in the wall above the harnesses immediately slid open, revealing the clear face-covering mask with two filtration units affixed to their sides. "Toxins out there are a bitch; that goes without saying. But I need to warn you, even with this thing on, you won't want to be out there for more than twenty minutes without something more advanced."

"I can shield them," Kumiko said. "No need for masks."

"Better safe than sorry," Snow said with finality. "My ship, my rules. Put it on or don't follow. I'm not about to explain anybody's death to the Pirate Queen on my watch."

"It really is safer," Xerx said, seeing the scowl on the silver-haired girl's face. "Let's not piss the lady off. You did say she saved your ass, right?"

Kumiko, still scowling, hesitated for a moment more, then, with obvious reluctance, went to the open locker and grabbed the mask.

"Paraska, did Alexa give you the combination for the back door?" Snow asked, facing Xerx, who nodded. She'd sent it all during their last communique.

"Good." She glanced upward. "Noomi, how long 'til we hit atmo?"

No sooner than she finished the question, the ship began to rattle.

"Shall I give the calculations in negatives, now?" Noomi replied with as much cheek as Alexa on her best days. "Now's a good time to gied yoursel' up to the cockpit, ken."

"Sit tight, everyone," Snow said. "I'll give the signal once we land, and I'll open the airlock." She betrayed a sly grin. "With any luck, the wind won't be the kind that scrubs off your flesh."

Snow retreated back through the door and it closed, leaving them alone once more.

"She was joking about the wind scrubbing off your flesh, wasn't she?" Xerx said after a silence that felt especially awkward amongst mostly longtime friends.

"Not really," Kumiko said. "Storms get that bad on the surface sometimes. But only morons would be outside the cities during one."

"Good thing we have you, then," Xerx said.

"Not according to our host, it seems."

"Well, that's not like you," Xerx said teasingly, "letting someone get under your skin like that. What happened to everyone's favorite ice queen?"

He received yet another sourceless *thump* on the back of his head. But rather than anger, there was an indecipherable grin on the silver-haired girl's face ... which quickly transformed into a look of surprise as she noticed the starfish-shaped device on Xerx's chest.

"You have a personal shield?"

"Biraknu let me borrow it," Xerx explained.

"Seems I won't have to look after your troublesome ass quite so much, then," Kumiko said.

"You say it like you're more disappointed than relieved," Xerx joked.

"We'll see."

The turbulence on re-entry was just as bad as Xerx expected. Mobola had given him a report about the local weather, and it seemed more like a hurricane than anything normal. But Zynj was a new kind of normal.

"Deeper atmo's gonna be a beast," Noomi said over the PA. "Gi' yer belts on."

With no need to be told twice, Xerx and the entire company slipped into the harnesses just in time for the jostling to feel like the time when he and Neela had escaped Siberna with the corax pursuing them to the *Reckless*. He'd felt his teeth rattle for an hour afterward.

"I hope I didn't make a mistake going down in this ship," Xerx said, more to himself than anyone.

"Snow's calm," Kumiko assured him. "So is Noomi. I'm sure they've done this kind of stuff before."

"No doubt," Xerx said. "I just wish they could make it a little smoother."

"Tell that to the planet," Paige said over the din of noise. Maria laughed, while Indira grinned and Miranda remained stolid.

"Okay, people, seems we've got an ion storm mixed in with the weather conditions. It fortunately didn't disrupt the cloak. I'll be landing you a hundred yards out from the dome's edge in about a minute. Head down toward the big door at the end and hop into the ugly vehicle; I'll join you in a sec while Noomi touches down. Check your weapons, check your rebreathers, then once I open the airlock, good luck."

Xerx and company slipped on the masks and tugged at the straps that held it securely in place. He pressed the seal check button to its side, and a green light flashed across his vision, signaling that it was well in place.

"Everybody good?" he said, speaking over the comm connection. He looked over at Paige, who gave a thumbs up, along with her crew, Indira, and Kumiko.

In a moment, the ship gave a final rattle as all motion came to a rest.

"This is our stop," Xerx said, unstrapping and heading toward the door at the opposite end of the corridor, which opened to a small hangar bay, where a six-wheeled monstrosity awaited them. It resembled the land crawlers that he'd seen in museums, which the first generations of colonists used to explore moons and asteroids for potential habs for mining and commerce, only it was more streamlined, with seating compartments protected by individual domes of armored glass. It was painted with a coat of silver and blue, which he suspected the outside conditions would quickly scuff off.

"Hop in, ye bunch o'crazies," Noomi said as the hatches opened, along with the hangar door, which opened to a hurricane.

"Lovely day," Xerx said, mounting the ladder that led to the passenger compartment.

"I should've tied my hair in a bun," Kumiko groaned.

The base of the city dome was straight ahead, though a mere silhouette in the dull, shrouded daylight, creating an immense, foreboding shadow.

Everyone slipped inside with relative ease, and a minute later, Snow hopped into the driver's seat, then switched on the ignition at her console.

"Well, this ought to be fun," she said, frowning at what Xerx thought had to be the view from inside a tornado. She bit her lip and turned back toward the passenger compartment.

"Looks like we'll need that shielding, madam," she said to Kumiko.

"Indeed."

Kumiko closed her eyes. Now, with much-needed extra protection, Snow punched it forward.

The vehicle didn't rattle and bump quite as much as Xerx had expected with its extreme suspension. And Kumiko's psionic shield worked like a bubble that was a buffer against the worst of the wind and debris, which he suspected would have indeed turned the vehicle to shreds in spite of its apparent sturdiness.

It was a short trip to the service hatch, which would need to be manually opened. From there, the trip would circumvent the city's main thoroughfares and Paige would navigate the way to the Council chambers. But the entrance would still need to be coded by hand. When they arrived at the wall, they noticed the canopied entrance door. Snow nodded at Xerx. At least with Kumiko, they wouldn't have to wait out this storm before they could head inside. He opened his dome to the island of calm in the midst of chaos, while Kumiko did the same and floated over to him. Their domes sealed back, and they made the rest of the way to the door. Despite the lack of wind due to Kumiko's shielding, the rocks and debris strewn across the blasted gray-brown landscape made for treacherous footing, regardless. Twice, he nearly tripped and landed on rocks that looked like they would have done their own share of cutting before they arrived at the outer air-lock that lay at the end of a wide tunnel that protected against the worst of the wind conditions.

Once within the tunnel, Kumiko let down her shield, and a burning scent of combined rust and petroleum assaulted Xerx's nostrils, which even the filters could not keep out. More reason to hurry and get everyone's asses inside.

The keypad was set beneath a handprint ID scanner and behind a separate panel. As if no one had bothered to check it in ages, it took some finagling to get it open with the help of his knife. Xerx had half expected Alexa's code to not work, but immediately after he punched it in, the door slowly slid open into the yawning maw of safety that was the city.

Once inside, a large screen flashed the word STOP in the middle of what otherwise was pitch darkness. The door behind them shut, and Xerx and Kumiko boarded the vehicle yet again, just as the screen flashed DECON in bold blue letters, and the room transformed into a car wash. A fine mist covered the vehicle, then was sprayed off by powerful air currents. The process lasted for over a minute before a series of fans activated and cleared the air. A sign above the second door that slid open read PROCEED as the room was flooded with overhead lights, and a door on the opposite end opened to a shielded corridor. Its makeup seemed to be made of glass, which shielded one end. On the other, piping of all kinds, along with the stone of Zynj's crust, flowed into the city.

"Overlapping city map," Snow said, and immediately, the view switched to an AR display indicating a wireframe image of the warrens that composed New Valis.

"The course we take should run parallel to a nearby maglev," Snow said. "It'll take us straight to the government district. How you deal with them will be up to you."

Through the glass side of the service tube, Xerx and the team received a view that few in the colonies had seen. Zynj had always been a reclusive world, and very few people would have bothered with it outside of the pirate clans, had the ruins of its old surface cities not been such a wealth of recyclable raw materials for construction on other worlds. But it was clear that the people of Zynj at least had an eye for aesthetics. The corridors of New Valis were like a contiguous series of massive branching overpasses, with signs and holographic maps indicating location and landmarks. It wasn't some sterile concrete warren like Xerx had imagined; rather, plants of different kinds carpeted the walls and sides of the passageways, mostly small groves of ginkgo, grass beds, and modified curtains of kudzu flowing over sculpted concrete buildings inset into the walls that ranged from single-story to nearly five stories tall. Walkways ran above the street, connecting to buttressed balconies extending from the higher floors like upper-level sidewalks. Electric lamps were set at regular intervals below painfully bright halogen lights hanging from the ceiling high above, where a maglev ran into and out of a series of tunnels hanging from its rail. The city was alive with life, just as bustling as they were in downtown Siberna Prime, though nowhere near as crowded as the megacities of Xiao. And of course, no one sported weapons, which were a ubiquitous thing on both worlds, just not allowed in most establishments.

"Reminds me of the training grounds where I began my service," Maria remarked. "So weird to see only humans here, though. Not a single tank, Felyan, or hybrid."

"Normal for them, though," Paige said.

"I'm pretty sure the sight of a Felyan or hybrid would be a great deal stranger for them," Xerx quipped. "Makes me wonder what they'd do if they knew that Kumiko was a tertiary."

A neon green line marked their course through the branching twists and turns of the service corridor, following the much faster maglevs, which snaked through tunnels parallel to their own. All the while, Snow steered her way through excellently. In the end, the final maglev tunnel brought them to a standalone cavern.

"Your stop," Snow said as everyone disembarked. "I'm following I/O signals, but Noomi's trying to help me get specific so I can ferret out where Helix's mainframe is. If I find it first, I'll comm you."

"A hundred credits says we'll find it first," Xerx said. To this, Snow gave him a smug grin.

"We have records about your gambling prowess," she said, "or should I say, lack thereof."

"That sounds like a challenge," Xerx said.

"Good luck," Snow said. And nodded as the hatch shut and she continued into the corridor, leaving Xerx and his team to take the service hatch to the cavern where the Council chambers lay.

Xerx and his team, however, froze where they stood once the hatch had opened. Immediately, the *Shadow Star* crew and Indira drew their weapons as several military-looking officers stepped into the corridor, wearing gray-black camouflage fatigues. Xerx's hand went to his pistols, still holstered as Kumiko rolled up her sleeves, the dark lines of the nano implants writhing beneath the skin of her forearms.

However, he noticed one thing kept him from drawing.

"Hold up!" Xerx shouted, waving Paige, Maria, Miranda, Indira, and Kumiko down. "I ... well, I'm surprised to say this, but they're not drawing weapons."

"Chook, what are you saying?" Paige said nervously.

"I'm saying I don't think they're here to hurt us," Xerx replied.

"You sure about that?"

"Not completely, but I think that if they'd wanted to open fire, they would've done it by now." He glanced toward Paige, then inclined his head toward the soldiers. "Don't you think?"

In fact, outside of the fact that they held on real firearms, the only weapons that Xerx could see at the soldiers' hips were nerve scramblers: not exactly nonlethal or legal in the Colonies; some deaths had resulted from their use at higher settings on people with weaker constitutions. But he guessed that in a hermetically sealed environment, they were a safer substitute than what anyone on their team was carrying.

One individual, clearly more decorated than the others, stepped forward into the midst of the soldiers, eyeing Xerx's team with a look of relief, as if they'd taken some kind of massive gamble and won. He was a swarthy man with slicked-back black hair and a HUD affixed to his left eye.

"Which one of you is Xerxes Paraska?" he said.

Hesitantly, Xerx stepped forward, hand still casually resting atop his holstered pistol, ready to mow them down at the first sign of treachery.

"I'm Sergeant Kent Del Arco," the man said. "In conjunction with the Council of Elders and Pirate Queen Alexa, I've been ordered to escort you to the Council chambers post haste." He waved toward the door through which they entered. "Please come with me."

"Anyone notice that none of them asked how we got this far into the city?" Xerx whispered to Paige, Maria, and Indira.

"First thing to cross my mind, as a matter of fact," Paige said. "Something's definitely up."

"They're under orders," Kumiko said, breaking into the conversation. "They won't ask much, but Snow might run into company before long. If things don't go well with the council, she's the wild card, and may have more trouble here than we will."

"I'll plan a rendezvous point once we know more about where we're going to be headed next," Xerx said. "I get the feeling we're gonna need to get the hell outta Dodge once this blows over."

"I think we can handle that without a problem," Maria said, as Paige agreed. Indira, listening intently, nodded her head while Miranda seemed to not hear at all.

The two-story Council building presented a Romanesque façade, carved out of the stone of the cavern wall, from which the flag of Zynj hung: a blue background with a white stripe and a golden glyph shaped like a backward "Z".

Their military entourage led them inside at a brisk pace, which quickened as they entered the building, moving past an empty receptionist's desk and then a series of halls that led to a grand wooden door.

"Nice display of importance," Maria observed, taking in the door's polished surface. "Wood on a planet where it's rarer than gold."

"The Council is waiting for you," the commander said, and gestured toward the door.

"After you," Xerx said, repeating the commander's gesture. He fixed him with a look that telegraphed his suspicion in no uncertain terms.

"Even now, you don't trust us?" the commander said.

Xerx raised an eyebrow. "Afraid?"

The commander gritted his teeth as if he wanted to fling every last expletive in the standard lexicon at him, but he showed an amount of decorum that cast doubt on Xerx's misgivings. Still, he wanted to be sure.

"Hey, Lex, a bunch of mooks led us to the Council's doorstep," Xerx said, switching the team's open comm channel to the *Wraith*. "You sure there's no chance of this being a trap?"

"I assure you, love, I smoothed things out for you," Alexa replied. "Time is now of the essence; don't waste theirs."

"The queen has spoken," Paige said.

"Indeed," Xerx replied, and opened the door, stepping boldly inside.

The council members numbered 22 in all: a group of men and women who appeared in their 50s and 60s. Each of them wore gray cloaks that were similar to the robes of magistrates on Siberna, but more elaborate, hearkening to the cloaks he remembered seeing in pictures of nobles from the First Imperium. All in all, they were a sad throwback to one of humanity's least humble eras. In their midst, a younger-looking council member kneeled on the ground, staring his way. Whereas the rest of the Council held cold glares at him and his team, the look in this individual's dark eyes and the way his jaw set below his thick mustache betrayed a smoldering hatred that seemed to project from the core of his soul.

"So we're here," Xerx said, and gestured to the man on his knees. "What fresh hell is this?"

"Hopefully, the Pirate Queen will be happy with this tribute," one councilman said. He stood behind the kneeling man like a hunter holding his dog to heel. "When she identified Mr. Singh by name, we couldn't believe it ourselves. But it seems he's been collaborating with Helix for many years now."

"Has he, now?" Paige said. Xerx noticed the *Shadow Star* captain nodding intently behind them. Xerx glanced that way and noticed that their military escorts had not followed them.

"Was this a private party?" Xerx asked. "I can't help but notice our hosts didn't follow us inside. I find it hard to believe that you trust us that much."

"I'm sure you understand how delicate a matter this is." One councilwoman, who looked younger than the rest, had spoken up, though her words of reason were tainted by a scowl that made her look like she'd drunk straight-up vinegar. "We can't afford terrorist factions in our society, so it's best that as few as possible know."

"They're hiding something," Kumiko whispered to him; Xerx gave a soft snort.

"Don't need to read minds to figure that out," he subvocalized, thinking the words rather than speaking out loud.

"It's a lot bigger than you think." Xerx saw Kumiko cast a very meaningful gaze across the entirety of the Council. "Ask them how they were able to confirm that this Singh person was the collaborator."

"Way ahead of you," Xerx said. "Good thing Alexa had me do a little research before this mission." He then shifted his attention back to the Council, a wicked grin now growing on his face.

"Terrorists..." he said the word as if he were tasting it. "An interesting choice of words, council members." He nodded to Singh, still on his knees in what appeared to be a very uncomfortable position. "Tell me, how did you figure out that Her Majesty's accusations were true?"

In response, the councilman behind Singh, rolled down the collar of the sullen-looking man's shirt, revealing a very prominent scar in the shape of a double-helix, in the same fashion as the insignia that adorned the Helix banners from Xerx's dives into the history of the organization. He stepped up to both men, inspecting the scar closely, making approving noises.

"Okay then," Xerx said. "I'm convinced." He then looked into the eyes of the councilman who'd just revealed that very scar. "Now show me yours," he said.

A look of utter incredulity, bordering on rage, flared up in the councilman's face.

"I beg your par—"

In a split second, Xerx drew his pistol and shot the man in his shoulder, sending him tumbling back into the dais that held the benches of his fellow councilmen, making a dent in the priceless wooden framework.

Now, Kumi, Xerx thought, and Kumiko leaped backward, behind Paige and the rest of their company, who stood in equal shock at what Xerx had just done. She pressed her hand to the entrance door, then stepped back in preparation. As expected, someone had access to a silent alarm that set the soldiers beyond the entrance in action. As the doors burst open, Kumiko swung her arm out in a swift, sweeping motion, scattering the guards. A collective thud rang out as the men hit walls and furniture. Nanotubules burst from Kumiko's forearms as she focused her power, and the guards struggled against an invisible force that pinned them to the ground.

"Get up," Xerx said, waving his pistol at the downed councilman. "I hit you with a dumb round. You're not dead; it only hurts enough to make you wish you were." He waited for the man to scramble to an upright position: a task he performed with visible pain against the point of the round's impact.

"Your scar," Xerx repeated. "Show me. Now."

With the impotent fury of a man who knew the pro-verbial jig was up, the councilman rolled away the collar from the portion of his shirt that was visible beneath the gray cloak. As expected, he bore a similar helix scar, the same as Singh.

Xerx stepped back, still keeping a tight grip on his pistol, and cast a very calculating gaze across the assembled Council, who had quieted down after this exchange. The captain of the *Reckless* shook his head, feeling yet again weighed down by the events of the day.

"I've been dragged halfway across the galaxy to pro-tect a baby that racist assholes want dead." He began in a sepulchral tone, but his words, as he continued, steadily increased in volume. "My crew and passen-gers have been shot at and forced to fight in a mission they have no part of; we have been chased across half of known space, and I've been in the crosshairs of a socio-pathic tertiary. And now I have to go ferret out a ter-rorist group that, in a fair universe, should have died with half the Colonies during the Imperium Wars, two hundred fucking years ago!"

He aimed his pistol at the Council assembly, who began to wail, ducking and dodging his, as of yet, unfired rounds.

"Those with helix scars had better show them to me right now, or I start making everyone hurt as much as Mr. Gonna-have-a-huge-ass-bruise down here."

The entire council froze in place, staring at Xerx with eyes the size of dinner plates.

That was when Indira, to everyone's surprise, stepped forward.

"Did he bloody stutter?" Indira yelled out, speaking for the first time. "And understand your place. Paraska is, for all intents and purposes, the mouth of the Queen! His words are her orders, and you *will* respect them, now!"

Her words were returned by a resounding silence.

"Do we need to make yet another example? I said *move!*"

Within moments, Xerx and the entire team saw that two-thirds of the Council were marked.

"Sit your sorry asses down," Xerx commanded. He was satisfied with the situation, but no less pissed. "I have a date with the real problem. And we'll be using Mr. Singh as a guide."

Kumiko released the guards, and they rolled onto their sides, groaning as the otherworldly pressure on their bodies melted away. Xerx then stalked up to Singh and dragged him to his feet. He then shoved him carelessly over to Kumiko.

"Does he know where Helix is?" He asked.

"Let's find out," Kumiko said, then reached out and spread her hand out over Singh's head, flattening his bouffant hairdo. Singh stiffened, then began to shake, the veins in his neck erupting into his skin as he appeared to be putting up some terrible kind of resistance.

"It's only going to hurt more if you do that," Kuumiko said. A moment later, she sighed. "Have it your way, then."

Another moment later, Singh screamed, blood flowing from his nose. Kumiko let him go, sporting a grin on her face that was just this side of sadistic as he fell limply to the ground.

"Thanks for cooperating," Kumiko said as Miranda checked Singh's pulse, nodding her head to Paige, much to everyone's relief. "Follow me; I know the way."

SIXTEEN

Even from orbit, Zynj looked like the place where happiness went to die. While the *Wraith* waited on the opposite side of the planet, the *Shadow Star* floated beside them with the same eerie silence, except for the banter between Mobola and Pip from her console below.

Orbital traffic was hypnotically clockwork, mostly automated, with the exception of delivery from Zade, of new "labor personnel"—a poor euphemism for slaves. Zynj and Zade were, in fact, the only two worlds in the Alliance where slave labor was still tolerated. This, plus the fact that its government had been harboring a human supremacist cult, made it even more a planet where Neela did not want to be.

She'd been passing the time by reviewing operations manuals for the bridge that Mobola had dug up from the Alliance archives on Siberna. Her *msaidizi* expedited the data exchange, but it didn't make things any less boring.

Mobola stood up and stretched at her console beside a holo of Pip.

"It's times like this that I wish something *would* happen," she said, her words reflecting Neela's thoughts, though it surprised her to hear them coming from her less-than-assertive crewmate.

"Careful what you wish for," Pip warned as Neela looked on with a grin. "Your captain is down there right now, probably dodging bullets. I don't think you want any of that."

"*That* is fun for him, though," Neela reminded the diminutive tank, leaning over the railing at the edge of the dais and sighing. "My husband thrives on adrenaline."

"Drives you crazy, doesn't it?" Pip asked.

"You have no idea."

"But you wouldn't have it any other way."

"We rarely speak, and yet you know me well," Neela said, hearing Mobola snort out a repressed laugh.

"Like the captain and Kairen," Pip said, "except he's you, and she's the crazy one."

"You do realize you're talking about your own boss when you say that?" Mobola said. It was a warning to which Pip merely shrugged.

"Not like she doesn't know it," Pip said. "'Sides, this ship is like Wonderland. Everyone's mad here."

"You seem ... well-balanced," Mobola said, now sounding slightly awkward from Pip's confession.

"Honey, I just let you know the parts of me that wouldn't scare you away," Pip said slyly. "Maybe one day, I'll tell you more when I'm sure you can handle my crazy."

Now, it was Neela's turn to laugh as Mobola sat back down.

"Ah, thanks for not giving me more than I can handle ...?" she said, sounding even more unsure than before.

"Anytime!" Pip gave a goofy grin—which quickly transformed into a look of distracted surprise. "What the—? Oh, shit! You got barnacles on your hull! Must've had a low sensor profile; not even I caught 'em until now."

"Barnacles?" Neela asked, now standing straight as a rod. For a moment, she worked to recall how to bring up a hull integrity sweep, then punched it in. "What are those?"

"Boarding vessels cobbled together," Pip explained. "They're usually used by raiders."

Incredulity and fury both flared inside of Neela's gut as the anomalies flashed across the neon holos in front of her. "So you're saying they *still* haven't given up?"

"Seems that way," Pip said. "You got a plan? They'll be cutting their way in any second."

"*Dada*, confirm the hull integrity sweep," Neela said to Mobola.

"Confirmed," Mobola said, sounding several times tenser than moments ago. "Four unidentified objects on the ventral side, attached through induced covalent bond."

"So an electrical discharge won't dislodge them," Neela thought aloud. Clever bastards.

"I'm getting hull breach warnings from the points of contact with the objects," Mobola said as a shrill alarm erupted from her console.

"I'm going to try to find out where they came from," Pip said. "You gonna need help if you get boarded?"

"We're prepared for that now," Neela said, then opened the comm to the *Wraith*. "Alexa, I think your Council is trying to double-cross us. We're being boarded."

Alexa's holo appeared. "I'm not reading anything that would read as an incoming vessel. Did they gamble on us passing through the field? Brave. Certainly foolish, but clearly effective."

"I'm not reading anything on the spectral distortion scans," Pip said. "There's nothing big out there, but I am reading a lot of encrypted comm signals in the debris field."

"Then we teach them a lesson," Alexa said. "I'll be making some pretty lights in a few minutes. I can't flush them all out, but I can certainly make sure any raiders left in the debris field don't get 'brave' again."

"And I'll prepare a reception for our guests, on my end," Neela said, satisfied that things were getting done. "Keep me posted." She then turned to Mobola. "Where specifically are the hull breaches?"

"Lower decks," Mobola said. "Two on port; two on starboard. Looks like they want to sweep the ship."

The transmission ended, and Neela notified her guests and crew for an emergency conference call. In moments, everyone aboard the ship, from Mobola to Ramirez, appeared in holos surrounding her.

"Looks like the raiders got savvy," Neela said. "We've got barnacles on the hull. They're burning through the outer skin as we speak, so that means we're about to have company. Salt, Pepper, remain at your posts until the danger has passed; engineering will be locked down to prevent access, so you should be safe. We'll need the ship still running when Xerx gets back."

"We'll keep her purring for him, boss lady," Salt said.

"Var, report to the sickbay in case we have injuries."

Var nodded and his holo vanished along with Salt and Pepper.

"Mobola will be using garrison mode to trap the intruders," Neela said to the assembled guests. "This is where I hope you'll come in."

"Say no more," Tyger said. "All I need to know is where they are."

"As do I," Akiko said.

"The moment they started cutting through the hull, they signed their death warrants," Ri'Kela said. "We're ready to assist."

"As long as they draw breath, there's potential danger to the princess," Biraknu said. "We will do our duty."

A sigh that Neela didn't realize that she'd been holding escaped her lips. Though she had no real worries that they would have refused to help, she nevertheless felt a palpable tension leave her chest at her guests' assent.

"Alright, then," she said. "Thank you all for your assistance."

"It is my pleasure," said Akiko, "I'm always ready for adventures with my furry fighter."

"Good to hear." Neela then switched over to Mobola. "How long before they fully breach the hull? And what are we looking at in terms of numbers?"

"About five minutes until full hull breach," Mobola said. "Life signs are hard to determine, but I think that there will be six in all. The barnacles seem to be big enough to only fit two at a time, and the mass readouts show greater mass than one normal human in each craft."

"Maybe they're a bunch of fatasses," Tyger quipped.

"One can only hope," Neela said, feeling even more relieved by Tyger's levity. "Ramirez, I'll need you to join me on the bridge. Bring the princess; you'll both be safe here." She then betrayed a shrewd grin as an idea formed in her head. "Plus, you'll make excellent bait."

"I beg your pardon?" Ramirez said. Neela stifled a laugh at the look on the ambassador's face, as well as the possessive way he clutched the infant.

"Just come to the bridge; you'll see," Neela said. "Everyone else, we'll direct you to the spatial recursion once garrison mode is set up."

"It already is," Mobola said.

"I see you're being proactive," Neela said. "Good for you."

"I didn't do it."

"What do you mean?"

Mobola sputtered for a moment, then inhaled. "It, ah, seems the ship did it for us. Spatial recursion indicative of garrison mode has occurred in a region measuring ten meters, starting at the hull breaches."

"I'm not sure if that's a good thing or a bad thing," Neela said. "Will you be able to retrieve anyone who goes in?"

"Lifeform differential exception protocol is still active," Mobola said.

Neela stopped and blinked, the jargon going completely through her head and out the other ear.

"*Dada*, pretend that I understood any of that as Alliance standard," Neela said, letting a tinge of impatience slip into her voice. "Now translate."

"It, ah, means yes," Mobola said contritely. "It seems the ship has learned from our previous encounter with intruders. It's been boarded before. Now, it's ready for them."

"It can do that?" Neela asked. She wasn't even sure if her husband knew this.

"Apparently so," Mobola said. "We've only been able to reverse engineer bits and pieces of First Imperium tech, and a lot is still a mystery."

"It looks like things have prepared themselves," Neela mused aloud, then spoke one last time to the guests. "Good hunting, then."

"So this is what garrison mode is like," Tyger said as the hologram ran several feet ahead of them into the maze of corridors. Neela had created an almost perfect likeness of the ambassador and the baby and had Mobola program them into the ship's holo emitters, which usually served the purpose of guiding guests and soldiers unfamiliar with the ship's layout to their destinations. "It's like we're trapped in that effect when you put two mirrors in front of each other."

"It is something like that," Mobola said over the private comm.

"Interesting." Akiko stalked ahead of her mate, crouched down and her rifle trained ahead. "But couldn't you have had us enter at a point closer to the breach?"

"The second they came in, they were prepared for a fight," Mobola said. "It might've put you in a hail of gunfire."

"Point taken," Tyger said. "No use in getting pinned down."

"You weren't afraid of being 'pinned down' last night," Akiko said, casting him a playful grin, which Tyger returned in kind. As close to her backside as he was, if she'd been a Felyan, she probably would have playfully brushed his face with her tail.

"Head in the game, *li-ah*," Tyger said.

"Yours too," Akiko replied. "My ass is not the current target, though."

A shot rang out and left a furrow in the corner just behind them. Tyger felt something electric shoot through him as all his senses went into full fight-or-flight mode. The same thing happened to Akiko as well, as both of them dashed into the opposite wall next to the corridor.

"It's a fucking hologram!" He heard the raider snarl with impotent rage. It was at that exact moment he knew he was distracted. Akiko was closer, and she turned the corner and fired multiple rounds. Tyger took this moment to run across the path, firing as he went. His eyes caught the target. Akiko's rifle rounds had stunned the man, but his spidersilk tac vest had absorbed the worst of the shots. His head, however, remained uncovered. Taking a chance, he leaped into the hallway, bouncing off of the walls like a parkour runner. The raider, snapping out of the pain from the rounds, fired wildly, but couldn't match the hybrid's randomness and speed. Tyger closed the gap and slashed at the man's face, ripping through the flesh of his bald head like paper. The raider screamed, dropping his rifle as he grasped for his mutilated pate. Tyger quickly put a stop to it, firing twice into his stomach, the rounds striking him like two well-placed two-by-fours, doubling him over, allowing Tyger to finish the job.

"One down," he said to Neela over the comm. "Looking out for the oth—*GAH!*"

Unlike the raider, Tyger was not wearing a tac vest, and the round from further down the hall went clean through his arm, a lance of pain and force tossing him in agony to the ground, leaving the world a blur.

He heard an exchange of fire and then smelled the scent of his mate as she touched his face.

"You got him?" he asked, teeth bared against the pain.

"What do you think?" Akiko's laugh was marred with tears.

"We ... still have one more," Tyger said through gritted teeth. Akiko shook her head as she removed a tube of nanogel from the tac vest that she wore and applied it to Tyger's wound. He gasped at the sudden spike in pain, which quickly dissolved into a dull ache as the nanos began their patchwork job. Var would make his pay in sickbay when they were done.

"These weren't very bright. They stayed close together; I got 'em both."

"Let's hope the others will dispatch them as easily as we did."

"You got shot, my furry fighter."

"Okay, as easily as *you* did."

The sounds of gunfire echoed from somewhere a lifetime away.

"Seems like they're having their fun."

"Should we split up?" Ri'Kela asked.

"Not a good idea," Biraknu replied, sniffing the air ahead of them. "They're close, but moving fast."

He magnetized the glaive to the dorsal plate of his armor and loped along on all fours, following the spoor created by the invading raiders. Even the most fastidious of humans had a musk to them, but this lot was hygienically negligent to the point where he could fish them out in his sleep. Besides, it gave him focus in the maddeningly recursive corridor where they were tracking their prey.

Abruptly, he paused, and rose to his two feet, making a halting gesture. The refracting hallway had hit an inexplicable t-section.

"The scents go both ways," Biraknu said, sniffing once again. His lips peeled from his muzzle, exposing his sharp teeth. He growled with delight. "They're close."

He prepared to move, but Ri'Kela grabbed his arm before stepping forward and coming to his side. She had reconstructed her usual attire of elegant jacket and dress to a black and green armored nano suit and moved with almost feline grace in contrast to her normally rigid gait.

"Wait," she said as she stepped ahead of her. She stretched out her opposite arm and threw two spheres into the air. They levitated and hovered in the air until they were slightly higher than her eye level.

"We could've used the drones sooner, you know," Biraknu said.

Ri'Kela shook her head. "They're not armed drones," she said as they flew off in either direction down the corridors, "just searchers." A wicked half-grin grew on her muzzle. "And they were hoping to surprise us, no doubt."

A chirping noise sounded from her wrist. She brought it up to her chest, and the holo emitter produced a map of the surrounding corridors: endless refractions of the same hallway, displaying their position, and now, two red icons close by, down both paths.

"We're lucky. They're just a few meters away," Ri'Kela said, her voice tense with excitement, "And they're probably swatting at my drones as we speak." She reached into the mass reservoirs at her hips and removed two daggers. "Which means it's time."

"Time to die, you mean?" said a voice behind them. This was followed by the very distinct sound of a weapon powering up. This one, however, wasn't MAG-based.

The two Felyans, snarling in frustration, stood up slowly, showing their hands. They turned around to face the raider, wearing what looked like a streamlined spacesuit, yet aiming a plasma concussion rifle their way. Ri'Kela's eyes widened at the sight of it. Either he was crazy, or maintaining hull integrity was not a priority for this one.

"Damn, it feels good to be the smarter one for a change," the raider said with a wicked grin on his scarred face. He took aim—

—Then dropped the rifle as a tiny object began to spin about his head. With a shriek, he swatted at it, as if it was a particularly overzealous insect, ducking and weaving out of its path, performing a maddening, yet oddly hilarious dance. Var took this opportunity and released his glaive. He charged forward and sliced laterally, painting the walls with the man's blood as his upper and lower half slid away from each other.

"You want left or right?" The massive Felyan gestured back down the hallway as the drone reconnected to Ri'Kela's sleeve and absorbed itself back into the nanomaterial.

"Left," Ri'Kela said, then swung around the corner before speeding down the hallway. With the same alacrity, Biraknu turned the right corner and let his sense of smell drive him down the repeating path until he saw the blade of a sword swinging and missing one of the governess's silver spheres. Immediately after, the raider chased it into the adjoining corridor, and right into the massive Felyan's path.

He was a fast one, despite being outclassed in weight and strength, and managed to shift his attention just in time to ignore the drone and slash at Biraknu with the hand that held his sword. It glanced off of the Felyan's armor, but the force of the blow managed to throw off his trajectory, causing a glancing blow to the wall.

"Baby-killing scum ..." Biraknu growled, turning around and baring his teeth with the ferocity of a rabid dog. "Your companion found only death, and now, so shall you!"

Ri'Kela slid into the corridor where the raider had waited for her, wielding two hatchet-like blades instead of the guns she expected. She slid under the first two swipes and rolled into a crouching position, waiting for her prey to make the next move.

The raider screamed and charged at her like a berserker in old Earth period piece movies. Ri'Kela lunged forward, stopping both blades with her own, and kicking her prey across the hallway. Winded, but unhurt, the raider made a run for it.

The Governess grinned hungrily. She had not been in an actual fight in years outside of the palace training grounds and hardlight arenas; a good chase was what she needed.

"I wish there was a way we could see their progress," Neela said. Though Tyger and Akiko had lucked out and ran into their quarries earlier, Ri'Kela and Biraknu had only just now run into one lone raider. The other two were wandering about, after realizing that the image of the ambassador and princess had been a fake. Now they were trying to find an exit. She'd spent the last few minutes pacing the command dais with the Ambassador staring her way. She would have perhaps been even more on edge, but there was a slight calming effect in carrying a baby, which she'd volunteered to do in order to give Ramirez's arms a rest.

"This waiting is making me antsy."

"Garrison mode corridors are still technically connected to the ship's power grid, and are dimensional refractions of the same space," Mobola said. "So they can transmit video data."

Neela paused in her tracks. "It can?"

"The same as how it can give us lifeform readouts."

"Bring it up, then," Neela said.

The holo that appeared wove a view of Biraknu engaging with a raider who seemed to be wearing a patchwork pressure suit and seemed unusually agile despite its dense Kevlar weave, which stopped the burly Felyan's massive claws and slashes from his glaive. Biraknu's blows appeared to intimidate the raider, who lost ground in his attempts to block the repeated blows. Surely the pressure suit was compromised to the point where it would, by now, no longer support him in space, but the raider's injuries thus far were perhaps only bruises to his forearms and shoulders.

"Where's Ri'Kela?" Ramirez said.

"Chasing after the other raider," Mobola said. "He managed to squeeze his way out of the fight without her taking a pound of flesh and made a run for it, but she's gaining on him. I think the shifting ground may be confusing her, though."

"Can you guide her?" Ramirez asked.

"I'm trying to, but she's not responding."

"Dammit," the ambassador said. "She's always been like that. Laser-focused, even on the battlefield."

Neela returned her attention to the continuing fight between Biraknu and the raider for a moment more, a bad feeling rising in her gut as she thought back to the first raider they'd eliminated.

"Why was the first target wearing a pressure suit, anyway?" she said.

"Ah, I think I can tell you that." Pip's voice had broken into the bridge as her holo appeared, replacing the feed. "Seems you guys have another problem."

"What kind of problem?" Neela said, bracing herself.

"It looks like one of the raiders did an EVA from one of the barnacles while they were trying to breach the hull," Pip explained. "They placed a device about fifty meters away, magnetizing it to the ship's ventral side, right on the main loading ramp."

"God, no…" Neela heard Mobola quaver. She groaned. This could only mean one thing.

"It's a bomb, isn't it?"

"I'm sorry, *dada*," Mobola said. "I had to run a rare materials analysis. No wonder it didn't show up on earlier scans; it's lined with Octanite."

Neela cradled the baby, envying her miraculous ability to sleep soundly through all these last hours of sporadic bedlam.

"Shit," she whispered, then handed the baby back to Ramirez. "Looks like I'll have to suit up."

"Actually, we might be able to help you with this," Pip said.

"Are you sending someone over?" Neela said.

"Well, I could do that," Pip replied. "Brogan knows a thing or two about explosives, but he gets a little bit twitchy with the higher caliber ones. And I'm thinking that's a tactical nuke. Gimme a sec … Yeah, getting some readouts on our sensor array, but the Octanite's making it fuzzy. If I'm seeing this right, it's got a deadman switch rigged up to it. Looks like one of your guests made a one-way trip. He was counting on being killed."

"Oh, no…" Neela said, forcing down the rising panic in the back of her mind. She switched the comm. "Ri'Kela! Biraknu! Disengage! We have a situation!"

"They might not do it," Ramirez said. "Ri'Kela's in full huntress mode, and ... well ... you know how *Hara'Kya* can get when in a fight."

Neela glanced at Mobola, who was eyeing the dais. She shook her head.

"Hello!" Pip called out. "I said I can help, remember?"

"Then are you going to tell us or not?" Neela snapped. "Out with it!"

Immediately after, she felt like an asshole.

"Look, I'm sorry, but I'm sure you can figure that we're under a lot of stress here."

"Oh, trust me, I know." Pip's demeanor didn't appear ruffled. The diminutive tank merely nodded. "Besides, the captain's said worse things." After a pause, Pip spoke again. "Okay, I think I can cut it off of your hull. It'll be tricky; we're gonna have to use a tight beam laser. We'll cut a teensy section of the ramp away; explosive decompression will blast it away from the rest of the ship in milliseconds. Just gotta try not to trip any detonation switches."

"Wait," Neela said. "You're going to fire on my ship?"

"Better than waiting for the folks on your ship to kill those raiders and set the bomb off, don't you think?" Pip replied dryly. "'Sides, you got a better idea?"

Neela exhaled, suddenly feeling exhausted. "No. No, I don't. But what if you miss?"

"Oh, please." Pip's assurance was spoken with a confidence that Neela envied. "Have a little faith, people! Just make sure your ship doesn't decide to return fire on us, okay?"

"I think it heard you; weapons just went offline," Mobola said.

"Alright, everybody, hold on to your socks and your jocks!"

The bridge alarm for incoming fire sounded. Mobola shut it off. A few seconds of silence.

A prayer from Neela, who heard Ramirez recite the Lord's Prayer.

A breath.

The holographic scene before showed the *Shadow Star* moving into position. One of the myriad panels opened on its sloping dorsal hull and a red beam lanced out toward them.

The ship shuddered.

"Like removing a tick!" Pip said with a squeal of victory that startled Mobola.

Neela sighed perhaps the longest she'd ever sighed in years. Immediately afterward, two bright flashes erupted in the surrounding holos: one close and caused the ship to give a slight, but sudden lurch. The other seemed to be coming from the planet's polar region.

"Looks like the bomb went off," Pip said. "Though I don't know if it's from what I did, or if the dead man's switch was triggered."

"What was the other explosion?" Neela asked, and was answered with Alexa's posh tone.

"Just the pretty lights I promised," Alexa said, popping back into the transmission. "I found the location for most of the comm traffic and set off a tac nuke of my own." She sniffed, a look of mild disgust flashing across her features, as if she'd just killed some particularly unpleasant bug. "Never underestimate raiders; you eventually get some with a modicum of brains that actually come up with something without using crayons."

"We should've been wiser for it since the pulsar," Neela said.

"This is Ri'Kela," the governess's soft voice spoke at last, her words punctuated by panting breaths. "Biraknu and I have neutralized the intruders. I scored a clean kill, but Biraknu ... well, he will certainly need a bath."

Neela wanted to admonish her for ignoring her instructions, but she was no commanding officer. And she could not help but laugh at the last part of her message.

"Thanks all of you," Neela said. "Var, you have one incoming for sickbay."

"Acknowledged," Var replied.

However you do it, my kidege, Neela thought, at last feeling true relief, *I'm glad I can somehow do it too.*

SEVENTEEN

Xerx had had a good mind to contact Alexa again to ensure that there wouldn't be any kind of interference, but Indira had minded him to trust his cousin-in-law. Besides, if the Council was as cowardly as she'd said, they wouldn't want to piss her off more. They'd just uncovered that nearly a third of the lot had been in bed with Helix the entire time and were willing to throw one of their own under the bus. That, as far as he was concerned, was grounds enough for her and the pirate clans to pull the plug on every operation they had going here.

"I'd still shut it all down if I were her," Xerx said, "just to make an example of them."

"They're not the only colony that is less than friendly to nonhumans," Paige said. "If we could do that everywhere, we'd be on a fool's crusade to upend legitimate governments in the Alliance and Imperial territories for centuries."

"To err is human," Miranda recited.

"What she said," Paige said, pointing at the enigmatic tank.

"What's to keep them from jumping us with their military once we get to Blue Point?" Xerx asked as they boarded the maglev for the entertainment complex that Kumiko had gleaned from Singh's pathetic mind.

"Aside from the Council believing that they're skating on thin ice as it is?" Paige said.

"Aside from our guns?" Maria asked with a self-satisfied chuckle.

"And the fact that we've got both a tertiary and one of the largest fuck-off ground tanks I've ever seen," Kumiko added, "including two other tanks, one of which has injuries that imply that not only did she get into a fight with a bear, but the bear probably came out looking worse?"

"Good point," Xerx said, holding back a laugh at the look of indignation that Indira had cast her way.

"Rude," she said before turning her attention back to the window.

Blue Point looked like the last place for a terrorist group to hold staging grounds unless they truly wanted to look like something out of an old Earth spy novel or vid. The entire place looked like a never-ending carnival, complete with holographic systems in the ceiling to simulate a daytime sky with high, wispy clouds.

"Reminds me of that shore leave I took on Dionysus Minor," Paige said as they followed Kumiko from the maglev platform down through the crowds among the stalls and rides. The smells of a thousand restaurants assaulted them. "Almost a shame we're here on business."

"There are better places," Xerx said, "chiefly places that actually allow Fel—"

"Somebody's following us," Kumiko said, stopping in her tracks. She glanced from her left to her right, her eyes narrowing as she scanned the crowds that, like when they'd first arrived, parted like the Red Sea, eyeing them with a mixture of curiosity, shock, anger, and near panic.

Among them, a woman dressed surprisingly like a nun, remained, seemingly rooted to the ground with surprise at the sudden recession of crowds.

"Well, at least I know we're on the right track," Kumiko said, not taking her eyes off of the woman. "She's got the same place on the brain as what I got out of the Councilman's head."

"I thought you knew where it was."

"I got the general location," Kumiko said. "He passed out before I could get it all."

"So you were hoping we'd find someone here who knew?"

"Always have a Plan B."

Xerx pursed his lips as he eyed the nun, whose body, though tiny, suggested a very buxom form that didn't seem to fit well into the habit—at least not in the way of the nuns from his old private school on Siberna. Even strands of her long brown hair stuck out of the wimple, meaning it hadn't been shaved down like the hair of a proper nun.

"So you're saying this nun is in cahoots with Helix?" Xerx said, casting a shrewd gaze at the woman. "She's got some *cajones* standing there like that when everyone else is bugging out."

"She doesn't have a choice," Kumiko said, finally making her approach. "I'm keeping her from moving."

"I should've known she looked a bit stiff," Paige said, following Xerx up to the silver-haired girl, who now looked as if she was going to soil her habit clean through.

"You," Xerx said, addressing the nun. "Show us your collarbone."

"Couldn't be any less discreet?" Kumiko said.

Xerx snorted. "I'm tired of wasting my time here."

When the false nun shook her head, Xerx gave the silver-haired girl a nod. She then sailed ahead of him, gliding a few inches off the ground, closing the gap between the team and the petrified girl. This had the additional effect of breaking up the remaining crowd of morbidly fascinated onlookers, as someone screamed and everyone scrambled away, leaving them alone.

Now face to face with the now-shaking woman, Kumiko gestured, and the habit appeared to unmake itself, unraveling away from her shoulder and neck, revealing her collarbone, where the helix scar sat, marring her otherwise perfectly pale skin.

"As expected," Xerx said as Kumiko undid the process, and the fabric repaired itself. He looked the woman in her wide eyes.

"We need to have a little talk with the ones who gave you that scar," he said. "And you're going to take us to them. Understand?"

A stream of tears flowed from the girl's eyes as, still panting with unbridled terror, she nodded.

"Let her go," Xerx said to Kumiko. Immediately, the woman dropped to her knees but remained where she was. He glared at her, placing his hand on his pistol in a very conspicuous and telling way.

"Now get up and let's get going," he said.

The woman was too afraid to do anything else but lead them through Blue Point's seemingly endless bazaars, concert venues, and theme park grounds until they reached an edge to the cavern that Xerx would never have been able to tell was there, as overgrown with kudzu vines as it was. But jutting out from the stone was a series of columns and arches that led to a square stone building with sculpted patterns that reminded him of masonry, all with neatly trimmed hedges.

"Looks like ... a church?" Paige said, slowing down her pace after Xerx had Kumiko put a renewed leash on their guide.

"It's a church," Kumiko confirmed. "Religious thoughts are coming from inside."

"And I thought that getup she was in was just a Halloween costume," Xerx said. "She really *is* a nun after all."

"A racist nun..." Maria said, shaking her head.

"So what now?" Kumiko asked.

"Is there a service going on in there?" Xerx asked the girl, who had exchanged her initial fear for despondency.

"We hold services daily," she whispered. "The Father presides over them."

"Funny place for a church," Paige remarked.

"Blue Point is a den of sin. We offer refuge and a better way."

"As long as you're human," Xerx sneered.

"Grace was given to the children of Adam and Eve," the girl said. "Defiling ourselves robs us of that grace. And when does holy scripture speak of any others?"

"Okay, enough proselytizing," Xerx said, and gestured toward the series of arches that indicated an entrance. "Let's go meet this Father."

"But ... Weapons aren't allowed in the church," the woman said, noticeably alarmed and reticent to enter with them, despite her situation.

"Nice try," Xerx said. "Besides, I'm pretty sure that God knows we won't use them if we don't have a reason to. That reminds me, though. You got something to detect data signals?"

"I have it," Maria said and removed a device from a pouch in the side of her tac vest. She switched it on and nodded. "Yeah, there are some pretty hefty data loads being transferred, probably to a ship somewhere. I'll let little sis know."

"Well, if they're being transferred to a ship, then we probably won't need the boosters," Xerx said.

"It should make it easier for decrypting, and harder to hack from this end," Paige said. "So better safe than sorry."

"Ready as we'll ever be, then," Xerx said, and gestured toward the church entrance. He nodded to the girl, who clearly wanted to be anywhere but here. No surprise there; if it turned into a firefight, she'd be fodder for the crossfire. He almost felt sorry for her.

Then he remembered the symbol that she'd allowed to be branded into her flesh.

The scent of incense struck Xerx's nostrils as the doors swung open—wood, like those adorning the Council chamber entrance. Asceticism be damned.

The interior was cavernous, with stone above carved into buttresses and beams, from which candelabras of reddened glass hung. Panels of backlighting illuminated red stained glass windows lining the walls of the nave, each featuring a long double-helix strand. The combined effect filled the place with crimson-tinted, subdued light. The immaculately rowed pews were empty, and a massive crucifix behind the altar, but with the icon of the Savior in red robes and with arms open in a commanding pose, not broken in crucified agony. From the crucifix flowed banners of crimson. Between each, they draped downward, featuring more black helix symbols with bold prominence.

Xerx wanted to burn the place down.

"His holiness will be in the sacristy," the girl said.

"Actually, Sister Calliope, I was expecting these wayward souls."

The voice belonged to a man who appeared from behind the altar, rising to his feet from a kneeling position behind what appeared to be an open Bible. He was a beanpole of a man, appearing to be well into his seventies, Xerx assumed, with slicked hair almost luminously white, exposing a helix symbol tattooed in bright red in the middle of his forehead, directly above a hawkish nose that appeared to dip below his upper lip when he faced their way. He wore a priest's frock with a crimson sash and a cuff on his left arm that was reminiscent of what some mated *Hara'Kya* Felyans wore. Only instead of jewels at its center, there was yet another damnable Helix symbol.

It appeared that Kumiko's hold on the girl was relatively light as she was able to drop to her knees as the frocked man rounded the altar and came toward the edge of the sanctuary.

"F-forgive me, Father Muldoon. They forced me."

The man—Father Muldoon—kneeled down to the girl's level. He then placed his hand atop her head, a gracious smile on his face.

"I said it's alright, child. God works in mysterious ways. And he has brought these souls here at the appropriate time." He then faced Xerx and his team for the first time, eyeing them with blue-gray eyes whose intensity was almost staggering.

"Would you still keep this child against her will?" he said.

"Let her go," Xerx said to Kumiko.

Immediately, the girl, finding that she could move again, shoved past Xerx and his team and fled out of the church.

"Gracious of you to allow her to leave," Father Muldoon said.

"We're not thugs," Xerx said.

"So says the pirate?"

Xerx rolled his eyes. "All this doesn't change the fact that you just expended a lot of resources to kill a child. It just makes you look like you're sticklers for attention."

Father Muldoon rose to his feet, at last showing his age, as he performed this act with some difficulty and painful slowness, now that he had nothing to hold on to for added strength.

"You see, Captain Xerxes Paraska of the *Reckless*—yes, I know who you are—this is where you and I differ," Father Muldoon said after several moments of catching his breath. "You and I have a differing idea of what a 'child' is. You see, it would have to have a soul if it were a child. Does holy scripture even mention life beyond the world of our origin? Or a redemption plan for them? You don't appear the religious sort, so I'll tell you. The answer is no. Why else would he not tell us of these other souls? Does he not wish to redeem them? And yet the Book is silent. Assuming they have souls, therefore, is mere conjecture. Art? Law? Emotion? Civilization? These things do not a soul make. So why care what happens to them when we were the ones whom God gave redemption to?"

A look flashed across Father Muldoon's face that sent a chill like a trickle of water straight from the freezer down Xerx's spine. The intensity of Muldoon's eyes was like that of a supplicant in a religious trance, right until a cold, dark rage glanced across every last one of his facial features.

"And yet we have welcomed them as brothers ... and even committed the insanity of laying with them in the bed of marriage." The rage then collapsed into something akin to a heavy weight of grief. "We have even accepted as normal their commerce in the sale of their bodies to us. How far have we fallen? But God is merciful and redeems his chosen. Here in the ruins of the old Empire that withstood this wickedness and after over a century of living under the charity of the soulless, we have become its own pure testament to what we can become. Here, I fight my battle with the principalities and powers of this age that seek to make us lapdogs of the chosen for the soulless."

His face returned to the beatific smile that he held for the false nun as he concluded what Xerx was fairly certain had been his attempt at a sermon for them.

"And so, these so-called 'children' are not children at all. Not in the way we are to God, and our pure children are to ourselves. These cross-bred aberrations are little more than a product of an unholy union of humanity and beast." He cast a glance at Kumiko. "Like this one, whom I only tolerate in this sacred sanctuary."

Xerx was grateful that he was not the only one on his team who stood in disbelieving silence after hearing this man's asinine word vomit.

"So, disrupting the ceremony at Tophanavar … what does it gain you?" he asked.

"Freedom from the taint of the soulless," Muldoon replied. "Humanity built a glorious empire over two centuries ago, without their help. We can do it again."

"I don't know if you got the memo," Xerx said, "but there's another empire out there. The Second Imperium took over one of our worlds, has another under siege, and wants to eat us alive. We're on the cusp of a war that no one will win. We need all the help we can get!"

"Whoever wins is irrelevant to me," Muldoon said. "The Second Imperium isn't interested in religions. It wants living space. And if they win, then those to whom grace has been given will have a unified purpose."

"Well, at least we know why he was giving weapons to the raiders," Xerx said, flicking the strap off of his holster. "That's all the explanation I need."

The moment he finished his sentence, Muldoon shot out a stern hand, the look on his deeply wrinkled, thin face now glowering.

"It would truly be a mistake to use violence here," he said.

"Paige, did you scan for any weapons in here?" Xerx called to the *Shadow Star* captain over his shoulder.

"Right when we came in," Paige said. "Nada."

"Tell her to scan again," Father Muldoon said.

Without Xerx needing to say anything, Paige checked the device built into her wrist.

"Shit."

The expletive, softly spoken, seemed to echo in the church's sepulchral silence ten times louder. She spun around, rifle drawn, while her tanks followed suit. Xerx was last, along with Kumiko, whose hesitation confused him. Out of the corner of his eye, he could see that the silver-haired girl was genuinely surprised. She stepped back from the black-clad soldier who had dropped in from a zip cord that dangled from the stone beams above. Several of his companions had arrived in the same manner and now had several blades that resembled the one that Paige carried, trained directly on their throats.

"Something's ... wrong," Xerx heard Kumiko say, her voice quavering.

"A problem with your soulless companion?" Father Muldoon said, stepping with ease down into the aisle between the pews. "Can't move, perhaps? Couldn't detect my praetorians coming?"

"The hell did you do?" Xerx said, his hand still on his pistol despite the blade poking him uncomfortably in the larynx.

"Me?" Father Muldoon sounded almost hurt. "*I* didn't do anything. My ace in the hole, however, is my own little private insurance against the soulless ones you call tertiaries."

From the shadowed narthex beyond, a small form stepped forward into the dim light, accompanied by another black-clad soldier. She was clearly a child, with dark skin and pale hair of an almost silver color like Kumiko. Her gray eyes were large and ... glowing?

Shit.

She was another tertiary.

"I suffered much to acquire this asset," Muldoon said. "They tend to travel in packs, you know, to prevent whatever clandestine purpose the soulless that call themselves 'Seekers' have in store. Ensnaring this one cost me more men than I care to contemplate. And I was forced to make a bargain with a woman who was as close to the devil as I've seen any poor wayward soul. But her inventions were indeed helpful. Especially a chip that shuts off higher brain functions. All I needed to do afterward was to find a tertiary to test it on."

"Scratch a racist, find a hypocrite," Xerx said, his mind racing in the background to try to figure out some way, *any* way out of this predicament. "Your benefactor wouldn't happen to go by the name of Hayashibara, would she? Pale skin, a lot like yours? Black hair? Glasses? Kinda androgynous?"

"It seems you two have crossed paths before," Muldoon said.

"We've met."

"Believe me, I take no pleasure in even putting the soulless out of their misery," Muldoon said. "But I do what I must. Now, I would advise you to drop your weapons. Besides, my associates in orbit will be bringing down the soulless one we require soon enough."

A spike of fear stabbed through Xerx's guts at this.

"Neela!" He breathed. "Ramirez ... the baby!"

Quickly, he forced calm into himself, swatting away his rising fear as if it were a fly on a sandwich. One wrong twitch, even to switch on the comm would probably set these fanatics off, and he had no wish to get his throat slit today. As things were, he knew that he had to trust his crew to take care of whatever Muldoon had thrown at them. Besides, they knew how to take care of themselves. The princess had seasoned warriors for bodyguards, including Tyger and his tank companion, and Mobola knew Garrison Mode inside and out. Anyone who would try to board his ship now had something far worse than just a red-assed beatdown waiting for them.

It was at that moment that Pip's voice broke in on the comm.

"Um ... captain?"

"Not really a good time, Pip; we're ... in a bit of a spot," Paige said, standing just as stock still as Xerx was, both her real and artificial eyes trained on the blade aimed at her neck. Xerx glanced at the three tanks, all sharing the same situation. He knew that the only reason that Maria didn't snap that pig sticker in half was that she wouldn't be able to get to everyone in time before at least one got a do-it-yourself tracheotomy.

"But you told me to tell you if Pinkie found the tracker, and ... well ... we found the tracker ... in her underwear ... which she left near a jettisoned escape pod."

There was a pause, then Maria spoke up, moving only her lips. "Pip, sweetie ... do you know exactly when the pod jettisoned?"

"Funny you should ask," the diminutive tank replied. "It's actually hard to tell ... since we found that nano-goop smeared on the controls. It sort of fucked up the interface between it and the ship's systems. For all I know, she could've popped off immediately after you guys left."

At this news, Xerx began to laugh. In a moment, Paige did as well, joined in quickly by Maria. Soon, their combined laughter crescendoed into a near-manic cackle.

"Why are you laughing?" Father Muldoon said, with a new tone of disconcertment.

"Hey, you think she made it here yet?" Xerx said, desiring nothing more at the moment than to wipe the tears from his eyes.

"If she did it when I think, then she's been following us the whole time," Paige said.

Xerx imagined Father Muldoon's face beginning to redden with confusion and repressed rage. And it was all the funnier.

"And going commando to boot!" Maria said, stirring them into renewed peals of laughter.

"I wish you three would let me in on this private joke," Kumiko said, speaking with effort against the force that held her at bay.

"If we guessed correctly, I think you're about to find out," Maria said, finally regaining her composure. She then called out into the shadowed beams above. "Little one, if you're there, you can come out. We could really need your help now!"

Xerx was certain that, except for Paige, with her artificial eye, no one had noticed the shadowed shape that dropped down behind the little girl and her handler. The armored figure went rigid, his body twisting at an odd angle as he fell to the ground, not making a sound. Then the shadow moved behind the girl.

"Wait!" He heard Kumiko whisper. It was barely audible, but from the way the shadow paused, he surmised that she was communicating with her mind.

"Not the little one. I know her. Don't kill her."

The shadow moved more slowly, and the girl then silently collapsed, but in a far less jarring manner than the soldier. Xerx swallowed, hoping to God that the aptly named "Angel of Death" had been more discerning with that one and had left her alive as Kumiko had asked. Nevertheless, the results of the girl's unconsciousness were instantaneous. Kumiko jerked forward, clearly freed of whatever force had restrained her. Before the soldier holding her at swordpoint could realize what happened, he split cleanly in half, as if sliced through by an invisible blade. With little more than the sound of blood splattering on the ground.

"You guys are so fucked now," Xerx said with a sneer. Though he wasn't a man of faith in the conventional sense, he normally wouldn't have used such language in a church, but whatever twisted idea of God these people worshipped was hardly worth his reverence. And so he watched with morbid bemusement as the small form ran silently behind each soldier, who had only just now begun to notice what had happened, but too late. Leaping back, a flash of pink pigtails winked into the dim light as each of the remaining soldiers' heads rolled free from their bodies.

Only then did Artemis step into the light, joining Maria at her side.

"Thank you," Paige said, turning back around with Xerx and company to face Father Muldoon, now free and ready to kick ass with no need for bubble gum. The scarecrow of a man now had become the one who was frozen in place, the confidence gone now from his wide, pale eyes.

"You want me to take this goofball out?" Kumiko said.

"I'd rather do the honors here." Xerx chambered his main rounds. "To be fair, he's more useful to us alive, but I'd like to teach him a lesson first."

Xerx fired, but the shot rang off a glint of light that spread across Muldoon's body at a skin-tight level.

"Co-opting Felyan personal shield tech?" Xerx said, ruefully shaking his head. "You really are a fucking hypocrite."

"As I said, I do only what I must," Father Muldoon answered. "Any true priest must keep himself pure of the tainted outside." Just then, his formerly panicked face smoothed back out into a look of smug self-satisfaction. "And I'm sure you figured that those subjects whose bodies you desecrated this sacred ground with weren't the only members of my flock?"

"You mean this one?" Kumiko said, then reached into what appeared to be air. Immediately, the façade pixelated away, revealing another black-clad soldier, the light-bending effects of the diffraction cloth peeling away from his body. Kumiko tossed him into the far wall beyond the aisle, where it crumpled and lay still amidst showering debris.

"Wow, they're using a ton of Felyan tech here," Maria said, brightening as she gazed upon the device she'd removed from her tac vest yet again. It was now emitting a shrill chirping noise. "Proximity detector didn't even pick up their life signs, just like those other guys."

Immediately after, she swung her fist to the right, bringing another cloaked soldier into view—whose neck she snapped with careless ease. "One by your side, sweetie," she said to Artemis, who leaped into the air and brought her knives down. For a moment, it appeared as if she was riding an invisible bucking bull, until the cloth deactivated, revealing the unfortunate soldier who would have checked her. Artemis held on tight, then once she had a proper angle, pulled his head back with all her strength and let the knife do its work.

Xerx watched on for a moment more, as Miranda and Indira dispatched several more formerly invisible soldiers at Maria's direction. Indira struggled only for a moment as one placed her in a bear hug, but underestimated her strength and speed, putting him quickly at the business end of her vajra, and writhing in his death throes in a pool of his own blood. Turning back to face Muldoon, Xerx gasped as Paige seemed to aim her rifle at him. But the shot missed him by nearly a foot, instead downing a soldier whose hand he had only just begun to feel on his arm.

"Sorry it took a moment," Paige said with a casual salute. "Had to readjust the old eye to see through that shit. Now be a dear, and stop goofing off with this clown so we can finish our bloody job."

"Right," Xerx said, and in one move, unsheathed his knife and threw it squarely into Father Muldoon's shoulder. As Biraknu had warned, the slower velocity knife ignored the shield's counterforce and sank deep into the man's flesh. He didn't think it was possible for the false priest to turn paler, but he staggered back, casting a look of utter disbelief as he grasped at his wounded arm. Though injured, Father Muldoon still had the strength to scramble away, his face now a mask of incredulous rage.

"Oh, I wouldn't remove that, by the way," Xerx said, gesturing casually to the handle and blade still pro-truding from the twisted priest's wounded shoulder. "Arty can stabilize you with her nanos—that is, if she wants to do it. But you'll need to be touched by her 'tainted' hands. Oh, and before I forget, we're gonna need you to show us where you keep your little cult's files. We've got the Alliance incoming, and they're gonna need evidence."

Father Muldoon began to shake with weak laughter.

"Something funny?" Xerx asked.

"You think we didn't know what you'd want here?" Muldoon quavered. "Whatever misadventures you experienced could only have led you here if you found out the whole truth. So I've had my flock diligently working to purge our data. It either leaves with us, or we don't leave at all."

Xerx snarled, reaching down and ripping Muldoon's black shirt open, exposing the shield device, which he ripped from his chest without regard to its dermal adhesive. Father Muldoon wailed in pain. It was not secured to his flesh strongly enough to rip it off, but it still would leave a long-lasting mark. The device curled up like the starfish it was shaped to resemble and folded into a small orb with a square groove in its chromatic surface.

"You didn't get the memo, Father," Xerx said, pocketing the shield device and feeling a particular sense of satisfaction in the act. He then aimed his pistol at the helix symbol branded into the twisted priest's forehead. "This isn't an option—well, let me rephrase that. It *is* an option, but you're not gonna want option two." He pulled the hammer back. "Unless you feel you've accomplished enough to be seen a as martyr? I mean, your flock seems to have gone to greener pastures, if you ask me."

Muldoon, wide-eyed at having the tables turned on him yet again, opened his mouth to speak, when suddenly, Xerx felt himself yanked several feet away from him by an unseen force, then dragged back to Kumiko's side.

"Kumi!" he shouted, spinning around to face the silver-haired girl. "What the hell—?"

"It wasn't me," Kumiko said, then gestured to the little girl, who now stood by her, coming up to only just above her hip, but Xerx could practically feel the white-hot rage emanating from her as she stalked up to the twisted priest, eyes glowing the same as when she'd first appeared beside her handler. But now, there was a freedom in that glare and a righteous rage that belied her age.

Xerx stood transfixed at the tiny girl, enraged in a way that made so many people terrified of tertiaries. But the anger was clearly aimed at only one person.

"Stop!" Father Muldoon wailed, staggering back, eyes wild with abject terror at the realization that she was no longer under anyone's control. He gesticulated wildly with his uninjured arm. "Stop, I tell you! Obey me!"

"*BAD MAN!*" The girl screamed the words in a voice like a tinkling bell, but at the same time, the thought resounded with a psionic backlash, creating a shuddering resonance that flared up as a sudden pain in the back of Xerx's head. Even Paige and the other tanks were not immune.

"*BAD, BAD MAN!*" the girl screamed out, tears now streaming from her glowing eyes. This time the words seemed to carry a force of their own, which launched Father Muldoon as if he'd been stuffed into a MAG pistol of his own, then fired into the massive crucifix, which fell from its moorings and splintered into pieces which rained down along with stone and pieces of the severe-looking Savior icon. In the midst of the cacophony, Indira shouted something, which Xerx was almost certain had been yet another curse.

The silence afterward was palpable, interrupted only by the little girl's sniffles. Kumiko was the only one who dared to approach her, and kneeled at her side, pulling her into an embrace. She spoke softly to the child, barely audible, her words soothing: the entire action taking Xerx completely aback with the rare moment of tenderness she'd just now shown—something he thought her incapable of.

"You know her?" Xerx said, his tone making it sound more like a statement than a question.

"Her name's Riju," Kumiko said. "I helped her family awhile back with a Seeker." She ran her hands through the tiny girl's hair. "Though it seems there are worse monsters out there than even them."

"That's for damn sure," Xerx said.

"She ought to be safe on the *Reckless*," Kumiko said. "She needs to get out of this environment. I think it's traumatized her enough."

"Shit," Xerx whispered, remembering Muldoon's not-so-veiled threat. He switched on his comm. "*Kipenzi*, are you there?"

"I'm here," Neela sounded tired, but the sound of her voice was more of a relief than he imagined. Immediately, Xerx felt as if he'd exhaled after holding his breath for a long time. "Look, we were told that the ship was boarded."

"It was," Neela said grimly.

"You still handling it?"

"No, it's been handled." There was a significant pause, then, "But you'll find a few additions to the ship that will need removing once we can find a suitable dock."

"Small stuff," Xerx said. "We've got things under control on our end. Frosty's about to head on over, with a plus one."

"Understood."

"Gotta wrap things up here now. I'll fill you in on all of it once we get back."

Xerx nodded to Kumiko. "Just make sure she doesn't do to my ship what she did to Muldoon, okay?"

Kumiko smirked, then, still holding the weeping child, vanished in a crackling flash.

That business done, Xerx turned to Paige, indicating the mess the little girl had made. "So, do you think ...?"

"Only one way to find out," Paige said, and made her way to the rubble, waving away at the cloud of dust. The tanks and Artemis followed, with Artemis the first to reach the twisted priest's motionless form, which was surprisingly uninjured.

"He's breathing," Artemis said, then drew a knife. "I can stop it."

"No, leave him alive," Xerx said. "Paige, you got some shiny bracelets?"

"When do I ever not?" Paige said, reaching into a compartment near her back and removing a set of cuffs. Xerx slipped them over Father Muldoon's uninjured arm and slipped the other over an exposed pipe. "Hey, Arty, could you do something about his other arm? I kinda want my knife back."

Artemis stepped up, then glanced down at the unconscious priest with a scowl. She crossed her arms, seeming to consider it, then returned her gaze to Xerx.

"You owe me," Artemis said, then squatted next to the fallen priest. With a single yank, she freed the knife, then quickly spat into her opposite hand and pressed it against the wound before it could begin to bleed any more profusely. The priest's eyes flew open as he gasped, his body shaking in spasms as an acrid smoke stemmed up from where Artemis had placed her hand. After several seconds, his eyes rolled back, and he lay still once again. Artemis removed her hand, revealing a black mark surrounded by fresh scar tissue.

"Call it a Jerry rig," the pink-haired woman said, handing Xerx's knife back to him. "It'll last long enough for a proper medic."

"Good enough," Xerx said, then narrowed his eyes. "Um ... by the way, Pip says she found your underwear by the escape pod hatch. Is that ...?"

"Tracking beacon was itchy," Artemis said.

"In ... indeed." Xerx snorted, biting his lip against laughter before he turned to Maria to switch the subject.

"You still getting those signals?" he asked, coughing away the remainder of his suppressed laughing fit.

"Loud and clear," Maria said, checking the device she'd used outside the church. "They're coming from a level down below."

"My guess is that the sacristy leads down there," Xerx said. "It's the only other entrance we've seen."

"Good idea," Paige said, then removed a tiny drone from a compartment in the shoulder of her artificial arm. She threw it in the direction of the sacristy door, and it floated on a set of antigravs into the chamber beyond. Paige's holo emitter began to display a map that grew as the drone performed a sensor sweep, revealing a stairwell leading to a small set of chambers beyond, encircling a larger one.

"The door's shielded from sensor sweeps, giving us any further information," Paige said. "I'd bet my month's salary that this is where we're gonna find what we're looking for."

"Any life signs?" Xerx asked.

"Door's blotting that out, too."

"Then let's saddle up."

EIGHTEEN

Xerx sent a standby notification to the *Hammerfall II* before beginning the descent. Indira, silent as ever, chose to take point with him, filling in Kumiko's place. Just as Paige's scan had indicated, the sacristy wasn't a sacristy at all, but rather, a stairwell leading down deeper below ground. The walls at the top landing looked like they had been filled in, rather than part of the natural stone of the planet's crust, however, suggesting that this had been an actual sacristy of an actual church at one time. Banners of the Helix symbol lined the descent into the chamber below. If it wouldn't have made their descent more hazardous, Xerx would have gladly set them all on fire on their way down.

The stairwell terminated in a large metal door. Paige stepped up and hovered her hand over its control panel. Several wires extended from her hand and within moments, the door swung open.

It turned out to be a much larger door than they expected, perhaps two meters thick as it rolled on grooves set into the floor. Xerx watched the process, bemused.

"Seems Helix had a lot of spare time on their hands when they came here," he said.

"And the Council seemed to welcome them with open arms," Maria added.

"I wonder just how deep their claws went on this planet?" Xerx mused, more to himself than anyone else.

"I don't think we'll ever know for sure," Paige said.

"*Shit!*" Indira hissed, and shuffled backward from the door.

"What's going on?" Xerx asked. "Is something—?"

"To arms!" someone in the room shouted. "Finish the purge as per Father's orders! Humanity is all!"

"Humanity is all!" came a reply from several voices, which were then drowned out by the crack of several MAG rounds, which sent the entire team to the ground.

The head of the apparent leader of the group suddenly exploded in a shower of bone, blood, and brain. His body collapsed to the ground as what appeared to be a white shadow dropped to the ground behind him. Xerx froze, just as stunned as everyone in the room, not believing what he saw, as the white shadow became more opaque and three-dimensional, revealing Snow's pearlescent form.

"So what are you waiting for, an invitation?" she said.

"Now you're speaking my language," Xerx said. Adrenaline surged into his limbs as he twisted himself upright from his prone position, then slapped the activation switch on his personal shield. He tucked into a roll and fired into two of the soldiers along the room's wall. His shots were first absorbed into his armor, knocking him back. He reached for his pistol, but Xerx found the seams, which broke with more precise shots.

Afterward, he fell like a toppled mannequin with no supports, and stayed down.

The room then opened into a sea of crossfire as everyone hit the ground.

"I'll draw their fire," he said to his team. "The rest of you be as precise as possible. Try not to damage the computers."

"Got it," Paige said as Xerx removed the second shield device from his pocket. He tossed it Paige's way, and she caught it. "You know how to operate one of those?"

The *Shadow Star* captain laughed. "I've always wanted one of these," she said, unfolding the device and placing it on her chest.

"It's only on loan," Xerx said. "You're gonna have to get your own."

With his shield switched on, Xerx stalked boldly into the hail of ammo, which had quieted down when he and his teammates didn't try to push through immediately. Now, it transformed back into its prior killzone.

Now, it was time to thin the herd.

The inside was composed of several rows of terminals, connected to a mainframe server behind a massive pane of what he hoped was armored glass. Above the consoles was a holograph that read, "SYSTEM PURGE/ COMMENCING 00:02:29." The lighting was dim otherwise, but it seemed like every person in there had been given a gun and was well-trained in its use. His shield absorbing the majority of the fire, Xerx went for the black armored soldiers first, aiming for the respective seams in their armor and taking them out as Snow used her rifle to do the same on the room's far end. A few soldiers dodged his shots with inhuman speed that could only come from bionics.

Paige provided cover fire to the opposite end from Snow, while Artemis didn't need bionics to match the augmented soldiers' speed and perform her usual magic. Maria and Indira moved up and demonstrated precisely why it was unwise to engage ground tanks in close combat. With a speed that belied her size, Indira swept her vajra around her, cutting and thrusting in a flurry of limbs and blood. Maria, meanwhile, shoulder-charged another, her momentum turning his insides to paste beneath the armor. He collapsed like a bag of mashed-up fruit. Miranda hung back, using her sniper rifle to make a strategic mess. Xerx, meanwhile, danced with two more guards, avoiding the sword that one brandished instead of a gun. The guard swung the sword and faltered as a knife appeared in his throat. Xerx glanced in the direction from which the knife had traveled and saw Artemis staring back, holding a limp body in her right hand. She discarded the corpse and smiled. Xerx nodded back in thanks.

Xerx removed the knife from the soldier's neck, then realized that the noise had ceased. He stood stock still, weapons still aimed as adrenaline still surged through his nerves. He gave it a moment to ebb as the reality of his surroundings set in. Was it over already?

"Everyone still breathing?" He turned around and found that he hadn't needed to ask. He noticed Snow, now standing relaxed, and grinning for the first time.

"Job well done," he said.

"I have definitely got to get me one of these," Paige said, tapping her shield generator. She then clapped her hands. "All right, everyone, the clock is still ticking. Let's put these signal boosters in place."

"No need," Snow said. "I have it all set up."

"And just how long have you been here?" Xerx asked, to which Snow grinned yet again, this time with all the cheek she seemed to be able to muster.

"Long enough to get the boosters in place in the ceiling girders," she said, gesturing to the metal network in the darkness between the light fixtures up above. "That covering fire was perfect. But I think it still looks like you owe me."

"Seems I might," Xerx said, and handed her a bank note, grumbling the entire time.

"Well, then," Paige said, "if everything's set up, let's see if we can salvage what they didn't dump."

Pip and Noomi joined in the conversation soon after Maria and Miranda had set up the signal boosters, at first wanting to spill the whole story about the adventure that had just happened aboard the *Reckless* with a gusto that rivaled Tyger's storytelling prowess. But Paige had reminded her that there was work to be done first.

"You'd think that they would've had more followers," Paige said several minutes into the download.

"That kinda worried me too," Xerx said, giving a glance toward Indira, who, along with Artemis, kept a silent lookout into the stairwell that led back into the desecrated church. She'd even volunteered to bring Father Muldoon back down with them now that the area was clear. He sat slumped over on the landing, arms still shackled. "I was expecting a mob with pitch-forks to come running in after the first gunshot went off."

"Ye sound like you actually want these nobs t'come and give ye all the malky," Noomi commed in. "Ye're a bunch o' dafties, ken."

"I'm sure he thinks that this is much better than a ton of action, Noo," Snow said. "Paraska's just an adrenaline junkie."

Xerx opened his mouth to protest, but then closed it. She wasn't wrong, after all.

"Well, that just makes me realize how much of a right bunch of cowards the Council really is here," Paige said. "They're more afraid of the Dragon Bitch than us coming in and wrecking shop."

"Scratch a racist, find a coward," Xerx said, casting a disdainful look at the unconscious priest. "Personally, I'm thankful that it's been so easy. But I'm pretty sure that assholes like this one didn't put all their eggs in one basket."

"Had to piss in my porridge, didn't you?" Paige said with a rueful chuckle.

"Hey, boss! We got a nice clean upload here," Pip said.

"Are the *Wraith* and *Hammerfall II* picking it up as well?" Paige asked. "We'd like to get out of here sometime this year."

"Steady on, now," Noomi said. "Picking up some right weird shite on my end."

"Yeah, I'm getting it too," Pip said.

There was a heavy silence that hung in the air, then Pip spoke, sounding frantic.

"Shit, they weren't manually trying to delete the files! It's a program that's doing it. The purge is still going on!"

"Can you stop it?" Snow said before anyone planet-side could speak.

"What d'ye think we're doing?" Noomi snapped.

"Damn! She's fast!" Pip exclaimed. "Trying to get ahead of the data wipe. But it looks like it was designed to work in a fractal pattern, expanding the data sets in multiple dimensions, eating it faster and faster—"

"Oi! Less yap, more work!" Noomi yelled.

"I'm workin'! I'm workin'!" Pip yelled back.

The line went silent for several moments, creating a tension that made the air feel increasingly heavy. Only every few moments, Noomi punctuated the silence with her colorful patois.

"Oh no, you dinnae be keeking at mah system specs, yah binary bastard."

"Ah pish, youse not got enough power behind that surge ta kick me out, ya nobby!"

"Aye that's why ya get, you're no takin a shite in my kettle, ya bawbag!"

In counterpoint, there came the crescendoing sound of a power spike in the computer, setting Xerx's teeth on edge. That was never good.

"Uh, guys, you sound like you might be making it worse," Xerx said.

"Shut up!" Both Pip and Noomi snapped back, and Pip finishing with, "We almost have it! Don't pull the plug!"

"He wasn't planning on it, dear," Paige said, leaning against one of the consoles and strumming her fingers. Xerx had connected to a dermal interface system and had a glimpse of what techies and tanks like Noomi, Pip, and even Mobola saw once, but it was too much for him. System environments were an entirely different universe, with a language that made him wonder how they could understand it. Whatever they were doing, it was more complex than he could imagine. Just then, the sound of footsteps came from the entrance to the chamber. A guard rounded the corner, but a thunderous crack rang out and he flew backward in a spray of blood and armor fragments, landing on two more guards following behind. Miranda ejected the spent cartridge from her rifle and chambered another in readiness. Wisely, the two others grabbed the body of their fallen comrade and hid around the corner. But it didn't save them from Artemis, who charged through the door, leaping against the doorposts and tackling the first guard whom she'd caught unsuspecting, her knives in hand. Making short work of him, she bounced off his body and used the moment of the other guard's frozen terror to make sure he joined his comrade. In less than a minute, the danger went from resurgent to nonexistent.

A spark shot from one server rack as Artemis skipped back into the room. The noise of surging power quit, giving a sound of an engine cycling down. Xerx felt a bead of sweat run down the side of his face. This could be good ... or apocalyptic.

"Okay, it looks like we managed to isolate the program's command lines," Pip said. Though not winded, she did sound suitably tired. Xerx let out a breath he didn't realize he'd been holding.

"Ain't never had a go at something like that 'afore," Noomi said in a tone that sounded even more exhausted than the diminutive tank.

"So she's fine now?" Xerx ventured to say. "Is it safe to speak?"

"Yeah, sorry about that," Pip said. "It was a bit hairy for a moment."

"Speak for yoursel'," Noomi said. "When I tell a bloke to shut his gob when he's talking shite, I mean it."

Xerx heard Snow sigh, and he couldn't help but smile.

"Anyways," Pip said, "the data's somewhat fragmented, on account of it being partly purged, but mostly intact. What I'm getting is pretty useful, if I do say so myself. I'm pretty sure Her Majesty will be especially interested in the juicier bits."

"You hear that, Lex?" Xerx said into the comm.

"It's still coming in on our end, but Pip's quite the time saver," Alexa replied, then let out a sudden gasp. "Oh, dear. And you said you have this Father Muldoon on ice?"

"Pretty much," Xerx said. "You want him on white bread or wheat?"

"Oh, sweetie, if what's coming in is true, then what you caught him doing on Zynj is the least of his sins."

"Told you he'd been busy," Snow said.

"Trafficking Imperium tech through raiders is bad enough to get him hanged and flayed on Rhoma," Xerx said. "And he admitted that with his own mouth."

"Trust me, chicken. It's far worse than that. He'd better hope his soul is right with God. Otherwise, at the pearly gates, he's fifty fruit flavors of fucked."

"Will you be taking him to Rhoma, then?" Xerx asked.

"As much as I'd love to see him subjected to the tender mercies of my husband..." A wistful tone crept into the Pirate Queen's voice. "Sadly, we need our fingers in the Alliance's respective pots so much more than we need to satisfy our pride. Besides, there's a nice, juicy bounty out on him on the StellarNet."

"Really?" Xerx said.

"Bet there aren't any connections to Helix, though."

"That Helix tattoo on his forehead wasn't a giveaway?"

"No tattoos on the mugshots," Alexa said. "But they are from a good ten years ago. Full name is Benjamin Richter Muldoon. Wanted for insurrection and terrorist activities on several orbital habs. Statute of limitations almost had the bounties run out."

Xerx gave a grunt. "Well, Helix did a good enough job of hiding itself over the past century. Still, looks like it's our lucky day."

"Data transfer's finished," Pip said. "Everybody got their piece of the pie?"

"Download complete on our end," Mobola said.

"Done here," Alexa said.

"Good, then," Xerx said. "Next item of business is getting the hell outta here."

"I used the ventilation ducts to get here," Snow said, "but I parked near a service elevator that leads to an emergency spaceport where Noo can pick us up. It's about a quarter mile away from where we are, along the outer wall, going away from the fairgrounds. It's protected by an environmental force field, but I don't know how often they test those systems, so you'd better get a move on."

"Ah, and it looks like we've got a stroke of luck once again," Alexa said brightly. "I got in touch with the Alliance garrison. They acknowledged my communique, and a shuttle just happened to be patrolling near this system. They'll be here in about twelve hours."

"Lucky indeed," Snow said. "I suggest we hurry, then."

Xerx never tired of Maria's talent for variety when it came to tactical armaments. This time, she decided to test one out on their departure: an enzyme warhead. It was usually used to down aggressive leviathan whales in the oceans of Columbus, but it made short work of most heavy mobile turrets. Once, he'd even seen one transform a derelict Gestalt in the jungles of Sepra into a pile of sludge. He figured that this would perhaps be overkill, but everyone else on the team had figured that bombs might have been particularly dangerous for this habitat, leaving Maria as the only adventurous one.

Besides, Blue Point was too deep underground to cause a breach. And the computers would be destroyed either way. So Xerx basked in the warm sense of satisfaction he felt as the unholy church melted like hot candle wax upon their departure, collapsing in on itself in a pile of acrid-smelling waste.

Too bad the trash couldn't take itself out. But Maria's little toy definitely helped.

They made the rest of the way to the service corridor and elevator on foot while Indira carried Father Muldoon slung over her back. The ride in Snow's six-wheeler was brief, and the service elevator fit the vehicle's entirety, making the rest of the journey easier, if a little snug, for his team with two extra bodies to fill the back seats.

The elevator opened into a dark hangar, which lit up once they stepped inside. Even if the elevator hadn't been working, it was built in a way that shielded it from the worst of the outside storms. Also, there were not only masks inside, but full-on environmental suits waiting for them, hanging on hooks in the wall, with several others in a stack of boxes near a row of benches.

"What's your ETA, Noomi?" Snow said into the comm.

"Half past 'get tae fuck, ahm here already!'" Noomi said, just as the gate ahead opened to the *Hammerfall II*'s open hangar bay. The ship extended its docking ramp, past the at first invisible force field. Xerx could see the shards of rock and gale-force winds that battered the ship's hull, thankful once again that everything was holding together as Snow led the way aboard and to safety.

"Enjoy the ride," Snow said as she hurried back toward the cockpit. Xerx performed a quick head count once his team had filed back into the corridor, then sat heavily down on the bench, buckling himself in. Wearily, he watched as everyone else did the same, and Father Muldoon was shackled to a fixture in the wall at the corridor's far end. The ship lurched in an upward angle as it launched into orbit, and Xerx let the motion lull him into a half-sleep, only awakening when Snow had announced their imminent docking with the *Wraith*. By this time, Father Muldoon had woken up. There was no fight in his eyes, however, as he seemed to accept his situation. Once the airlock had opened and Alexa's soldiers stepped through, he boarded the ship without hesitation or protest while he and Paige stood behind him, weapons trained. But the poisonous look he shot Xerx shook the captain of the *Reckless* to his core, making him supremely glad to be rid of him once the airlock door had finally closed.

At least the bounty would be nice.

The next stop was the *Reckless*, and he had been about to suggest Snow come and work with them when he saw the "kill that thought" motion from Paige. Clearly, this blank tank was not one to defect. Rather, in the end, he shook Snow's hand, who in turn, gave a cordial incline of her head.

As he turned to step through the airlock, Xerx looked up and grinned mischievously.

"Och aye the Noo!" he yelled, chuckling as the response came over the comm system.   "A h h h get tae fuck ya wee bawbag, 'fore I disengage the seals while you're halfways across, ye ken?"

Neela waited for him at the airlock, then began crossing the gap between them, falling into his arms and nearly laughing as he kissed her.

"Mission accomplished," he said.

"Have we all got a story to tell you, *kipenzi*," Neela said, still touching her forehead to his own.

"As do I," Xerx said. "But I'd like to hear yours first."

"And deprive Tyger of his favorite pastime?" Neela said, shaking her head. "I wouldn't dream of it. Let's go meet him in sickbay."

"Wait, he got hurt?" Xerx stopped in his tracks. "How badly?"

"He wants to tell us a story," Neela said, and Xerx caught the twinkle in her eye. "Despite being shot with a round that went clean through his shoulder, he's doing quite well, I should think."

"And that girl that Kumiko brought on board?"

"What girl?"

Xerx's expression went blank at first, then he switched on his comm. "Hey, Mobola, is Kumiko on board? And do we have any unauthorized passengers?"

"She's with me," Kumiko replied before Mobola could answer. "We're in sickbay."

A second later, klaxons blared, the sudden noise startling both Xerx and his wife. The phrase, INTRUDER ALERT sounded off in the corridor for several seconds before Mobola cut it off.

"I just remembered, I have to take a rain check on meeting with Tyger," Xerx said. "Gotta conference with the captains back on the bridge, so lemme go take care of that." He started off in the bridge's direction, then paused to switch on his comm one more time.

"Just wanted to tell you that you did good back there, Kumi," Xerx said. "I owe you one."

"Yeah, you do," Kumiko replied, though she sounded more playful than her usual haughty self. "And ... well, thanks."

"Looks like we all got what we came for," Xerx said.

"It doesn't exactly make things better, though." Alexa leaned forward, resting her elbows on her knees in the holo. "Now we're going to see if we even want to keep doing business with Zynj. But that'll probably be stuck in parliament for the next few months to more than a year."

"Well, our bosses will be thankful for the free intel," Paige said. "But if what Pip gleaned from the data is true, it looks like we're in quite a bit more of an arms race against the Imperium than we thought. The only saving grace here is that they've been kept in the trenches on Tantagel IX."

"There's more, I'm afraid," Alexa said. "From the looks of it, the raiders weren't being supplied by Helix from Zynj, but rather, they were coordinating the supplies. We have locations, so we'll be ferreting them out for awhile." She pursed her lips at Xerx. "Looks like you gave the pirate bloods yet another job."

"And what about Snow?" Xerx asked.

Both Paige and Alexa shrugged their shoulders.

"She jumped out as soon as she finished dropping everybody off," Paige said. "And God only knows what her side will be doing with the data."

"Guess there's no use pitching a fit over it," Xerx said. "I just hope that what happened has left the raiders confused enough to ignore me for right now. We have a ceremony to get to on Tophanavar." He then smiled, as much to himself as Paige. "The Empress did tell me that the Felyans would be more open to sharing their tech with us after this, so things might not be so bleak after all."

"Let's hope my bosses share your optimism, love," Paige said, then straightened up. "Now, if that is all, I have a massage pending by a man whose hands go everywhere."

Just then, Pip appeared in the middle of the conference.

"Um, guys. There's a problem."

Xerx's stomach began to hurt.

"God, what now?"

"Well, we got a response from the Alliance garrison," she said. "And ... they said that they would be sending a ship within the hour."

Alexa looked up, visibly confused. "That can't be right. Indira handed Muldoon to them in our shuttle bay less than an hour ago. Right brusque lot they were too, not very chatty and surprisingly eager to get out of there, it seemed to me."

Then her face dropped.

"Oh, fuck."

The debris field with the remains of the Alliance ship lay at the edge of the system. Pip and Mobola's combined analyses showed the exact same thing. A reactor breach in the ship's hyperspace drive. Neela, recalled to the bridge, stood beside Xerx, observing the wreckage, just as stunned as he was.

"Long-range sensors picked up the explosion right after the Alliance contacted me," Pip said. "I'm sorry. There's no way we could've detected or stopped it."

"Shit," Xerx said, shaking his head at their turn of fortune. "Hey, Lex, was that bounty marked dead or alive?"

"Makes no difference without a fucking body to prove it; does it now?" Alexa said.

"A quick death was more than that bastard deserved," Paige remarked, her tone heavy with the frustration shared between all three of the captains.

"I say this is too convenient," Neela said.

"It's a puzzle, that's for sure," Xerx added, shaking his head. "Should've known he'd have something up his sleeve."

"No other engine trails," Pip said. "And an explosion like this would've atomized any organic matter within about a hundred meters. There's nothing here."

For the longest time, Xerx stared at the surrounding holos of space, with the floating remains of the ship that they'd turned Father Muldoon over to surrounding them, with no evidence of any other ships involved, just an astronomically improbable mishap and its fallout.

"I can't accept this," he said at last, then released a long, reluctant sigh that almost sounded like a wheeze. "But I have no choice, do I?"

"Alliance military will have some investigators coming to do a cursory evaluation of the wreckage," Pip said. "But you'll never find out the truth, honey—especially if they don't want to share it."

"Well, that bloody sucks," Paige said, then began to slightly fidget. "But nothing any of us can do about it."

"Yeah," Xerx said, his tone sepulchral. "Still, thanks for your help, Paige."

Paige gave a sad smile. "Anything for you, Chook. Now, if you don't mind, I, myself have an appointment for some ... treatment."

"Have fun."

"Lucky bitch," Alexa quipped as Paige's holo vanished. She then sighed. "Too bad my little boy toy is preoccupied with his first love, or I'd have convinced him to come fly with me for a bit of stress relief myself. Anyway, love, safe travels."

"You too, Lex," Xerx said.

The conference ended, and Xerx slipped back into his captain's chair, sighing. To his left, the entrance door opened, and Pepper stepped through. He saluted, then waved at Mobola as he stood by her side.

"Hey, Captain, don't you think she deserves a little break now that we've got a chance to breathe?" the young Felyan said.

"Does she ever?" Neela replied, and cast a pleading gaze Xerx's way. Xerx smiled as he stood back up. He was reticent to put the ship on autopilot, but he expected things to be much calmer on the way back to Tophanavar. Ramirez had communicated his relief that they were now safe to conclude their journey. Besides, he wanted very much to head to the sickbay to hear Neela and Tyger's stories. At least that was something to be happy about.

"Go ahead and set course for Tophanavar, Mobola," he said. "Then go take a rest. You've earned it." He turned toward the captain's chair and sat down heavily. "We all have."

EPILOGUE 1

The news feeds on the monitors that peppered New St. Louis' market district were festooned with news about the newly signed treaty between the Alliance and Felyan Empire amidst puff pieces on how adorable the princess was, with endless shots of her, both sleeping and wide awake in the arms of her father and Ri'Kela, with Biraknu standing watchfully by. In the background, she even caught a glimpse of Xerx who looked both haggard and relieved beside his wife. Equally endless were the commentaries that prattled on about how this treaty would open up a wealth of resources and tech that would revolutionize life in the Colonies. And yet, some were not so optimistic. Humanity's penchant for distrustfulness produced pundit after pundit who weighed in with skeptical takes on possible alternative agendas of the Empire, regardless of the paucity of evidence. And some were at least in the middle of the road. One headline ran the particularly intriguing tagline that read, A RETURN TO THE FIRST IMPERIUM JUST OVER THE HORIZON? It was a bit hyperbolic, perhaps, but only time would tell how things would ultimately pan out.

But Kumiko was someone who always curbed her optimism. Besides, it was better to focus on the here and now. And right now, she could relax over a job well done. On Haven, she waited for Riju's family, who had been, as usual, notoriously difficult to reach.

"Are you sure you want to stick around here, mum?" Kumiko said to Akiko as they waited by the market district on New St. Louis. The little girl standing by their sides licked happily on an ice cream cone that she had bought for her. "I can take you anywhere you want to go, you know."

"It's okay." Her mother's smile was a comfort, despite the fact that she clearly wanted to spend more time with her, sans Tyger. Perhaps it could have probably even been quality time now that her father had thankfully remained aboard the *Reckless*. "I contacted a Space Hippie fleet that will be coming 'round in a few days for a farmer's market. They need reliable security. Besides, you have other places to go, right?"

"Must I?"

"Well, you'll be back on An'Re'Hara anyway," her mother said. "Doesn't the Empress have to formally dismiss you?"

"Yes, but—"

"No." Kumiko knew the finality in her voice all too well. Whether she liked it or not, she would be meeting with her father on An'Re'Hara after leaving the palace, and he would be introducing her to his mother—her Felyan grandmother. She would endure it, if only to please her mother.

"You've gotten better with your father," Akiko said. "Really, I think that your reactions to him are more reflex than anything. You know he looked for you as persistently as I did."

"I know," Kumiko said, her voice straining with annoyed tolerance. "I really don't feel the same way about him as I did before. I believe you now; I really do. It's just that I wish he didn't act so much like a shiftless hobo."

"Please don't speak about him that way," her mother said in a brittle tone, then smiled wanly. "I know you'll never like him, but I know you love him. He's braver than you think. Or do you think I was lying when I told you how he went leaping into that corridor when the ship was boarded?"

"I *know* you aren't," Kumiko said, tapping a finger against her temple.

Leaning back against the archway, Akiko crossed her arms. "I think when you meet his mother, you will understand him a little better."

"Don't expect me to hold my breath," Kumiko said. "But we'll see."

"Kumi..."

She hated when her mother used that tone of voice. Soft, almost cajoling. Subtly manipulative ... motherly. She could sense the intent behind it, and for some reason it made her want to turn and run away.

"You need to understand what it means to belong somewhere." She grinned knowingly. "You went back to the place again, didn't you? That pleasure house?"

It was always amazing how non-psionics could be so accurate without the ability to read minds. She hadn't even told her about her trip to the old neighborhood, though she had mentioned where she'd lived.

Mentioned Remli. She never told her about their semblance of a relationship, but that was something that could easily be figured out.

"He wasn't there," she lied. "Not that it matters. He took a lifemate. The old place was made into their home. They even have a kid."

"Would it hurt to talk to him?" Akiko asked. "Never hurts to keep up with those dear to you, you know."

Kumiko frowned. "I'll ... think about it."

Suddenly, Riju's tiny bell-like voice shrieked with a joy that broadcasted to both women in the way that only a tertiary without full control of her psionics could. It made both Kumiko and her mother giddy as they turned down the road to see a tangle of youths, ranging from their late teens to children around Riju's age, of varying ethnic backgrounds, running toward the little girl, their faces alight with happiness and relief.

"Those kids are her family?" Akiko said, her surprise amusing Kumiko.

"Tertiaries usually stick together in groups," Kumiko explained as she hurried behind the little girl, herself grateful that this particular family had not become victims of any Seekers. "I ran with them for a little while before we were reunited. And we run into each other from time to time."

Riju, dropping the remnants of her ice cream cone, which a nearby sweeper robot hurriedly disposed of, closed the gap between herself and the small herd, and ran into the arms of the oldest woman: a tall, slender young lady with fair skin and dark eyes, wearing what looked like a slightly tattered private school uniform. Kneeling down, she hugged Riju as if she never wanted to let her go, and the rest of the group fell into the hug as well. How she was not smothered by this puzzled even Kumiko. But her momentary confusion was quickly drowned out in the warmth of joy and relief the group—tertiaries all—shared amongst themselves. And the tears that flowed from their eyes made her own eyes burn as she sensed that sense of familial belonging. She had never been close to anyone, except perhaps to her mother, and even she knew that it was not as close as Akiko would have liked. This was almost overwhelming, and she found herself fighting off a sense of jealousy that threatened to burn like her eyes.

"We got the message from Yana and Yumi," the oldest girl said, standing up. She wiped away the tears that formed twin streams down her cheeks. "I can't ... I can't thank you enough for this." She tousled Riju's silver hair, as the little girl clung to her with the tenacity of a baby opossum to its mother. "We thought the Seekers got her. We took our eyes off of her for one second on Dionysus Minor and—"

"Don't worry about it, Cin," Kumiko said, waving her hand and trying to keep a poker face in spite of the emotional spillover. "Good thing is that you won't have to worry about the asshole who took her ever again."

The girl nodded, becoming more serious in her expression as she picked Riju up into her arms. "This one's always been giving us the slip. She's about as independent as Tessa but far less able to take care of herself."

"Tessa's not with you?" Kumiko said, eyeing the colorful group. She had only now realized the lack of the unique timbre of the eccentric girl's mind among the group, and a sense of worry began to creep into the back of her mind anew.

"Off looking at the universe again," Cin said. "She always comes back. She's probably back home again, sleeping in the cabinet under the sink."

"Seems like you adopted a cat more than a human," Kumiko said, forcing herself to choose not to worry until there was actual reason to. She had enough worries of her own, after all.

"Well, she adopted us more than us adopting her," Cin said. "So she really is more like a cat. And Riju follows her like a lost puppy. When we see her again, we'll need to give those two a good talking to."

After the business with Riju finished and having left her mother at the poshest hotel that she could afford, Kumiko made her way down a familiar path, down a familiar alleyway, and into a familiar neighborhood, where she stood before the familiar place she'd passed by all too often.

At least the bodies had been cleared out.

Mr. Pickles meowed at her feet and she reached down to pet him as he rubbed happily against her legs beneath the skirt of her pinafore. She stepped up to the front door of the old pleasure house-turned-home ... then again paused.

She thought about it.

She smiled, surer now that she had been the last time she'd been here. Then walked away.

Mama Gold threw the door open to an empty porch. Aura'Li cooed in her arms, biting on her fingers. Remli came to her side, confused.

"You heard something, *Li'ah*?" he asked.

"No, I felt someone," Gold said. "Someone was here. It felt ... familiar."

Remli sniffed the air and smiled. It was a familiar, nostalgic scent. At once, he knew it. He glanced downward, where Mr. Pickles, the final gift she'd given to him, sat. Beside him was a tiny cat sculpture. At first, he thought it was made of glass until he picked it up, and realized that it was ice.

"It was familiar," he said, holding it up for his lifemate and daughter to view, a wistful look in his eyes, despite the happiness he had found.

"I wonder why she didn't stay?" Gold asked. Remli shook his head as they closed the front door.

"She never was big on goodbyes," he said, and brought the sculpture to the freezer.

EPILOGUE 2

"Thank God he's alive," the man said, checking the environmental controls of the coffin lifepod.

"Lots of bruising, and a few cracked bones," his companion said. "You think she'll be okay with that?"

"Not our fault; not our problem," the man said. "We did as asked—track it and grab it." He gestured to the beanpole of a man in a tattered priestly frock sleeping inside. "She said he'd know what to do after we got here."

A deathly wail shook both men to their cores, and they stumbled to the floor of the ship's deck, scrambling away from the pod. Wide-eyed, they gaped at the man, now sitting bolt upright, at first gasping in something resembling an apoplectic fit, then twisting in pain, collapsing back into the pod, where he groaned.

"The nanogel!" the man whispered sharply to his companion after regaining his composure. The device was pressed into his hand as both of the deck's occupants rose awkwardly to their feet, still shaken.

"Hold still, old man," the man said as he grabbed the arm his scans said had not been damaged. "We need to fix the rest of you."

"No..."

He reached down with his free hand and pinned the man down, jabbing the injector into his skin with the other. The man screamed, but only for a moment, as the pain momentarily locked even his jaw and vocal cords. He twisted in the pod and howled in agony. Moments later, he settled down, panting, but looking less banged up as the multiple cuts across his body healed and the bruising began to fade.

They stepped back as the elderly beanpole rose from the coffin pod, slowly and painfully.

Aside from the weird twisting tattoo on his forehead, he looked like a priest.

"H-how ... long?" he quavered.

"Ah, how long were you out there?" the man said with trepidation.

"What else could I mean?" beanpole replied tersely. There might not have been much to him physically, but the man quickly realized the tone of authority in his voice. Whoever he was, he must have been someone important.

"Well, if the timer on the pod wasn't damaged, it looks like three months," the man's companion replied. "Montgomery and I got orders to locate your pod a couple of weeks ago, but we had a lot of higher-priority jobs and couldn't get to you until then."

"He doesn't need to know all that, Whit," Montgomery snapped. "You're always oversharing."

"Three months..." Beanpole muttered the words, resting his forehead against his hand. "She couldn't have sent out anyone sooner?"

"That's above our pay grade, I'm afraid," Montgomery said. "But we're headed for Columbus like she wanted.

You hungry? I know cryo can make people sick to their stomachs, but others come out starving. Which one are you?"

"Do I look like I need to vomit?" Beanpole growled. "No, I need to use a comm. I need to get in touch with my benefactor."

"Ah, right," Montgomery said, and indicated an exit door. "This way."

He led Beanpole to the cockpit and spun up the comm system for him.

"Leave me," he said.

"Can't do," Montgomery said. "I—"

The poisonous look in Beanpole's eye made him regret his objection.

"Just ... come out when you're done," Montgomery said. "And the ship's on autopilot; don't touch anything else."

Moving backward, the man slinked out of the cockpit, leaving Father Muldoon alone. Immediately, he dialed in the code.

The androgynous image of Dr. Hayashibara appeared.

"It is good to see my employees were able to deliver," she said with a catlike grin.

"Three months?" Father Muldoon said, letting his frustration bleed through. "You had the pod's signal for all that time, did you not? Do you know how many of my flock I must attend to? How many plans I have to see to? Three months may as well be thirty!"

"I have my own priorities as well," Dr. Hayashibara said, "plus dwindling resources that I needed to consolidate since my own failure at Tophanavar. Nevertheless,

I held my end of the bargain. You'll be arriving at Columbus soon, Fissure Island, if things don't go any further awry. Your ... flock is tending to the gifts I left them, keeping it well, I should think."

"So it's done?" Muldoon said, brightening. The labs had only been a year into the research and were just nearing peak growth.

"A lot happens in three months' time," the Doctor replied, resting her fingers together. "Have a little faith in me. All you need to do now is relax and come join us. We have a great deal to talk about, as well as how to secure my end of the bargain. *My* particular plans are no good if the entire Felyan race goes extinct, after all."

"I keep my promises," Muldoon said, and recalled the comfort of scripture. "Let your yay be yay and your nay be nay."

"Indeed."

The elevator continued its descent. It had been descending for a long time.

Now I know why there's a bench in here, thought Snow as she shifted her feet, discomfort growing in her calves from where she'd remained standing.

Through the mesh walls, she could see the industrial heart of the arcology she was passing through, intersected by the supports of the elevator shaft. Occasionally patches of daylight and a view of outside would flash past. Snow had never been this deep or even this low within the Xiao megacities before. She found it discomforting.

More pipes and gigantic cables rushed by as the elevator descended further.

Eventually, it came to a stop, and the doors slid open. Snow was hit by a breeze of stale, musty air that reeked of dust and metal filings. The whole place was covered in gloom, pierced only by harsh strip lights overhead and orange, caged sodium lamps on the walls. It looked like it had been carved from solid concrete.

The gloom seemed to dull the sound of her footsteps as she stepped out of the elevator car, the lack of echo giving the whole place an unnerving peacefulness. Gently, she reached down and quietly unhooked the strap on her MAG holster.

As she moved further down the corridor, faint noises began to work their way toward her ears. The musty smell began to yield to scents of food and a refreshing breeze replaced the stuffy closeness that surrounded the elevator.

Snow stepped out into a wide atrium; huge pipes reached skyward, disappearing into a faint white glow far above. There was a gentle misty rain that fell whilst steam vented from various vents and drains. Before her was a market. The noises were people shouting, advertising their wares, and trying to attract customers. She noted how the various exchanges consisted of goods rather than money. The fact that people even lived down here, let alone had a thriving economy—albeit one based on barter rather than currency—was surprising to her.

She shook her head; she was getting distracted. Agent Four had told her that the target location was not far from the elevator but hadn't specified how to find who she was looking for.

"Don't worry," he said. "They'll find you." He then slapped her on the arm and gave his customary smirk before taking his leave. His words weren't very reassuring.

As she scanned the barter market, Snow noted an exit in the far-right corner. Above it shone a bright green neon arrow. *It couldn't be that obvious*, she thought, *could it?*

Regardless, she decided to follow the sign and made her way through the narrow passage. It was dark, but Snow made her way easily to its end, where a beaded curtain covered the exit. Gently brushing it aside, she found herself standing in what appeared to be a domed room made of cables and steel supports. She looked over the space and turned to face the way she'd come. Snow started when she turned back and a short, white-haired tech tank was standing in the middle of the room, staring at her. This tank, though just as petite as her kind, was different from what she'd encountered before. She wore a long, black, thick weather beater coat, which, in turn, was covered in numerous cables that fed into a device on her back. Two cables fed from the woman's mouth and ran down and around her neck to the device. Her cranial implants were covered in aerials of all sizes. Black tattoos adorned her lower jaw, making abstract circuit patterns across the skin and neck. She had bright, scarlet eyes that remained fixed on Snow.

"Hello," Snow said, her words seeming to be too loud for the room's apparent silent sanctity. "I'm assuming I'm in the right place. I was sent by Agent Four to locate the, erm, 'Coven,' I believe they're called."

The woman cocked her head to one side but said nothing. And Snow felt a distinct sense of frustration building in the back of her head.

"Look, it is really rather important that I find them. I need their unique skills with a delicate matter."

The tank continued to stare, unblinking, still not speaking. Snow sighed and her shoulders drooped.

"Can you help me or not?" She snapped, "Or do you just get a kick out of staring at people all day?"

At that, the woman finally blinked. Suddenly, Snow heard a crackle in her implanted comm unit. A female voice suddenly broke through the white noise, machine-like in its intonation.

"Yes, I believe we can help. I needed to make sure that you were the one we expected. You may proceed."

Snow blinked and shook her head, disbelieving. Her internal comm was meant to be only accessible through wired contact. Still, this was the right place. She reached into the pocket of her jacket and pulled out a portable memory unit.

"I need these files decrypted. Normally my shipboard processor would do it, but it's complex, and she'd need a week to break it. And in all honesty, we need it done as soon as."

The crackle returned, and the voice spoke once more.

"Give us twelve hours and return to this place. Please leave the device with my colleague."

Snow jumped again as suddenly on her left a second tank had appeared. This one wore a light blue hoodie and black shorts with fishnet tights and large trainers. She did, however, share the same artfully arranged multitude of cables and devices as the other.

Snow handed the memory unit to the hooded individual and nodded to both. The red-eyed mistress in the center returned the nod and gestured for Snow to return the way she'd come. Snow heeded the gesture and took her leave.

She sat on the bench as the elevator ascended, rubbing her chin in thought. The world was changing and for the stranger, it seemed. It certainly wasn't getting any better...

THE END

COME FOLLOW THE NORTHWEST
PASSAGE WITH US!

SUPPORT US ON PATREON!
www.patreon.com/WildSpaceSaga

WILD SPACE SAGA CONCEPT AND COMIC ART
BY TERENCE PEGASUS AND BRANDON HILL:
wildspacesaga.deviantart.com

ART BY BRANDON HILL:
brandonhill.deviantart.com

FOLLOW BRANDON HILL'S FACEBOOK PAGE AT
"AuthorBrandonHill"

Follow us on Twitter!
@DecKrash
@WildSpaceSaga

Be sure to check out Brandon Hill's other e-books, paperbacks, and hardcover books, available on Amazon Kindle and Nook:

<u>*Wild Space Saga:*</u>
Wild Space Saga, Book 1: Between the Devil and the Dark
Wild Space Saga, Book 2: Wrath and Redemption
Wild Space Saga, Book 3: Twisted Faith
Tales of Wild Space, Book 1: Lifemates
Tales of Wild Space, Book 2: Rites of Passage

<u>*The War of Millennium Night:*</u>
From Slate to Crimson
Double-Cross My Heart

<u>*The World of Five Nations:*</u>
The Hidden Meanings
Elven Roses

<u>*Virtual Law:*</u>
Reunions

COMING SOON

Wild Space Saga, Book 4: Tech Support

During a brief layover on Xiao, Shadow Star captain Paige is called to test pilot new Gestalts outfitted with exotic and potentially revolutionary tech, and brings Xerx Paraska in on this lucrative opportunity. Meanwhile, Pip, the Shadow Star's pint-sized extroverted "tech tank," is netted along with Kairen, the ship's medic and her constant cynical foil, into the affairs of the coven: a secret nest of abandoned tech tanks like herself. Resorting to eccentric means to survive in a world that runs contrary to their own formerly safe electronic world, they request the endlessly bickering duo's assistance to locate one of their own. This leads them into a dangerous adventure that uncovers a deadly secret in the city world's labyrinthine lower levels that not only puts the lives of both Paige and Xerx on the line but may spell destruction on a scale never seen before.

BOOK CLUB QUESTIONS

1. Do you feel that there was good development for Kumiko as a character? If not, what would you like to see in that development?

2. Did the history behind Kumiko and Amira's falling out make their animosity seem genuine? Why or why not?

3. Do you feel that Kumiko is a character you would like to see more of? How about Riju or the tertiary children in the epilogue?

4. Were the missions in the story overall clear?

5. Do you feel that there were character(s) that felt under-used? What would you have done to make them more integral to the plot?

6. Did you feel that Neela seemed to grow as a captain for the *Reckless*?

7. Did you believe that the *Reckless* and *Outlaw Star* crews teaming up with Snow for their mission to Zynj made sense?

8. Was Kumiko's relationship with her family believable?

9. Did you feel that Kumiko was unnecessarily cold? Where and how?

10. Would you like to see Alexa presented more often as a character?

11. Was Father Muldoon a convincing villain?

12. Did you feel that Father Muldoon's character needed more fleshing out?

13. Did Zynj seem plausible/real as a world?

14. Which member of the *Reckless* crew would you like to see more of?

15. Did you feel like Noomi and Snow's relationship was realistic/relevant to the story?

16. Did you feel that things were wrapped up properly at the story's end?

17. Did An'Re'Hara feel like a living world to you?

18. Did you feel that Xerx and Kumiko have good chemistry together?

19. Did the enemies' motives feel clear and understandable?

20. Did the story put together a comprehensible tale to you? Why or why not?

AUTHOR BIO

Brandon Hill is a native of Louisiana and an avid reader of science fiction and fantasy, who began writing in the eleventh grade. Of himself, he says, "I am a 'classic nerd' and prolific writer who has had dreams of authorship since childhood. I sketch perhaps even more prolifically than I write, and have drawings of just about every character my warped imagination has come up with. I hope to continue sharing these ideas, characters, and stories with others for years to come."

Terence Pegasus is a native of Northampton, Northamptonshire in the United Kingdom. Sharing the same love of science fiction and fantasy, he enjoys making kitbashes of various Warhammer 40K parts. Sharing the same love of sci-fi and fantasy and having forged a friendship with Brandon that began in the mid-90s with a mutual interest in 80s cartoons and sci-fi series, he and Brandon began their work on Wild Space Saga, eventually sharing his unique characters and integrating them into the story and providing his concept and technical work to its ever-expanding universe.

Discover more at
4HorsemenPublications.com

10% off using HORSEMEN10